**REA**

P9-BHR-323

*"Looking for someone?"*

Maria turned in the direction of the rough-toned male voice and almost replied, *"You. I'm looking for you. I have been all of my life."*

In a near daze, she dragged her eyes from his lopsided grin. She'd never thought to meet a man who could actually make her heart jump into her throat. But to happen tonight of all nights! Swallowing her instincts to flee, she answered, "Randy Searle. Is he here?"

Head cocked to one side, he gave her a once-over that was almost insolent in its laziness. "Too bad," he drawled. "I'd hoped you were looking for me."

"Is—is he here?" she stuttered, watching the only guy ever to make her mind crash come closer, moving with all the lethal grace of a male confident of his own attractions.

ROMANCE

Dear Reader,

Welcome to another month of excitement and romance. Start your reading by letting Ruth Langan be your guide to DEVIL'S COVE in *Cover-Up*, the first title in her new miniseries set in a small town where secrets, scandal and seduction go hand in hand. The next three books will be coming out back to back, so be sure to catch every one of them.

Virginia Kantra tells a tale of *Guilty Secrets* as opposites Joe Reilly, a cynical reporter, and Nell Dolan, a softhearted do-gooder, can't help but attract each other—with wonderfully romantic results. Jenna Mills will send *Shock Waves* through you as psychic Brenna Scott tries to convince federal prosecutor Ethan Carrington that he's in danger. If she can't get him to listen to her, his life—and her heart—will be lost.

Finish the month with a trip to the lands down under, Australia and New Zealand, as three of your favorite writers mix romance and suspense in equal—and irresistible—portions. Melissa James features another of her tough (and wonderful!) Nighthawk heroes in *Dangerous Illusion*, while Frances Housden's heroine has to face down the *Shadows of the Past* in order to find her happily-ever-after. Finally, get set for high-seas adventure as Sienna Rivers meets *Her Passionate Protector* in Laurey Bright's latest.

Don't miss a single one—and be sure to come back next month for more of the best and most exciting romantic reading around, right here in Silhouette Intimate Moments.

Yours,

Leslie J. Wainger
Executive Editor

Please address questions and book requests to:
Silhouette Reader Service
U.S.: 3010 Walden Ave., P.O. Box 1325, Buffalo, NY 14269
Canadian: P.O. Box 609, Fort Erie, Ont. L2A 5X3

# Shadows
# of the Past
## FRANCES HOUSDEN

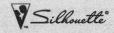

INTIMATE MOMENTS™

Published by Silhouette Books

America's Publisher of Contemporary Romance

If you purchased this book without a cover you should be aware
that this book is stolen property. It was reported as "unsold and
destroyed" to the publisher, and neither the author nor the
publisher has received any payment for this "stripped book."

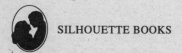 SILHOUETTE BOOKS

ISBN 0-373-27359-2

SHADOWS OF THE PAST

Copyright © 2004 by Frances Housden

All rights reserved. Except for use in any review, the reproduction
or utilization of this work in whole or in part in any form by any
electronic, mechanical or other means, now known or hereafter
invented, including xerography, photocopying and recording, or in
any information storage or retrieval system, is forbidden without
the written permission of the editorial office, Silhouette Books,
233 Broadway, New York, NY 10279 U.S.A.

All characters in this book have no existence outside the imagination of
the author and have no relation whatsoever to anyone bearing the same
name or names. They are not even distantly inspired by any individual
known or unknown to the author, and all incidents are pure invention.

This edition published by arrangement with Harlequin Books S.A.

® and TM are trademarks of Harlequin Books S.A., used under license.
Trademarks indicated with ® are registered in the United States Patent
and Trademark Office, the Canadian Trade Marks Office and in other
countries.

Visit Silhouette at www.eHarlequin.com

**Printed in U.S.A.**

**Books by Frances Housden**

Silhouette Intimate Moments

*The Man for Maggie* #1056
*Love under Fire* #1168
*Heartbreak Hero* #1241
*Shadows of the Past* #1289

## *FRANCES HOUSDEN*

has always been a voracious reader, but she never thought of being a writer until a teacher gave her the encouragement she needed to put pen to paper. As a result, Frances was a finalist in the 1998 Clendon Award and won the award in 1999, which led to the sale of her first book for Silhouette, *The Man for Maggie.*

Frances's marriage to a navy man took her from her birthplace in Scotland all the way to the ends of the earth in New Zealand. Now that he's a landlubber, they try to do most of their traveling together. They live on a ten-acre bush block in the heart of Auckland's Wine District. She has two large sons, two small grandsons and a tiny granddaughter who can twist her around her finger, as well as a wheaten terrier who thinks she's boss. Thanks to one teacher's dedication, Frances now gets to write about the kind of heroes a woman would travel to the ends of the earth for. Frances loves to hear from readers. Write to her at P.O. Box 18-240, Glenn Innes, Auckland 1130, New Zealand.

I'd like to dedicate this book with love to my mother, Annie Gibb, as well as the late Frank Gibb, my father, and to his father, John Gibb, who used to make up stories just for me. And to thank Barbara and Peter Clendon, who sponsor The Clendon Award, aka *Finish the Damn Book*. The win sent my work to the right place to get published.

# Chapter 1

"**V**anity, thy name is woman," Maria Costello told herself, even as she snapped the clasp of her evening purse closed over her glasses and ditched the last particle of her normal librarian look. If there was one thing she didn't need tonight it was anything that smacked of timidity.

No, if she was to face up to her bête noire, then she had to look as if all the power was in her hands, whether it was true or not. She took a deep breath, tilting her chin, and stared after the lights of her departing cab. Without her glasses they were just two fuzzy red balls zooming into the deep blue of a New Zealand summer twilight.

On any other day, the soles of her feet would have itched to dance to the music pouring out of the early New Zealand colonial edifice that housed the Point restaurant, but tonight nothing could distract her. Not even the song rocking off the overhanging verandas that sheltered sidewalk diners. Tonight the tables were empty. All the action was taking place inside at the party she intended gate-crashing.

Of course, if Mamma knew what she was about to do, she

would think Maria's sense of proportion had gone haywire. An opinion that would be voiced in a mixture of English and Italian, the exact mix dependent on the level of her excitement.

Somehow, Maria was positive tonight it would be Italian all the way. One look and Mamma would know she'd gone over the top with her plum-colored dress. Its nunlike high neckline and long sleeves fooled everyone until she turned around.

She'd needed a confidence boost and this was the first time since buying the dress she'd hauled it out of the wardrobe and worn it outside her bedroom.

All her best glamour products, and for what? For the sake of turning the tables on the man she believed was stalking her.

Some people might think she was taking a gamble denouncing him with no more proof than he'd been the only person she'd recognized when the sensation prickled up her neck. But it hadn't started until just after she'd been called to reception at Tech-Re-Search and Randy Searle had handed her some documents from Stanhope Electronics. Nearly every time she turned around quickly, she'd caught him dodging out of sight.

She shuddered, switching her thoughts back to her mother before fear could sneak in a low blow and turn her away from her goal.

The way Maria looked at it, in this life you either had to laugh or cry and she was done crying and ready to do battle.

Clenching her back teeth so hard it hurt she walked into the pool of light spilling from the restaurant door. The happening inside was the Christmas party of Stanhope Electronics, the firm that employed Randy Searle. She'd convinced herself that by confronting him face-to-face, even if he tried to bluster his way out of it, people would know, and in future he'd leave her alone.

Her shoulder-length hair, caught up in butterfly clips,

tugged as her scalp prickled, the way it did when she felt him around.

Watching.

No! No more letting her mind take that track.

One more indrawn breath, one more step, and she crossed the threshold into a world of pure sound.

A quick sidestep helped avoid a collision with the couple leaving. Laughing over their shoulders, they waved goodbye, calling out, "See you next year."

At the last moment they noticed her. "Oops, sorry." The tall blonde's blue-eyed gaze held hers with the soft bleariness of someone who'd had just enough to drink.

"No harm done," said Maria, standing to the side to let them exit, hoping the smile on her face hid her apprehension.

The male half of the couple endowed her with a sloppy grin, and just when she thought she was safe, shouted, "Hey, Franc, hang about, we've got a live one here."

A live one? What kind of party was this?

As she hesitated, he said, "Go right on in. Better late than never, it's one hell of a party."

His blond companion tugged at his sleeve, snagging his attention. "And it can only get better."

A look passed between the two. A look of naked need and desire that pinched at Maria as she watched him practically carry the blonde down to the street in their haste to be alone.

Distracted, she wondered what it felt like to want someone so badly you didn't care who knew.

Mentally reproving herself to get back to the task at hand, she let her eyes adjust to the soft glare of candles reflected in the old-fashioned white-and-black tiles that had first adorned the walls when it was a butcher's shop.

"Looking for someone?"

Maria turned in the direction of the rough-honed male voice and almost replied, *"You. I'm looking for you. I have been all of my life."*

Uh-oh, was her mouth gaping? She shut it with a snap. In

a near daze, she dragged her eyes from the guy's lopsided grin. A grin she'd thought exclusive to her favorite movie hero. Now she knew better. And for worse.

It was as if someone had played a sick joke on her. She'd never thought to meet a man who could actually make her heart jump into her throat. Truth be known, she'd hadn't been sure if she wanted to. But to happen tonight of all nights! Swallowing her instincts to flee, she answered, "Randy. Randy Searle, is he still here?"

Head cocked to the side, he gave her a once-over that was almost insolent in its laziness. "Too bad," he drawled. "I'd hoped you were looking for me."

Her hands fisted tightly round the strap of her purse until her nails dug into her palm. Real life intruded on her fairy-tale moment and let loose the beast to steal her peace of mind. Hopefully a crowded place would keep her safe.

"Am I too late?"

He turned his wrist to check. Dark hairs showed above a gold watch where the cuffs of his white silk shirt folded back. "Not that late, nine-thirty."

"Is…is he still here?" she stuttered, watching the only guy to ever make her mind crash come closer, moving with all the lethal grace of a male confident of his own attractions.

His glance caught hers. Brown like her own, but more intense in color—bitter chocolate—his eyes held hers until she forced herself to look away.

Franc had never seen eyes quite that color before, never been one to play favorites, but then…times change. Dark brown washed with violet, they were almost the color of her dress.

And if her eyes had stolen his breath, her mouth stopped his heart, the full top and bottom lips pouted naturally as if shaped by a kiss. Immediately the thought *my kiss* was born. A tiny black mole enhanced the top right-hand corner and definitely required closer investigation.

"Randy?" he replied slowly, snatching time to think of something other than how her mouth would taste, and stop him cursing that Randy had supped there first.

"Do you know him?"

"Sure. Just give me a minute to think where I last saw him." Which would make at least two minutes since he'd watched her halt in the doorway. One glimpse had sent him hurrying between the tables lining the miniature dance floor, praying she wasn't a trick of his imagination, brought about by a period of abstinence that had ceased to bother him, until now.

"Hmm, maybe he went upstairs, there are a couple of quieter rooms up there by the bar..." His words trailed off as he realized he *had* seen Randy heading in that direction, but he hadn't been alone. Kathy Gilbertson from the experimental electronics lab had been with him, and Franc wouldn't have laid bets on which of them was in the most hurry to reach the scattering of sofas in the secluded upstairs bar.

"Okay, I could be wrong. Randy is more likely to be in the courtyard out back where all the action is."

"Thanks. I guess I'll try there."

Her words lacked enthusiasm, and at the sight of one of her white teeth nipping at her bottom lip he decided to give her an out. "Then again that might not be a good idea unless you're wearing insect repellent. I heard some of the ladies complaining about mosquitoes. I'd hate you to get bitten."

*By anyone but me.*

He'd wanted to touch that honeyed satin skin bare from neck to waist from the moment she'd turned her back to let Hailey and Joel pass. At that moment he wouldn't have given a damn if the rest of her hadn't lived up to his fantasy that a goddess had come calling.

*Two days early, Santa, but who was he to complain?*

Her hair was as dark as his, but no butterfly could ever look half that good on him. She sported at least ten that seemed to flit around her head. Fists bunched, he held back

3 1833 04565 6698

from trying to capture one, but knew his resistance was almost shot.

Hell, what was a guy to do when he that knew up close and personal was never gonna be enough?

From the moment she'd turned to face him, Franc had known he'd been deluding himself. No woman so beautiful, fabulous eyes, generous mouth, not to mention that mole, could possibly be here without a partner.

Soon as she'd proved him correct he'd wished the words unsaid. Randy Searle? The guy was the last person he'd have predicted. And he'd say the goddess standing before him was the last person Randy expected since he'd bet any money the sales rep was more interested in Kathy at the moment. Maybe he could save both of them from an embarrassing situation and do himself and the goddess a favor at the same time.

Her grateful smile almost floored him as she said, "Then that's no problem, I never get bitten. Guess I'm the wrong blood group or something."

"Good for you, let me lead the way through the crush. How about I get you something to drink on the way out?" he asked, hoping delay would give him time to formulate plans.

Hell, Randy was in a jam. The least Franc could do was help him out of it. Too bad he couldn't claim his motives were entirely altruistic.

"Yes, I'd like that."

He got the distinct impression his goddess was just as eager to put off the meeting, and a spark of hope blossomed that all wasn't well in the house of Searle. "Okay, red or white?"

She rubbed the tip of her tongue over the spot her tooth had nibbled, his mouth watered for a taste of raspberries. What other flavor could lips that color be?

"A merlot would be nice, if it's not too much trouble."

"No problem, Ms...."

"Maria. Maria Costello."

She held out her hand…their fingers touched, skin sliding on skin…the world stopped spinning and threw him off.

He took a deep breath before he ended up with a foot between his teeth. He just couldn't get past the idea of Randy and the goddess as an item. The guy had all the inclination of a Casanova with none of the expertise. But filling his mouth with his own shoe leather wouldn't help his cause.

"I'm Franc Jellic."

Faint streaks of color fanned her cheeks. "Oh, I've heard of you. Nice to meet you at last."

"Heard of me?" He didn't like the sound of that one bit. It made her association with Randy resonate with words like *long term.* The back of his neck prickled. Funny place for a conscience, but he'd swear that's what it was, though he was a bit long in the tooth to start worrying about moving in on another guy's woman.

"I've read of your work in the business section of the *Herald.*"

He remembered the article; it had likened him to some sort of wunderkind. "I hope you took everything it said with a grain of salt. I'm not that good."

"Hah," she chuckled. "They always manage to get something wrong, and where I work, I tend to collect a fund of useless information. They never once mentioned modesty."

"Got me. Okay, now the introductions are over let me snag you a glass of wine." Guiding Maria through the crowd, he grabbed a full glass of wine from the small bar in the corner, hoping it was merlot. It was definitely red but he didn't have time to inquire. It would be just like Randy to arrive before Franc had time to hustle Maria out of the dining room.

"This way." Guiding Maria past the kitchen and out to the courtyard was both a bonus and a nightmare. He slipped one arm behind her and opened a passage into the courtyard with the other. The moment his fingers brushed bare flesh his heart jolted as if he'd touched a live wire.

"Sorry about that," he murmured. Sliding his palm closer to the top of her hip, which had no calming effect on his equilibrium whatsoever, Franc made a pretense of checking out the courtyard. Laughter and conversation were more prevalent than in the other room and most of the tables were occupied by more than two. Using the excuse of the music stealing through the corridor behind them, Franc leaned closer and spoke a bare inch from her ear. "I don't see him, do you?"

Maria took a step back as she turned to answer. "No, I don't." He saw her lip tremble as the glow of the Chinese lanterns highlighted the faint bloom of sweat beading her top lip and forehead. The step she'd taken pushed her close to the curve of his arm and through his shirtsleeve her skin felt on fire.

"You'll be better out here, where it's cooler than inside. I'll find you a table to wait at while I look for Randy." He found one overhung by ivy and a potted palm that filtered the pink lantern light.

A fat yellow candle burned in a ceramic pot and Maria motioned to it as she sat down. "I see someone took care of the mosquitoes."

"Huh?" he looked at her, his mind blank as she tipped up her glass and drank. Were his lies catching up to him?

"Can't you smell the candle? It's citronella."

The only scent teasing his nose was Maria's perfume and it reminded him of crushed rose petals. "You can be comfortable then while I send out a search party."

Sitting sideways, she leaned an elbow on the table, her wineglass swayed in the hand above it as she crossed her legs. "Don't go to too much trouble."

"I don't mind."

Her foot jiggled in midair, making a liar out of her. It was obvious she couldn't wait for Randy to arrive. Well, he'd see about that.

Her toenails were painted to match her dress and he found himself staring at them as he wondered if he could get Randy out of the restaurant before Maria became suspicious.

He flashed one last look at her toes as he turned. They would keep. "You just enjoy your wine while I go look for your boyfriend."

Boyfriend! Maria supposed that was the impression she'd intended—at first. Before Franc.

Quickly, she took her glasses from her purse, put them on her nose and glanced round the courtyard to make sure Randy really wasn't there. After taking them off, she took a sip of wine. It had the full-bodied flavor of a cabernet sauvignon. Maybe it would bolster her courage. Suddenly, the idea that confrontation would solve all her problems before she went home for Christmas seemed like the worst she'd ever had.

Wasn't it just like her luck to take a holiday on the night she met Franc Jellic. After years of knowing she had to keep herself safe from men, to meet a man who made her want to throw her heart into the ring and forget all her problems. He could almost pass for the description of the guy she'd told Mamma she was dating. She just hadn't believed such a man could be real.

But her imaginary man friend existed solely to prevent Mamma from insisting she go to Italy to pick out one of the nice Italian boys the family would parade in front of her. She'd acted secretive about the guy she was seeing, telling Mamma she wouldn't let him run the gauntlet of her family until she was sure of her feelings for him.

But, deep inside she was sure no other man could evoke the reaction she'd had to Franc. And in all probability, in a few moments he'd be ejecting her from the premises. What was it about him that called to her in this innately sensual way? Stirring her hormones. Filling her head with ideas about losing her innocence at last. Not that she'd dare give in to the devil prompting her imagination.

*Sometimes her imagination was her worst enemy.*

Her family was convinced that losing all memory of when she was abducted at seventeen was a good thing. They hadn't allowed for the scenes that ran through her mind each time she touched her scars and tried to picture how she'd gotten them.

More reason for her to confront Randy Searle tonight and put this stalking business behind her, once and for all.

She took another sip and another. The alcohol skipped her stomach and targeted her brain. She'd hardly eaten all day. Nerves. But if she were slightly numb, maybe giving Randy Searle his comeuppance wouldn't seem so daunting.

In the last few weeks he'd invaded her life, crushed her sensitivities with his grubby mind, violating her privacy. She was here to demand face-to-face that he *stop* stalking her.

Six feet and a crowded table away from the stairs, Franc's pores broke into a sweat at the sight of dark-clothed legs heading down them. He was at the foot of them before he recognized Brent, his general manager. "Hey, buddy, am I glad to see you."

Brent was almost as tall as his own six-four, but his slighter build made him look taller. "Whatever it is, no. I've done everything you've asked of me tonight, replaced every empty glass with a full one and danced with every wallflower until it feels like I'm wearing someone else's feet. I'd say that's enough favors for one night."

Franc gripped the banister and moved a step closer. "And it's all appreciated. But I kid you not, this one you'll enjoy. I want you to help me get rid of Randy Searle."

His friend's jaw dropped. "What? No way. You know I love you like a brother, Franc, but not enough to kill for."

Franc rolled his eyes, giving Brent a punch on the shoulder to emphasize his point.

"Idiot. I fancy the woman like crazy, but murder's too high a price even for a goddess."

"A goddess? I take it you aren't talking about Kathy, because that's who's with Randy. The pair of them were over each other like a rash. It got so bad I had to leave my bolt-hole and you know I'm a pretty tolerant guy, but man…"

Grinning, Franc said, "That's because you're a man of good taste, unlike Randy. No need to worry. That rash isn't catching."

He and Brent had been friends for years, working in the same line, electronic design, when the chance for a top job with Stanhope Electronics had come through a family connection—no nepotism involved. If he'd come up short on the qualifications, his new brother-in-law, Rowan McQuaid Stanhope, wouldn't even have considered him, or Brent, whom he'd taken with him.

"The guy's simply inconvenient. And what I'd like is Randy to leave and the woman who's called for him to stay."

"Let me guess. She's the most beautiful woman you've ever seen." Brent counted on his fingers. "How many times have I heard that?"

"A few, and not for at least a year, but this time I mean it for real. She's goddess material."

"That good, huh? So, it isn't just a coincidence that this is the start of the summer break. Or, that you have almost two weeks on your hands when Rowan and your sister have forbidden you to work."

"Never entered my mind."

"Bull! You've thought of nothing but the project for the last year, and as a workaholic you don't know how to switch off. Unless I miss my guess, you're looking for a distraction."

He couldn't pretend he wasn't already having withdrawal symptoms, Brent knew him too well, so he laughed, then said, "Wait till you see her. Just remember, you can look but you can't touch."

Brent ran his fingers through his sun-streaked brown hair, a habit that always made him look as if he'd just got out of bed, a woman's bed, which was usually right. So Brent had no need to point a finger in his direction. "I'm surprised you can even find the energy to contemplate a relationship."

"Okay, so you were half-right. I'm not talking relationship, just a holiday fling." He hadn't spent the last year working his butt off to blow it all now. If the project he and Brent were working on paid off, it would mean a partnership for him and a leg up in the company for Brent.

He caught a sigh building and pulled out before he could give breath to it. It was something he'd been aiming for since he was little more than a kid, to own part of something worthwhile. And as the son of a cop gone wrong there was no place to go but up. They hadn't been much of a family for a lot of years, but he was determined not to let his sister or himself down.

There were many ways of making money in the electronics industry, secrets to sell to the highest bidder, but that was the route his father had taken by dealing in drugs. Been forced to take, to Franc's mind because of all the mouths he'd had to feed on a cop's salary, and if he'd learned a lesson from his father's suicide, it was he travels farthest who travels alone.

Franc looked straight into the laughing derision in Brent's eyes. "What if I said I need this?"

"Tell me what you want me to do? Though I warn you, the last time I saw Randy, the only thought in his head seemed to be the quickest way to get Kathy out of her bra."

"How about you whisper a warning in his ear about the big guy downstairs looking for Kathy that could be her husband then show him the back way out through the kitchen?"

"So all's fair in love and war?"

"I don't think Randy's much of a fighter, and you know me." He shrugged his shoulders slightly, smiling as if he was about to tell a lie and wanted to lose the feeling. "I never fall in love."

"Just remember you owe me big-time for this one."

"Anything," he conceded. And before Brent could make any demands, he was on his way back to Maria as if his life depended on it. Which should have made him take pause. In all his adult life he'd never depended on anyone but himself. He knew better.

Everyone he'd ever loved had up and died on him.

A huge shadow slid across the table blocking off the light. Maria's heart bruised itself against her breastbone. She didn't look up. Instead, she breathed deeply, sucked up her courage and sat higher in her chair, trying hard to ignore the cold pulse beating in her temple as loud as hail on a tin roof.

Of all the foolhardy ideas in her life, tonight's had to be the worst. This was going to be harder than she'd first imagined.

Her hands shook as she lifted her gaze.

Franc slid into the seat opposite. His hands were full of wineglasses and snacks, the fingers of one cupping two glasses while he slid a plate of finger food onto the table.

"Thought you might be hungry." His mouth looked grim. "I hate to be the bearer of bad tidings, but it looks like Randy went on someplace else. Could he have gone over to your house?"

*God, she hoped not!*

Thoughts of Randy peeking in her window were the last thing she wanted. Now they'd entered her mind, would they ever go away?

"No, not my place."

For a heart-plummeting moment disappointment took her far away from the restaurant to a dark place inside her mind. When she'd calculated the risks of gate-crashing the party, Randy leaving early hadn't featured as a worst-case scenario. How would she get through the holidays with this dread hanging over her?

"Have a fresh glass of wine. These are nicely chilled." He pushed one over to her, and then picked up a lobster patty. "Delicious. You should try one."

This was awkward. She was here under false pretenses, how could she accept his hospitality. "I really should go. You must have better things to do than sit here with me."

"None that would please me more than sitting opposite a beautiful woman. I'm only human. Tell me about yourself. Do you work locally?"

"In the city, at Tech-Re-Search."

"I know the company, we have dealings with them. Is that how you met Randy?"

"Yes." How else had he latched onto her? Known her comings and goings?

"So you work in the city in a research library and your name is Costello. Were you born in New Zealand?"

"Of course."

His eyes flicked over her hair and face as he lifted the patty to his mouth and bit down. His teeth were white and even, and his face crinkled with laughter as his tongue captured a portion that broke off. He had an earthy confidence that exuded sexuality. Something reminded Maria of her long-ago visit to Italy, the way the men relished their food, wine and women.

"My roots in Enzed probably go back as far as yours."

His eyes glittered. "You wanna bet on it?" She shook her head. "I guess I could raise you at least a generation, maybe two on one side, if there was anyone I could ask, but my family isn't close-knit and the future interests me more than the past."

"Why is how many generations your family has been in New Zealand so important anyway, like we had some sort of *Mayflower* society?"

"It's a young country, how long ago your family arrived here is a sort of status thing."

She rolled her eyes at him even though she knew he was correct. "Well, my parents weren't born here, and probably because of that, in my family everyone likes to know what the others are up to."

Except this latest venture of hers. Wasn't a daughter obliged not to worry her parents? Maybe this was fate's way of telling her to back off. For now at least.

A stray drop of wine coated her lips as she chased it with her tongue. She raised her eyes and caught Franc's gaze.

"And what have you been up to, Maria?"

The question brought her back to the present with a start. What had she done to deserve Randy Searle stalking her? She'd only managed to catch a glimpse of him those few times, but she'd felt him. Felt his eyes on her and it gave her the creeps. It was as if her life wasn't her own anymore. Not that it had been anyone's idea of exciting. Her life had reached a plateau early on, what with studying for her degree by correspondence until she started work in Auckland three years ago, she'd only ever left home to take her exams at Massey University.

And if there had been little upswing in her social life since then it had been down to her own fastidiousness rather than a lack of opportunity. The friends she shared a house with were just the opposite. *God*, how she wanted to be like them, to be ordinary, to flirt, have on-and-off relationships.

The only bump in the even tenor of her life was being told she'd been abducted when she couldn't remember a thing about it. Post-traumatic stress amnesia, it had taken Randy Searle to flip her back out of her staid orbit.

She focused her attention on Franc. The flickering candle reflected in his eyes. "I expect since I had to think it over, you've gathered I haven't been up to anything exciting."

Franc leaned forward. "Well, I find you very exciting. Maybe it's the dress you're wearing. As if you're two different people."

The candle appeared to flare as he spoke, and her heart quickened when she realized the flame that leapt was confined to his eyes, and like the flash of light, she was out of place and way out of her depth. "Thank you, I think?"

"You got it right, it was a compliment, though I obviously made a hash of it since you didn't recognize it as one." His voice was low, husky, as if she really was the woman the dress had been designed for. As if with the fading of the light everything had changed and in the dark anything was possible.

"Then, I really do thank you." Had that sexy purr come

from her throat? Or was it the sophisticate she pretended to be? As soon as she'd seen the dress she'd known it was meant for her by the sheer ambiguity of the style. Full of half truths like her, it was perfect for a woman who didn't want to show her scars to the world. *Especially the emotional ones.*

Franc stood. He towered over her but there was no menace in him, simply the means to make her forget why she'd come here. "What if I said I'd rather have a dance than your thanks?"

She slid her fingers into his, her heart racing as she abandoned all thought of her previous goal. "I'd say, perhaps even two dances."

He pulled her to her feet. Even in heels her eyes only came level with his chin, perfect for watching his throat move as he swallowed hard. "Why don't we make that *all?* The rest of tonight's dances are mine."

His breath feathered across her eyelids. Made them flutter. Made them heavy, so heavy she wanted to close them and rest her head on his shoulder. The music grew louder as if it played in her head instead of at the other end of the passage.

Could this be her Cinderella night? What had she to lose but a slipper?

# Chapter 2

"I've had a wonderful evening." Maria's whisper reached Franc from somewhere below the level of his chin.

Soon it would be midnight. The lights were low, the music soft, and Maria was exactly where he'd wanted her from the first moment he'd observed her entering—in his arms, her body a mere heartbeat from his. Every few seconds her breasts brushed his chest, and on the turns his leg slid between hers. It was torture of the worst kind. And he never wanted it to end. "The evening's not over yet."

"But it will be, like all good things. That's life." Her voice sounded regretful, as if she didn't want to be wakened from the dreamlike state they were dancing in.

"I don't want to know that. I want to stay in the here and now and forget about tomorrow. This is a night for stolen kisses." He trailed one down her temple. "Soft touches." His fingers shivered down the skin covering her spine. "And secrets, lots of secrets."

"I already know your secrets."

"You what?" His head reared back, breaking the moment. Had Randy been running off at the mouth?

How the hell had Randy found out that practically before his dad's body had gone cold, his father's best friend and partner against crime in the New Zealand police had outed Milo Jellic as being a drug dealer.

As if Milo's suicide hadn't been bad enough.

"I'm sorry." She hid her eyes from him, but the way her white teeth pressed down on her lip was telling.

One look wiped his annoyance aside. "I hope Randy left me some secrets to share." His gaze dipped to the lip her teeth had left bee-stung. He'd taste that for himself before the night was over.

As Franc's face cleared, Maria's roiling stomach settled down. She hadn't ruined her night.

"It's nothing personal, just the new project." She galloped on, afraid to stop as his eyebrows met in a line. Perhaps personal would have been better? "I work on your project at Tech-Re-Search. It sounds so exciting to make a thread that carries…? Darn. I guess I shouldn't discuss it here."

Heavens, she'd just caught herself before she apologized again. Nothing was worse than sounding whiny.

"It's fascinating, but I'm not allowed to mention it at work…we have this Chinese wall deal…you know, no one can discuss the projects they are working on. But I think it's great that you guys are ahead of the game…" Was he never going to butt in and save her?

"So it's you who make sure we don't infringe on someone's copyright or spend a million dollars inventing something that's already out on the market. Somehow I had the impression that you'd met Randy through working on reception at Tech-Re-Search."

"No, I was called to reception since he wanted to hand over the envelope of data personally." She felt Franc's hand tighten round hers.

"Understandable. We don't just want anyone getting their hands on our data. That's why I was surprised you knew about our project." He hesitated then asked, "You don't discuss our research with Randy?"

Maria shook her head. So far, her only contact with Randy had been that day when he'd said he'd driven into the city specially to deliver the data to her at the research library. Heaven only knows what she'd done to spark off his need to stalk her.

"Good. This project is my baby, my idea. The research you're doing has saved us a lot of time but you understand, with its military applications, secrecy is vital." He huffed out a breath. "But of course you do. The only reason Tech-Re-Search got the contract was because of its security clearance."

"I hope your project succeeds." From the light in his eyes, and the determined thrust of his chin, she couldn't imagine him failing.

"You were right. This isn't the place to discuss it. One day, you can come see what we've done for yourself."

"I'd like that." Suddenly her mind was grasping at straws. Hoping her fairy tale wouldn't end with the ball. She had no illusions about forever, but even a little while would be nice.

Better than nice. Wonderful.

She allowed herself to hope.

Tomorrow, she'd start a new chapter in her personal journal.

Franc pushed out a long whisper of air. Spaced each breath, to slow his heart rate. He wanted her to himself away from the crowded dance floor. "Let's go out to the courtyard and dance in the dark. The stars are out. Do you know where to find the Southern Cross?" Next moment he heard Brent announce, "Last dance, folks, make the most of it."

"I should have thought of it earlier." Disappointment rocked him with intensity as he anticipated her departure. But he'd no time for soul-searching as nearly everyone squeezed onto the floor and space was at a premium.

The lights went out.

With Maria in his arms he stayed in the middle of the crowd, swaying slowly, feet barely moving. The slippery texture of her dress flowed like water under his palm. He let them drift lower until they slipped round the soft swell of her buttocks. He wanted to shape her curves with his hands, to pull her closer and rock her in the cradle of his hips.

He consoled himself with drinking in her perfume, brushing his cheek against the tiny whispers of curls escaping round her hairline. He had an ache in his groin hard enough to make a grown man cry. His teeth clamped down on a groan as her palms flattened against his chest and her head rested on them. Close, but not close enough.

He hoped the dance would never end. They circled one tiny spot on the floor in what felt like a dream, and in the dark no one existed but the two of them. His hard flesh throbbed and flexed unbearably against her hip. He wanted more than this tease. He wanted to be inside her, thrusting deep and fast till they both screamed their release.

His moan dampened her skin where the curve of her neck met jaw. *Damn, I'm thirty-four, too old for this, too old to be worrying about Maria knowing I want her. The hell with it!* His palms shivered over the silky fabric and curved round her slender shape, drawing her tight against his aching need just as the music stopped.

The song finished, ending the dance, ending the closeness. Maria didn't move, couldn't move. A fire blazed inside her, leaping the barrier of clothing to meld her to him. Could he feel her shake? If he moved would she fall? She hid behind closed eyes. It didn't mask the sound of people wishing each other Happy Christmas or good-night. Franc's lips skimmed her forehead as his hands loosened their grip, leaving her bereft.

"Merry Christmas, Maria," he whispered.

It was over. Time to go home.

The gruff timbre of his voice echoed in her tremors. Tilting her chin with one large hand, he sought an answer in her eyes. The pad of his thumb stroked her bottom lip and released a sigh. In that instant she changed her mind about the color of his eyes. Not bitter chocolate, bittersweet. Like the moment binding them. She wanted to remember this. She would remember this. *Always.*

The last time she expected she would see him. Tears blurred her vision. His face floated above hers like a mirage, until his mouth slanted and he took hers, blinding her with his nearness, his kiss, until only touch and sensation remained.

God! She tasted sweet; Franc had known she would. Her lips parted on a sigh and his tongue swept past them for a taste of the honey he knew lay within. Almost tentatively her tongue touched his and he felt her hands tremble and flutter like butterflies across his chest. It was more erotic than if she'd answered his passion with one of equal demand.

"Stay with me tonight. My apartment's just next door." The words grated from his throat as emotion took over. For one second he wished he hadn't said them. But only one.

As the lights came on she pulled away, her eyes huge, more violet than brown. They flicked from side to side, grounding her in the present. The party was over.

"No!"

Franc hesitated in mid-farewell-wave to a departing group. What did she mean, *no?* She couldn't mean it. Did she think he didn't know she wanted him as much as he wanted her?

"We shouldn't have done that," she said quietly.

Maria backed away, breaking the contact, taking her heat. Franc shivered. "Why?"

"We've had this evening. Why spoil it?"

"We could have tonight and no one would be spoiled but you. Let me spoil you."

His breath stirred long tendrils of her hair against her cheeks. She pushed them behind her ear, remembering how they'd gotten that way. Franc's fingers forking through her hair as he held her head still. "I need to call a cab."

She needed to get out of here before she did something stupid.

"I don't mind driving you home."

"No. I insist. It's better this way. Let me take a cab."

"All right. Tell me where you want to go and I'll call one."

Maria turned in her seat and watched out the back window of the cab, and without resorting to her glasses, she saw his tall figure soon blend into the shadows.

Franc Jellic was *almost* irresistible. And that six-letter word, *almost,* was her saving grace. She'd never met a man like him. Never been tempted until now, though she had been curious about her sexuality.

For a moment the answer to the puzzle had been within her grasp, until she banged into a wall of reality and the image of what might have been shattered as she hit. To bare her body, her scars would mean explanations. Explanations she couldn't give him. Explanations that wouldn't help her find the way out of the maze left by her abduction.

A sigh racked her body. She hugged herself to stop the tremors and tried to look on the bright side.

One thing for sure, she'd learned a lesson tonight. Learned how easily one could become trapped, brought to one's knees by a glance, both tender and wild at once. A glance that promised to teach all she wanted to know as it sent her body into meltdown and her heart into overdrive.

Yes, curiosity was all it would take. His kiss…how would it feel in the secret places where her body had throbbed as they danced? Would it ease the ache or sharpen the pain?

Christmas Eve had arrived with a bang. Heat sizzled in puddles of tar on the road and sunburned leaf tips spangled trees meant for the northern hemisphere with bronze. The only cloud in the sky was the leaden one hovering over Maria's head advertising her failure.

She mulled over her problems as she stood at the top of the driveway, waving to Tess and Linda, who she shared the villa with. "Bye, have a happy Christmas and a lovely holiday," she called, her thoughts nothing to do with the joys of the season. Soon she, too, would be hitting the road back to the bosom of her family.

*Bosom* being the appropriate word. There would be hugs all round. Papa and Mamma squeezed so tight, sometimes she could hardly breathe. It was their way of showing they loved her.

The word *suffocating* reared its head. Flushing, she pushed the thoughts away. Of course they were protective of her. They still tended to see her as the teenager who'd been abducted.

It was a weird situation. She couldn't remember anything. Yet it was impossible to forget the incident. Her family's concern kept it in the forefront of her mind.

Yes, *incident* was a better word.

It was real, yet unreal. A story told from someone else's point of view. Lately, she'd begun to waken in the dead of night in a panic from nightmares. It dated from the moment she realized someone was shadowing her footsteps.

A faint ping sounded at the back of her mind like the first warning note of an alarm. The impression sent her spinning round to scan the front garden and faded just as quickly when she saw the old man next door raking the pebbles on his driveway. Being unable to carry through last night's plans had left her jumpy, knowing Randy Searle was still on the loose, didn't realize she was on to him or that she knew his name.

Alone in the house, she cleared the festive lunch table where they'd exchanged gifts. The other girls had protested, but saw her logic, conceding her journey home was less lengthy than the ones facing them.

She pushed her glasses up on her nose, her spare pair. On

her way home this afternoon she'd stop by the restaurant to see if her others had been found where she'd placed them on the table. But before she left, since she had plenty of time, she'd walk around to the shop next to Northcote Point cinema and buy her mother a box of the handmade chocolates she loved.

As she washed up, flashes of memory from the night before filled her thoughts. Could any woman ever forget her first real taste of romance?

The trick would be to make sure no memories of Randy Searle were allowed to taint it. Thank heavens she'd made time to write it all down in her journal before sleep overtook her.


Franc wrote his signature on the check with a flourish. Stanhope's annual Christmas party didn't come cheaply, but it was worth it for the goodwill and camaraderie it engendered in the staff. He passed the check over the tall, narrow desk to the manager. "How much of this covers breakages?"

Paul Start, the manager of The Point restaurant, grinned. "You got off lightly, no more than two or three glasses." Always one for an eye to business, Paul winked. "Come back next year. You're the kind of customer we like."

Just as astute, Franc took his receipt, glanced at the figures again and said, "Next time, I'll ask for a discount."

Paul's eyes narrowed, calculated. "Do that. Next time, you might get one. But for now, how about having lunch? On the house."

"Thanks, I will."

He should have known that eating lunch in almost the exact spot he'd held Maria in his arms wouldn't aid his digestion.

He looked up at the entrance and relived his reactions of the night before when he'd watched her walk through it.

He'd likened her to a goddess, and when his ardor had carried him away, she'd spurned him. Didn't mean he was going to give up or take his rejection as absolute.

There had to be a way.

No sooner thought than found.

Paul slid into the seat opposite. "I forgot to hand over these." He twisted fragile-looking rimless glasses in his fingers so they caught the light. "One of the cleaners found them at the table by the potted palm."

Franc recalled how her pupils had been huge as they turned the lights on at the end of the dance. Could the look that had enchanted him been slightly myopic?

Taking the glasses from Paul, he slid them into the pocket of his thin chambray shirt. "Thanks, Paul. I'm sure I know who these belong to."

Mind made up, he tossed his napkin onto his plate and pushed his chair away from the table. "Her place is on my way, so I'll drop them off." He'd written the address down when he'd called her cab, though he'd been sure it was one he wouldn't forget.

"Good idea. I couldn't see a thing through them, so she's probably lost without them." Paul stood up, saying conversationally, "So where are you off to this afternoon?"

Knowing that Paul had often commented on his many lonely dinners, Franc just tapped his pocket. "Anywhere that takes me past where she lives."

Maria couldn't remember the last time she'd taken the car out. Working in the city, she traveled mainly by bus. It was convenient and less hair-raising than driving over the Auckland Harbour Bridge each morning and evening.

She unlocked the car and slid inside, placing her purse on the passenger seat along with the chocolates she'd just bought. If she started the car, she could leave it running while she went in to change out of her lilac crop top and shorts.

Key in the ignition, she turned it, pressing down on the accelerator at the same time. The starter engine turned over a few times then faded away. She turned the key again with less success than before.

Nerves tightening, aware there was no one she could ask for help, she gripped the key in a death lock. The third attempt ended in a couple of clicks.

She recognized that sound, it meant the battery was dead or the connection was loose. Her brothers were always on at her to turn over the engine occasionally between her visits home. Now she wished she'd taken their advice. In contrast to her vision, her hindsight was always twenty-twenty.

In no time at all, she'd popped the hood and stood blinking into its dark depths. The battery was easily recognized. She wiggled the connection. It seemed nice and tight apart from the green gunk sprouting from under the plastic cover.

Shifting her exploration to the trunk, she grabbed the tool kit and unrolled it on the concrete. The huge screwdriver looked handy, so she grabbed it.

As she stood, she felt the back of her neck tingle as if someone had laid a cold hand on her nape. Her stomach plummeted like a bird in freefall while the rest of her was shocked into immobility.

He was here.

As she began to take stock, Maria wrapped her hand round the metal shaft of the screwdriver, holding it like a club as she took a deep breath then whirled around.

The heavy frames on her old glasses slid down her nose as she spun. Great, now she could see nothing. She pushed the black frames higher on her nose with the back of an oil-smudged hand.

Over the last month there'd been times when she'd balanced on the edge of panic. Since the first day she'd felt someone's eyes on her, there had been other occasions with no one in sight when she knew he'd hidden to watch.

*Like now.*

The air bristled with static energy that prickled her skin as if a storm was brewing, but with not a cloud in the sky she knew that wasn't the reason.

On the edge of the garden, the bushes stirred between the

villa she and her friends rented, and the one next door. She started to shake. Why had no one put in fences? They helped keep people out.

Stop!

This is what he wants. Don't give him the satisfaction. A few deep breaths in out, in out, that's it. Calm down and find the courage you took to the party last night. He can't scare you if you don't let him.

The next-door neighbor's cat, Mimzie, sauntered out of the bushes, tail high. It looked straight at her, as if to say, "It's only me."

Only him. She wanted to believe that desperately.

But the creepy sensation she got when she felt *him* watching her hadn't gone. And to pretend that it had would be a cop-out.

"Everything all right, Maria?"

Her eyes lost their focus as her thoughts turned inward. Someone was walking up the driveway; he wore a white T-shirt and dark blue jeans. Not Randy, thank heaven. It was one of the young guys from a house down the street. "My car won't start.. Tony, am I right?"

He reached the top of the driveway and moved into the shade of the carport. One hand pushed a lock of straight surfer-blond hair from his eyes. His smile was cocky. "That's me, Tony Cahill, the one and only. What happened? Wouldn't that huge screwdriver scare the motor into submission?"

"I thought the problem might be the battery leads. I was going to try tightening them up with this." She waved the screwdriver at him. "Or if that didn't work, take the wooden handle and knock off all this verdigris that's growing out of it." She turned around and looked at the engine.

He was tall, which meant he had to duck to fit under the hood. "Let me have a look." He moved in close, his shoulder brushing hers. "You're right, it does look a bit of a mess."

Maria flinched as his arm snaked round her back. His arm sweated on her bare skin as his hand skimmed the underside of her breast and lingered before he reached under her arm for the screwdriver. "Let me see what I can do."

Maria was trapped, but she wouldn't let go of the screwdriver, What if she needed it to defend herself? She elbowed him in the ribs. "Creep! I think you've done quite enough. You can go now. Your kind of help I can do without."

Franc had parked on the road. He could see Maria and some lanky kid bending over the open hood of a car, arguing. Urgency lengthened his stride. "Is this a private tussle or can anyone join in?"

The kid jerked his arm away from Maria and a huge screwdriver bounced off the chrome bumper of the outdated Ford and onto the concrete paving, where it lay humming like a tuning fork.

Maria recovered quickly and literally threw herself into his arms. Not that he minded or needed reminding how she'd felt in his arms last night. "Franc! I thought you were never going to get here."

So they were into playacting. "Sorry, sweetheart, time got away from me." He took a chance and stole a kiss.

She moved into it like a true drama queen that had just heard "Lights, camera, action," but the sigh and the flutter of her eyelashes weren't put on. She was glad to see him. "My car won't start."

"I was trying to help her but she wouldn't let go of the damn screwdriver." The kid shook his head. His tow-hair shadowed the disgust in his eyes as he moved away from the car. "Women."

"Thanks for your help, but I'll take over now." Franc narrowed his eyes and gave the kid the once-over as he held out his hand.

Hesitating under the scrutiny, the kid stuck out his fist and took Franc's, saying "You're welcome."

As if to confirm the hours he'd spent in the gym weren't wasted, Franc firmed his grip. "See you around."

Tony rubbed his palm on the side of his thigh as he started moving away. "Sure, I got somewhere to go."

As soon as the kid turned his back, Maria laid into Franc. "You actually—" her voice shook as gave what for her passed as a growl "—thanked him!"

"Did I have any reason not to?"

"Tony touched my breast."

A curse not meant for women's ears ripped out of his throat. "I should have broken his arm!"

*From the bushes he watched them as he stroked the cat.*

*Watched Jellic's hands on her as he held her close then turned her back toward the car he'd taken such care to disable.*

*A new player in the game added excitement, but two was too many. If the young one came back he'd have to make an adjustment.*

*He almost smiled at the thought.*

*And at the same time he might use the modification to make sure Jellic didn't get too close to her. He'd recognized him straight away and knew his competition would be a force to be reckoned with.*

*Such care and attention Jellic took of her, as if she was fragile. But only he knew how truly fragile Maria was. Ten years hadn't changed that, or removed her look of innocence.*

*The innocence he'd taken for his own.*

Half an hour later when the jump leads from Franc's battery to hers made no difference, he threw in the towel. In fact, he screwed it up in a ball and chucked it in disgust. "We're going to have to get the car towed."

"Marvelous. It's Christmas Eve, no one's going to want to know. How am I going to get home?" Maria knew she sounded selfish after all Franc's efforts, but she'd been looking forward to a couple of nights at home with the family, the one place she knew she'd be safe from Randy Searle.

"Leave it to me," he said. "I know a garage."

Franc was as good as his word, as far as it went, but even he couldn't get her car fixed on Christmas Eve. Close on an hour slipped away as if made of water as they waited for a tow truck.

Business was obviously too good.

"I need to ring home. Maybe one of my brothers can spare the time away from the wife and kids to come and get me," she said as Franc drank his second cup of coffee.

She'd punched in the area code and the first two digits, when a shadow fell across her and loomed large on the wall. Habit sent a shiver to ice her spine, and she knew there was no way she could stay here tonight alone with only her fears to keep her company.

A glance was enough to dispel them for now. Franc filled the door frame with his shoulders, bracing one against the jamb while his hand gripped the frame overhead. "Leave that for now. I have a better suggestion. Let me run you home."

"That would be an imposition. I couldn't do that to you the night before Christmas. I don't even know why you turned up here in the first place, but I am grateful you did."

He tapped his shirt pocket. "Damn! I didn't return your glasses. I see now there wasn't a rush. In fact, the ones you're wearing look pretty cute. They're the kind that prove you can look like a librarian and still be sexy."

In the narrow hallway the atmosphere hummed with tension left over from the night before. It licked up the back of her neck in a way that made her head spin. It was all she could do to give him a sensible answer. "I keep telling you, I'm not that kind of librarian. I'm a researcher." The husky murmur she achieved was less than sensible, but she couldn't take it back.

He quirked an eyebrow at her to ask, "Does that mean you'll save me the research and tell me where you want to go?"

But it was his crooked smile that had her saying, "The

family vineyard is on the other side of Matheson's Bay. It normally takes about two hours from Auckland, but tonight the roads will be jammed with traffic both ways.''

No matter how much she wanted to get home, she had to warn him, ''If you give me a lift, I can't see you getting back to Auckland much before midnight.''

''No worries, I'm a night owl. Besides, didn't you say your brothers have kids? I'd feel bad about them missing out on all the fun, of hanging stockings and setting out the presents.''

Franc had just flicked the off switch on her original idea. She couldn't take her brothers away from their children on Christmas Eve, no matter how much she dreaded spending a night in the house alone. ''You're right. It wouldn't be fair. I accept your offer, but I hope you don't regret making it.''

''What's to regret?'' He made a joke of it. ''I'll do anything if it gets me an extra three hours with my favorite woman.''

Maria's eyes widened a moment then fluttered closed, leaving Franc with a picture of bruised violets crushed underfoot to tug at his conscience, because there was an element of truth in what he'd said.

''I know you're teasing since we only met last night, but I can't take *you* from *your* family on Christmas Eve, any more than I could take one of my brothers away from his family.''

*His family?* Hell, his sister was the only member of it he'd met up with in years.

''That's because you're judging my family by your standards. We're all pretty much loners. Or we used to be. My sister got married last year, so you can count her out, but my brothers will be working through the holiday. She's the only one of us who's married, the rest of us are married to our jobs.''

Drago, the eldest, would be up to his neck in his latest book on the wines of New Zealand. As for the twins, just above Franc in age, Kurt would be hip-deep in work on the lodge he would open next year at Aoraki, Mount Cook National Park, not far from Queenstown, a tourist resort that had two busy seasons, winter for the skiing, and the rest of the year for the tourists.

The other Jellic twin, Kel, could be anyplace on the Pacific Rim, investigating drug trafficking, as if he lived his life in a movie. But in his case, the danger was real. And so secret he hadn't contacted Franc when he'd been in town a few weeks ago. Kel had been in Auckland only last month and hadn't even given him a call.

"And tomorrow, what are your plans?"

"Much of them revolve around kicking back on my own, watching the Sports Channel and eating the giant turkey-and-cranberry pizza I have stashed in the freezer." Now that he'd said it out loud, he guessed it didn't sound like anyone's idea of a perfect Christmas, but after a year spent slogging his guts out, it had been his notion of hog heaven.

"Let's make a deal then. I'll let you drive me home if you will stay the night." Maria raised twin arched eyebrows over eyes that brought his protest stuttering to a halt. "You wouldn't want me sleepless through worrying if you made it home safely?"

Franc wasn't about to contradict her. The only way he wanted her sleepless was in his arms, in his bed, moaning because she couldn't get enough of him...

A sensation that prickled like a warning crept through the short hairs at the back of his neck. It followed the thought, *But would he ever get enough of her?*

What the hell was the matter with him? He'd been given about two weeks out of his usual routine. Twelve days max to indulge in a lighthearted fling, with one of those days already struck off and another well on its way.

With a flick of his wrist he checked his watch, reading the time past the scratches on the glass. For all it was gold, its slightly battered condition usually raised a few eyebrows until he mentioned it had been his father's. The nods of understanding this engendered always wanted to make him laugh. The timepiece wasn't worn to remind him of his father, its job was to remind him not to follow in his footsteps.

His father had crossed the line for money, but Franc would far rather be an honest jerk than a dead one like his dad.

"Isn't it a bit late to expect your parents to put up a stranger for the night."

"You don't know Mamma. For her, nothing is impossible. Please say you'll stay, then I can call and tell her you're bringing me home with a clear conscience."

"Okay, I guess one night couldn't hurt."

Maria shrugged as she put down the receiver. Her mother had sounded odd when she asked if Franc could stay the night. The inquisition she'd expected had been glaring by its absence. Instead, she'd caught a hint of relief in the brisk no-nonsense acceptance that Maria was bringing a friend home—for the first time. Although, it might simply be gratitude that Papa wouldn't have to drive all that way to fetch her.

"Point me in the direction of your bag and I'll carry it out while you make sure the house is secure."

"I was going to change first."

His gaze traveled from the tips of her toes to her face, trailing a flush of color in its wake where the blood rushed under her skin. "I don't see what's wrong with what you're wearing, but give me a whistle when you're ready."

This was the type of treatment her brothers dished out, they were as protective of her as Mamma and Papa. "If you insist, but my case really isn't that heavy."

The house was a Victorian villa with a shotgun hallway that ran from front to back. Like a lot of others on Northcote Point it had been built long before Auckland Harbour Bridge had been a twinkle in the designer's eye. She dashed into her room, grabbed her clothes from the wardrobe then dived across the hall into the bathroom, locking the door behind her. It wasn't that she had any reason not to trust Franc, quite the opposite. But the business with Randy had made her look at every man in a new light.

So, where were your senses this afternoon when you gave Tony a chance to paw you?

After changing with the speed of a catwalk model, she whistled for Franc as instructed and discovered he hadn't gone far when he appeared almost immediately, striding down the hall as if he owned the place. Some men carried an aura with them that made them at home anywhere. She guessed Franc was one of them.

She pushed back her bedroom door and pointed. ''That's my case on the bed. As you can see it's quite small.''

His eyebrows shaped a V above the high bridge of his nose. ''Are you sure you could get everything you need in there? We won't drive halfway and discover you've forgotten something vital that means we have to turn around and fetch it?''

Franc's question was a big giveaway to the type of women *he* was used to dealing with. For sure they weren't like her. If she forgot anything, *she* was the one who had to go back for it. ''Don't worry. I keep a lot of casual gear at home. Most of my clothes here are strictly for business.''

Franc's breadth made the bedroom walls close in on her. It was hard to be nonchalant about his presence beside her bed when what she wanted to do was quickly dodge past him to check that the windows were locked. She flicked a sideways glance at him from under her lashes, but his attention wasn't on her. Following his gaze, she was mortified to see a pale pink lace chemise hanging out of the top drawer of the dresser, next to the bed.

She was usually so tidy, tucking everything in place the way the nuns had taught her at boarding school. Franc's presence in the house must have flustered her.

And now her secret was out. Compared to the rest of her everyday wardrobe, her lingerie was *hot*.

It hadn't seemed to matter that no one knew as it meant no

one saw the scars her beautiful silk scanties were too small to hide.

Maria had been careful not to get into a situation that meant a man would expect to see her body, though the need to hide her scars hadn't bothered her until now. Until Franc.

"Nice..." She heard the grin in his voice though his face never twitched.

She shaped her lips into a fierce grimace that only broadened his grin. "You never saw that," she told him as she tucked the pink lace back where it belonged. "My mother would have a fit. She's inclined to be old-fashioned."

"When it comes to daughters, most mothers are," he answered, yet his eyes said more. Touched more. He was doing it to her again, taking her libido on a journey it had never traversed before. Something shifted inside her, a need, a wanting, an ache.

She did her best to ignore it.

Franc studied her single bed as he picked up her case to leave. Neat and virginal, with family photographs on the nightstand; under its flower-sprigged quilt was hardly the place to conjure steamy dreams in the middle of the night. Unlike in his bed last night. Dreams stymied until he confronted Maria and his bed in one and the same place.

It didn't seem to matter any longer that he'd first met her while she was looking for Randy. The last few hours made him certain that associating with Randy had done nothing to taint the innocence she exuded. How would it feel to have Maria surrender that innate innocence to him?

For Franc Jellic, it would be an unmistakable first.

Maria reached up to check the catch of the old-fashioned sash window closest to her bed. It was undone.

Newly formed ice, at odds with the temperature inside the room, slicked over her skin as she swiveled the small lever into place. Her gaze landed on the drawer she'd divested of its lacy adornment. She never treated her clothes that way or left her room untidy. Her training was too ingrained.

Her eyes searched the garden, focusing on the bushes Mimzie the cat had disturbed, unmoving now as if weighed down by the heat. Had someone been in her room? Randy?

Or was her imagination working overtime?

Wasn't her journal farther over on the nightstand than she could easily reach from in bed? She grabbed it and put it in her purse. Hurrying to leave before Franc came back to look for her, she glanced over her shoulder, scanning the room, remembering the position of every ornament, every picture frame.

No matter how terrifying the prospect, she just had to know if anyone came into her room and touched her things while she was away. Then, on an impulse, she turned back, re-opening the drawer to scoop up an armful of silk and lace underwear. Quivering, she tossed every last piece into the laundry basket.

Whether anyone had gazed at her ultrafeminine garments with lust in their heart she had no way of knowing, but the thought of it made her wonder what would happen if she told Franc. Would he help her see that Randy Searle got what was coming to him?

Or would he put it down as a flight of her imagination.

As she locked the door behind her, she remembered the cat next door sidling out of the bushes between the two properties. She still had the feeling she wasn't alone and she wasn't thinking of Franc.

Her last thought as she slid into the passenger seat was a prayer that he wouldn't follow her home.

## Chapter 3

The journey north hadn't taken Franc as long as Maria predicted, and because of that, he'd stopped the car on the brow of a hill at a scenic outlook where Maria said the view of the coast was at its loveliest.

"I wish you could see the view properly. From this distance it's muted around the edges, like an impressionist painting. I always think the best thing about going away is coming home again. How about you?"

"The view looks fine to me. As for going home, give me until tomorrow to see if that's true. This is my first trip away from my new apartment."

"Oh, I'm sorry." Maria turned to face him, and something like sympathy flashed across her perfect features. "Is that why you wanted to stay home for the holiday? How long have you lived at Birkenhead Point?"

"Three months. I haven't done much to the place yet. I bought it as it stood along with most of the furniture."

"So that's why it looks...?" She'd braved the kitchen and

dining room and lounge of Franc's apartment while he grabbed an overnight bag.

"Don't tell me it needs a woman's touch. It was a woman who designed it. Once I've had time to collect a little clutter of my own it will look different." Work wouldn't always be this frantic. One day soon he'd be able to indulge in the things he'd never had, like good paintings and pieces of furniture to his own taste that would take away the blank-canvas effect.

"I wasn't going to say that. But from the little I saw of the apartment when you picked up your gear, it didn't reflect your personality. It lacks your warmth."

He hadn't expected her be so perceptive, not when he'd been doing his damnedest to make sure their relationship was about sex, sex and more sex. Getting to know Maria better bore some considerations that went beyond trying to get her into bed with him. "Dare I take that as a compliment?"

"That would depend on how you see yourself."

This was a moment that called for a kiss. On the other hand, in his Porsche Boxter only a contortionist could achieve the desired effect with any elegance.

He settled for tucking a few errant strands of slippery black hair behind her ear. It gave him a better view of her profile, short nose, full lips and the small mole that drew attention to them. A slight movement toward him turned his gesture into a caress as his fingers grazed her cheek. He felt a short sharp jolt in his chest. Face on, her features became twice as heart stopping and he had to force his reply out of a larynx gone rusty. "Definitely a compliment then. Thank you."

"Don't thank me too soon. If I know Mamma, she'll want chapter and verse about you and your family. So don't say I didn't warn you."

"Warning heeded, but I doubt it's necessary, I'll only be there overnight." No way could he tell Maria's mother about Milo Jellic. Chances were if he did, his stay was likely to be of shorter duration. He'd learned that with some people of an older generation the sins of the fathers were still visited on their sons, especially with his father's dubious history.

Bile spiked in his throat, taking him back to a past he'd thought was well and truly gone.

Abruptly he spun the wheel and pulled the car out onto the road. The sun had nearly finished its plunge into the hills behind them, and ahead scraps of pink reflection were strewn across the sea like silk banners.

With distance to add magic, house windows shone out of a denser patch of horizon, draping it with festive lights, a scene undiluted by knowing the truth. "I take it that's Kawau Island?"

"Yes, it looks so different at this time of year. The population triples round the bays and inlets at Christmas. Home will be quiet in comparison. We ought to be there soon."

Maybe it wouldn't be so bad. He was used to meeting strangers, selling himself and his ideas, that's what had got him where he was today. What was wrong about spending one night out of a lifetime where, for a change, he had nothing to gain?

Except maybe their daughter? But then, he only wanted to borrow Maria, not keep her for good.

"How far to go now?" he asked as they sped down the hill and the lights on the horizon disappeared from view.

"We're almost there. Look, over to the left. Can you see the lights winking through the vines? That's the southern edge of our boundary."

The car headlights illuminated a two-story white house with a blue roof and matching shutters. Welcoming lights shone out from the front porch. Kids' picture-book stuff. And he was the guy whizzing the princess home. What did that make him, white knight, or wizard with evil intentions?

Only time would tell.

Rosa congratulated herself that when Maria had called earlier, to ask if Franc could stay the night, she hadn't let her excitement show. This was an event that required marking on the calendar after all these months; her daughter was bringing the man she was dating home. The mystery man she'd wanted to keep to herself for a while. She supposed she couldn't blame her; the Costellos en masse might scare away a prospective suitor.

Instead of the multitude of questions Rosa had wanted to ask, she'd simply said, "Yes, yes, bring him with you, we'll see you soon," and hung up.

From the window, she watched the sports car negotiate the gravel driveway. With its top down she could see Maria's friend was exactly as she'd described him all those months ago. The car's momentum blew his dark hair back from his forehead, a strong wide forehead. He looked reliable, the kind of man who wouldn't hurt her baby, she thought with relief. At last she and Papa could go ahead with their plans without worrying.

She'd probably taken her mother away from the stove. Mamma loved to cook and always overdid the food at the holiday season, but then that was Mamma.

Maria knew that when they got inside, the house would be filled with the delicious aromas of lemons, dried fruits and spices. And tomorrow morning, her sister and sisters-in-law would add to the feast till the house overflowed with people and food.

Mamma was out on the porch by the time they drew up. The shutters behind her had faded to a milky-blue and the wraparound porch was overgrown with jasmine, but Maria wouldn't change a thing. That's what made it home.

Franc helped her out of the car just as her mother made it to the steps. Tiny and plump, her dark hair liberally streaked with silver, it didn't stop her from leaping down the steps like an eager teenager.

Maria knew what was coming of old.

From one step up, Mamma easily reached her face, running

her hands over it, looking into her eyes. "You're so pretty, but why don't you get contacts and let people see your eyes properly?" Then before Maria could reply, she cut her off by asking, "Have you been eating properly? You look thinner."

"Never miss a meal, Mamma. I've been working hard."

She saw her mother look past her shoulder at Franc as he pulled their bags out of the trunk. "Playing hard too, maybe. You need your sleep."

"I'm okay, Mamma, don't worry. Come meet my friend."

"Franc, I'd like you to meet my mother, Rosa Costello." Maria pulled him over. "Mamma, this is Franc Jellic."

Franc held out his hand. He had expected someone more like Maria, but this little woman had hands like quicksilver, and their movement added emphasis to every word she spoke.

Maria finished introducing him. "Franc's family came here from Dalmatia." It was as if by telling her mother this, she created a bond between them that Rosa would approve of.

"Great, this year we'll have a United Nations. I expect you know Papa and I are from Italy, but did Maria tell you Kris, her brother-in-law, is German."

Rosa smiled up at him, her eyes sparkling as she took his hand. "I'm happy to meet you, Franc." Reaching up, she gave his cheek a gentle tap. "You be good to my girl."

"Oh, Mamma." Maria protested loudly, as if shocked.

Rosa just laughed. "Franc understands."

"You could say I got the message." Could this woman see right through him? He tightened his gut. What happened when he got inside, would they bring out the thumbscrews?

"See, I told you, he understands. I'm glad this daughter of mine has brought you to meet us at last. Welcome to our home."

Franc darted a glance toward Maria, waiting for her to correct the misunderstanding. When she didn't, he began to say, "No—"

"I know," cut in Rosa. "No time. People in Auckland are

always busy, but you're here now. That's all that matters. Come on inside and meet the others." To Maria, she said, "Papa gave me a moment to have you to myself."

"I bet he's just keeping out of the way in case you start weeping all over us. He knows how sentimental you are at Christmas." Maria stepped between them, slipping a hand through each of their arms, separating them as they climbed the steps to the porch.

Her mother chuckled, "No, if you hadn't come—then I might have cried. The others can thank Franc that it won't come down to that."

Rosa leaned forward and looked at Franc. "Maria doesn't come home often enough to suit me." She looked him up and down and winked. "But I suppose I can't blame her."

Franc lifted an eyebrow at Maria for guidance.

She scrunched up her eyes and mouthed the word *wait* then turned to her mother. "You said others, who else is here?"

"Everyone. It's a surprise, the whole family is here to spend Christmas together under one roof."

Maria had a premonition of doom. No wonder her mother hadn't been able to take the time to speak to her earlier. She wondered who'd be sleeping on the couch, her or Franc. But her mother hadn't finished. "I've put you two in the small rooms at the end of the house."

She looked at Franc again as if measuring him up. "Only single beds, I'm afraid, and the connecting bathroom is tiny, but I'm sure you'll manage. The children can all squeeze into one room for a change. I expect they'll like that better anyhow. I just hope we can put up with the noise." She chuckled. "This is going to be a wonderful Christmas."

For years after her abduction, her family had kept her close, their way of protecting her from the big bad world. Now, her mother had done an about-face with a vengeance.

What really bothered her was Mamma's willingness to throw her into the arms of the first man Maria had ever brought home.

For the moment, all she could do was go with the flow and explain to Franc later. She squeezed his arm as they entered the large sitting room. "I'll explain after," she whispered, hoping Franc got her message and that his sense of humor was in line with her own.

The moment he entered the sitting room Franc realized he was outnumbered. The words *enemy territory* flashed before his eyes.

The huge sitting room ran the full width of the house and was practically bursting at the seams, adults, kids...cats. In self-defense, he bent to pick up the cat, giving his hands something else to do other than drag Maria out of there and back into his own comfort zone.

As his brain worked on his problem, he counted six children, my God, *six,* and five adults, not including the three of them entering the room.

Everyone talked at once, and the snatches of conversation he managed to pick up made no sense. Rosa brought a tall slim man with dark thinning hair, who, from the looks of him, couldn't be anyone other than Maria's father. Franc let the cat spring to the floor as everyone stopped talking. And stared at him. Now he understood what it meant to be put under a microscope.

"Franc, this is Pietro, Maria's father."

Somewhere in the back of his mind Franc heard a clang of metal gates shutting behind him. Trapped.

Everything in the room, the people, the atmosphere, all the kids, were perfect reminders of why he didn't do the family thing. The urge to run a finger round inside his collar made his hand itch, but he kept it clamped by his side. It was all too much like sitcom material.

Pietro clasped his hand, shaking it heartily, with a hand that was as tanned as his face. His dark eyes creased into a hundred lines as his laughter kept time with the energetic pumping of hands. Hard calluses bit into Franc's knuckles. Lean and sinewy, like the hands of a man who had worked hard all his life, they carried as little meat as the rest of the older guy's body.

"Welcome. We thought Maria was never going to let us meet you. And tonight is the ideal time."

There it was again. The family had him confused with someone else. Randy maybe, though that thought stung in spades.

Why didn't Maria just come right out and tell them? Set them straight, for Pete's sake?

He glanced at her; she shook her head, and left him none the wiser. He read embarrassment, and maybe a little confusion in her expression at her father's effusive welcome.

As Pietro let go, Franc reached out for Maria, meshing his fingers with hers. For a couple of seconds he rubbed both sets of knuckles against his thigh on the off chance it would relieve the tension gripping him.

A damn futile course of action as it turned out. How could he have known it felt the natural thing to do, as if they often communicated this way?

His heart turned traitor, thudding against his breastbone as he found himself wishing it wasn't a lie.

*Escape.*

A wiser man would have turned on his tail and run. Franc caught the inside of his cheek between his teeth as if grounding himself in the present instead of cloud cuckoo land where all this junk was happening to him. "So? Apart from Christmas, what's so special about this evening?" Franc asked, before realizing he might have left himself open to some crazy suggestion.

Laughingly, Pietro slapped him on the shoulder. "You will find out soon, we've been waiting for you both to arrive. But first…" He turned to Maria. "Introduce Franc to the rest of the family while I open some wine."

Then he turned to Rosa, saying, "Wineglasses, Mamma."

Maria squeezed Franc's fingers, stopping him voicing the question at the forefront of his mind. "Don't let this lot scare you off, Franc. They can be a bit overpowering at first."

"Like this situation, you mean."

She studied his eyes. For all his abrupt statement of the facts, warmth softened their depths, making her knees go weak. "Can you wait until later for an explanation? Please? I don't want to embarrass my parents. Mamma in particular."

He released her hand, but the imprint of his remained as she waited to hear him say no. Instead, he looped an arm around her shoulders, stooping closer so no one else could hear, and whispered, "I intend to keep you to your word. And it had better be good." That said, Franc continued to hold her against the lean muscled strength of his body as they moved farther into the room.

Last night, they'd danced almost as close, so the combination of aftershave and his peculiarly male muskiness filling her head was already fixed in her memory. But she hadn't known a man's body could burn with such heat. A heat so strong it made her want to melt into him and over him till she couldn't tell where she began and he ended.

Her insides clenched and she almost cried out with the strangeness of the sensation. This was desire, and until Franc, she'd never known its effect could be so utterly physical.

The journey of a few feet seemed to have lasted a mile. Now, an arm's length away from the generations of Costello, born in New Zealand, she warned him, "Okay, take a deep breath and keep in mind most of us are of Italian descent. If they ask anything embarrassing, just pretend you didn't hear, and answer someone else's question."

He slightly pushed away, flicking her with a glance that said, "You've got to be kidding."

So, he was new to the game. He'd learn.

There didn't seem to be as many of them with everyone sitting down, now he'd gotten over the hurdle of meeting them all, and the shock of having two more adults appear from the kitchen.

Way past their bedtime, the children still rolled around the faded Persian rugs, pushing, shoving, laughing and squabbling over toys, but no one appeared worried.

The sitting room was comfortably, yet tastefully decorated, suitable for a big family. Long and narrow, open French doors led to a tiled patio at the far end of the room where a breeze drifted in, lifting the sheer curtains hanging on either side.

"Quiet, you lot," ordered Giovanna, a younger version of Rosa, who was married to Kris; she sat with a baby on her knee. Two of the older boys looked up for a second and went back to their game, and the noise continued.

Everyone, her sister, brothers and their various spouses were being very nice, too nice. Suffocatingly nice.

Look-how-good-it-is-to-be-married nice.

If it hadn't been his suggestion to drive Maria home, he could almost think he'd been set up. It was as if the Costellos were husband shopping for their little sister and his name was on the top of their list. All *he* wanted to do was find a big black pen and score it out.

Maria appeared to be going along with the charade that they'd known each other a lot longer than two days, when she deferred to his opinion. "What do you think, Franc?"

And she smiled a lot, touching him shyly, as if they were lovers in the first flush of discovery.

*Lovers.* The word took on more onerous connotations than ever before. He couldn't deny making love to Maria had been on his mind, but he hadn't planned on having her family around when it happened.

Franc took a quick step back from his thoughts. The aura of nuptial bliss had to be messing with his mind. Next thing he knew, he'd be breaking out in a cold sweat.

It was a relief to see Pietro come back into the room carrying bottles of wine—sparkling, from the shape of them.

Andrea, the eldest brother, commented, "Must be something special, Papa's had that wine laid down in his personal cellar for almost ten years."

The cold sweat arrived with a vision that played havoc with his imagination, of Pietro standing up and announcing his daughter's betrothal. To him!

No. Even Maria wouldn't go that far to please her family. As for him, was it fear of actually playing along with the charade that made his top lip damp?

As the wine fizzed in the background, Franc took stock of his reactions. There was no doubt about it, this was unfamiliar territory. And maybe he was actually shying away from discovering what he'd missed out on. He'd never experienced the close-knit structure that the Costellos projected as a family.

To make more space now that everyone was in the sitting room, Franc perched on the arm of Maria's chair. Around them the atmosphere sparkled like the wine frothing from the bottles. Pietro poured, while Rosa passed around champagne flutes, and when they were done, stood together before the fireplace.

"We wish to make a toast," Pietro announced, holding up his glass. "To our retirement." He clinked glasses with Rosa and they both drank.

They were going to sell the house! Maria couldn't believe it. A dull roar had settled inside the top of her head and it wasn't caused by champagne. Her tongue felt stiff and thick, and the words she wanted to say, questions she needed to ask, wouldn't come out. It was the shock. She'd never ever thought they would *sell* the house.

Andrea found his tongue first. "What about the vineyard? You can't sell that!"

Pietro lifted his hand in a calming motion. "Of course not. The vineyard will belong to all of you, and the work needn't change. I know three of you have your own vineyards, but maybe this is the time to expand and begin taking on the big vineyards. Of course, you will have to come to some agreement with Maria, she may want to sell her share."

"I don't want to sell." If she knew one solitary thing, it was that she could never barter her rights to Falcon's Rise Winery for money.

"We couldn't afford to buy you out anyway," her brother, Michel countered, frowning. She knew why. His vineyard was the least established, and he owed more money on it. He and Sarah had been in their house less than a year.

As questions buffeted her ears from every side, Maria piped up, "What about the house? Do you have to sell it?"

She wished it unsaid as soon as the words were out, but the others all had their own homes. All she had was a room for rent in the city. It wasn't the same thing.

This house was her home.

"Enough!" One word from Rosa and silence replaced their anxious questions. "We thought you'd be happy for us. We won't move far. We're thinking of Warkworth. But first we want to take a vacation in Italy." Rosa slid her arm round her husband's waist. "Drink up now," she ordered. "Be happy for us."

Franc carried their bags as they followed her mother upstairs.

Just as well. She didn't feel fit for anything as she trailed behind, her head ringing with the news. What was worse, she hadn't known it would affect her this way. Thoughts of selling the vineyard hadn't troubled her before because she'd been sure it would always be there. Always be her home.

"The rooms are at the far end of the hall," said Mamma to Franc. "You'll like the view, they look down over the patio."

Gradually, her feet slowed. Connecting rooms. How could her mother do this to her? It had to be because they were retiring. Nothing else could explain their eagerness to be rid of her.

"Tell him how nice the view is, Maria."

"It's very nice."

"Don't sound so enthusiastic," her mother chided as she opened the door on the right and flicked on the light. "You're in here, Franc."

He propped her bag against the door opposite his then shrugged through the narrow entrance to the room he'd been allotted.

She wished now that she'd said something and ended up with the whole family annoyed with her instead of Franc, who probably wanted to ring her neck right about now. She measured the space between the two doors. The distance could have been longer, say, about half a mile. While her mother showed Franc where everything went, Maria carried her bag next door.

The room was smaller than her one down the hall with its queen-size bed, but at least it was quite airy, and higher than the mosquito line, so the window could be left open at night. She smiled as she imagined her nieces and nephews sleeping top-and-tail in her bed. This she had to see.

Her good mood lasted until she heard her mother showing Franc the bathroom. "It's small, but it will give you more privacy from the children."

The door on Maria's side of the bathroom was flung open and her mother entered. "Maria can show you where the towels are kept if you need more. *Now,*" she said, looking as if she'd just performed magic, "I'll see you for supper in a few minutes. No need to unpack. Just wash up."

Maria turned her back on Franc, who was framed in the doorway, and walked over to gaze out the window. Her brothers and Kris were on the patio, watching Papa wave his arms around, pointing things out to the others. It didn't matter that it was dark; they all knew the vineyard like the backs of their hands. The way she did.

"No time for looking out the window," Mamma told her. "Get ready for supper."

*   *   *

Franc leaned against her bedroom door as if that would bar it against Rosa. Maria hadn't moved from the window. She glanced over her shoulder at him as though she wondered what he was doing there, in her room. Well, he'd soon set her straight. He wouldn't be here a minute longer than he could help.

He took a deep breath to center his thoughts and find some balance. Now he knew what they meant by culture shock. He was suffering from it.

"Why didn't you say anything?"

Maria shrugged. "It's no big deal."

"You should have told your mother we'd only just met. When I take a woman to bed, I prefer to do my own asking. I won't be forced."

"No force intended, we have separate rooms."

"Connecting rooms." He'd had enough. Maria was no help. "Look, I've no intention of stepping into Randy Searle's shoes. So what do I have to do to get out of this place? Should I come down with a virus, or do I have to break a leg?"

He felt as if he was coming down with a case of happy-families, a disease that came with a ton of mouths to feed and could only spell disaster for his ambitions. The chances of his taking Maria to his bed no longer seemed like a cure for what ailed him.

Although he sensed he might just die a happy man, if he was going to go down, he'd be fighting all the way.

# Chapter 4

$F$ranc raised an eyebrow, as Maria's response was an indignant snort. "Ha! Try that and you'll be here for a month, not just overnight. My mother would love it. She'd nurse you to within an inch of your life."

She lifted a hand to her mouth as her breath caught between a giggle and words. "Believe me, I've been there. I never want to be sick around Mamma again. So be warned, don't even sneeze in her direction, or she'll be looking out for an old remedy passed down from her great-great-grandmother."

Maria's laughter was unexpected and infectious; he joined in. It was a relief to do something normal, ordinary. Then he remembered. "But what is she going to think when she eventually meets Randy?"

"There is no Randy—in that way." She shook her head and released a sigh before carrying on. "My mother was worried about me being left on the shelf. She and her sisters married very young, but she forgets things change, a woman doesn't have to get married these days, not even to have a family."

She looked up at him from under the veil of her lashes. Her lips quirked and he had the darnedest urge to reach out and touch the mole beside it that seemed to say, "Kiss me quick."

"My mother was making noises—loud noises—about me going to Italy to meet some nice Italian boys." She shuddered. "And though I know she would never force me, the thought of Mamma's relatives lining them up for inspection was enough to send me running for the hills or composing an excuse. Sooo, to keep Mamma happy, I made someone up. It just so happens that his description fits you to a tee."

He'd thought this convoluted situation bizarre, but it was getting worse. "I gather that would make me your ideal man?"

"On the outside, but it takes more than good looks to make an ideal man."

It wasn't an insult as such, but his reaction must have shown, because she laughed, and it was enough for now to see Maria's eyes shed the dull flat look they'd held since her parents had made the announcement downstairs. "Yeah, he'd need to be able to commit, and my background lets me down there, but you still haven't explained about Randy."

"I just needed to see him, and your receptionist let slip where you were holding the party, so I visited the restaurant, looking for him."

An oblique answer that left him no wiser than when he'd arrived at Falcon's Rise and been catapulted out of his comfort zone. He grasped her shoulders as the truth dawned, and he gasped, "You mean you gate-crashed? The party?"

"If you remembered, I wanted to leave and you insisted I stay, but I never said Randy was my date. Besides, how could Mamma mistake you for him, you're nothing alike."

"I thought she'd forgotten his name or something. Grandma Glamuzina used to do it all the time with my brothers and me. Whoever she was looking at took the—" He broke off as one of the kids peeped in the door. "The blame."

"Supper time," the boy gurgled, as if it was a great joke that Maria had a man in her room that seemed about to kiss her. He was still laughing as he ran down the hall, but the noise he made bouncing down the stairs muffled everything else.

"Which one was that?" He'd be damned if he could tell them apart no matter that Maria had told him all their names.

"Ricky. He'll have gone to share with the others. At that age they're easily pleased."

"C'mon," he said, making good on Ricky's speculation by planting a fast hard kiss on her lips. "The rest of the explanations can wait until after supper, I'm starving."

Maria looked dazed for a second, but as he grasped her hand to pull her with him, she recovered her wits. "Well, I sincerely hope you like Italian food or you'll stay hungry."

He turned, trapping her against him in the doorway as he ducked his head, releasing a ravenous growl as he nibbled on her earlobe. "I thought you'd have guessed by now, I'm hungry for anything Italian." And to prove it he kissed her again, drowning in the sweetness of her, lifting his head only when the sound of childish laughter reminded him they had an audience. One that stifled his impulse to carry Maria to the bed and finish what they'd started in the doorway.

As always, his nearness had a startling effect on Maria's senses. She leaned against the doorjamb, her heart throbbing to a rhythm she was only beginning to learn. Fist clenched against her breasts as if that would soothe it, she called, "Shoo!" to the children hogging the top of the stairs, then turned back to Franc.

Without conscious thought, she brought her free hand up to lie on his chest, his large body seeming to surround hers again. Her fingers rasped against the knit of his shirt. Every breath he took, stilled and held, as she felt his heat seep into her palm, through his black polo shirt.

One big palm pressed her closer, the other cupped her

cheek as her gaze mingled with his. It felt so right, the closeness, the touching, breathing the same air. The connection she felt with Franc burned fiercely, making her mouth turn dry. Moistening her lips with her tongue was no help.

"Don't worry about me, hon. I won't do anything to spoil your Christmas." She felt rather than heard his reassurances. His voice scraped across her nerve endings like dry pumice stone. "I don't enjoy seeing people hurt."

"This will be our last Christmas in this house. We were all brought up here. There's a tree in the garden where we all carved our initials one summer."

He pulled her back into the doorway. "You'll have to show me sometime."

He gently caressed her cheek with his thumb. She wanted to close her eyes and wallow in the feelings his touch wrought in her body. But the newness of them, the brand-new sensation of letting another human being, and male at that, closer than ever before, made her want to see his reactions, as well.

Her eyebrows flicked up at the outside edge, dark and softly gleaming, like a tui's wings as it took flight. And the way she trembled, Franc wondered if the same thing, flight, was on her mind.

"I wish there was some way I could imagine what it was like, all this closeness, but my family—we couldn't wait to leave home." He hadn't said it deliberately to play on her emotions. Hadn't touched her to set her lips quivering. The lipstick hadn't been invented that could imitate the soft rose pink of Maria's mouth. And nothing under the sun could stop him from taking her face in both hands and running his thumb over the silklike surface, reviving the memory of its texture under his mouth.

That first kiss? Had it only been last night?

"You must have missed a lot, growing up. I wish you'd known us then. We'd have dragged you into the fold."

He thought about all the warmth he'd noticed downstairs

and shook his head, knowing it would never have happened. Was never going to happen.

"You're a much nicer person than I am, hon," he murmured against the swell of her mouth. Like the champagne they'd just drunk, her taste flowered on his lips, tingled on his tongue as she opened to its pressure, and lingered on his palate. There was no doubt about it. Maria was a gold-medal winner and far too good for a man like himself.

Franc's mood darkened on a twist of pain. For himself, for Maria. Especially Maria. She deserved better than him, but now he'd had a taste of her, he'd never let her go—not before he'd drunk his fill.

He sealed his compliment with another kiss. Her head bumped against his shoulder as he lifted his mouth from hers. His breathing grated past his larynx as he sought to control the hard ache in his groin. He'd been in this condition almost permanently since he'd met her. One touch and his hormones roared in agony, without a sign of relief in sight.

"We can't keep letting our emotions take control."

Typical Maria, always making him smile. "Hon, if I didn't have mine under control, you'd be on that bed right now. The only thing stopping me is knowing it's your parents' house and any moment some kid is going to come flying through the door."

"Well, it's a good thing one of us has control, because I'm feeling the strain. I confess I'm very attracted to you, Franc."

*There—she'd said it.*

"And I'm not exactly the kind of guy your mother *wants* you to need. Not the type who expects a relationship to end up with a husband, a home and a family. That's not my lifestyle. But that doesn't matter now. We should be thinking of a way for me to leave before I do something you're gonna regret."

"I've been thinking, am thinking. One thing I do know,

Mamma won't want you to go off on your own. Not right on Christmas.''

As she paused for thought, he walked away from her toward the window. Good. She needed the break as much as he did, needed her hormones to stop jumping, and they'd never do that while he stood close to her. He wanted a solution.

All *she* had to do was come up with one that sounded mature, sensible—and worked out exactly the way she wanted. Because she'd discovered she didn't want him to leave.

''Look at us—''

He came back to her. ''I'm looking. *I'm looking,*'' he said, but his eyes said much more. ''I don't know if we're seeing the same thing.''

''We're two mature adults. It's not as if we're in the same room. Lock your door.'' She bunched her fists at her waist and cocked her head to look up at him. She looked a long, long way up. His height had never been more obvious as when he stood alongside her father and brothers.

His grin curved higher one side than the other and reminded her again of one of her favorite movie stars. ''You think that all the problems are on my side.''

''No, you've got that wrong.''

''Like I didn't know the feeling was mutual?''

He slid his hands inside her arms and pulled her close as if he didn't want her to run away, so there was nothing she could do but slip her arms around his neck. At the moment, running away didn't figure high on her things-to-do-next list. It was running *to* him that made the situation hazardous. Yet, the more she thought of it, the better it sounded. She wanted to know him better. A good idea since she'd decided this was the man she would give her virginity to.

''Look, hon, all I've ever wanted in my life is to pit myself against all its caprices and win. I have a chance to do that, to become a partner in Stanhope Electronics if my work pans out. And I won't let anything or anyone swerve me off that path.''

He tilted her chin toward him as if she would read in his

eyes that he meant what he said. "But I have been forced to take a break. I have roughly twelve days left. If you like, we could spend them together, but that's all I'm offering, so don't think of holding out for more."

Franc was ideal. A fling was all he was after—not under her mother's roof, of course, but that was only for a couple of days—she knew she could never have forever…but at her age it was about time she had today.

Her lips quirked, and her eyes flirted, trying to dissolve his frown. "How does this sound? I promise not to take advantage of you, Girl Scout's honor."

"Hell, you've already discovered how to get around me. All right, if you think that will work. Just one more thing, were you really a Girl Scout?"

Supper, the crowded table, the crisscross of conversations that the family easily kept pace with, a blend of herbs and spices tantalizing her nose as the food passed from hand to hand—all of it meant Christmas to Maria.

The children had gone off to bed without protest, and now her parents were reminiscing, except this year the stories seemed more poignant. Franc appeared to be coping. It wasn't that the members of her family were impolite, but as she'd explained, they were all naturally gregarious and had so much to say since her parents' bombshell.

No doubt it felt like an alien world to him.

Maria was conscious of him sitting next to her, the warmth of his leg close to hers and the touch of his hand as he'd passed one of the many dishes.

The awareness between them had intensified into a hungry ache in the pit of her stomach that food couldn't assuage.

They'd built a wall between them on a promise, but the foundation supporting the wall was pretty shaky. Her nerves prickled as she tuned in to him. Of all of them at the table he was the quietest, laughing when necessary and answering questions, but not truly giving of himself.

"Have some biscotti with your coffee, Maria." Her mother pushed the plate in her direction.

"Honestly, Mamma, I couldn't eat another bite. Maybe Franc…" She flashed a quick glance at him. His crooked grin put her off her stride and she almost forgot what she'd been saying. He was so darn handsome she'd rather eat him than a piece of cake.

Darn and double darn. How would she sleep tonight knowing she could leave her room and be with him in a heartbeat? "Would you like some, Franc?" she asked, shifting the focus on to him.

"No more for me."

She slid the plate across to her mother. "Looks like you'll have to sell them to someone else. No takers over here." Her good humor died when she caught a snatch of Michel's conversation.

"We'll need to get a surveyor in. I know someone…I'll give him a call."

She couldn't control the urge to rail at him. It burst out of nowhere. The words tumbled out as she leaned across the table toward her brother. "You talk so easily of dividing up the property, as if it was only a piece of land and not our home."

Her brother's eyebrows rose as he gawped at her. "What's with you? You don't even live here anymore."

"Yes I do, but my work is in Auckland. I could be here—"

"Enough!" Her mother had the last word. "Take no notice, Franc. Siblings, they argue about the littlest things and then bang, it is over. Why don't you take Franc for a look at the vines tomorrow," she said, her eye on Maria, and changed the subject neatly.

Michel had to have the last word. "You always stick up for her, Mamma. She's not a baby now."

For the first time, Franc saw a flash of real annoyance in Rosa's eyes. "I think you've forgotten something, Michel. Wait till you and Sarah have a daughter."

Michel looked at his wife, who had to be at least six months pregnant with their first child. He touched his wife's stomach as if for reassurance. "Sorry, Mamma. You're right, I forgot. It's been so long."

The chattiness took a nosedive and smiles gave way to frowns as Maria's sister, Giovanna stood and began gathering up the coffee cups. Franc pulled Maria out into the hall away from the brooding silence as the others began clearing the table. "You feel okay? You've gone a bit pale."

"I'm all right, just tired. It's late."

"Guess you won't want to go outside for some air."

"No. I think I'll go up and get ready for bed, but you go ahead, get some air, it's a nice night. I'll see you later."

Then he remembered the sight of her lace chemise and imagined the feel of satin and lace in his hands. "You going to wear something like that nightdress you shoved inside your drawer? It would look great on you, make your eyes look like pansies."

The compliment was worth it just to see the color return to her cheeks. "You flatter me, my eyes are plain brown. And whatever I wear to bed, you aren't likely to see it."

"You can't blame a man for trying." He stopped at the foot of the stairs. Her hand was still in his and he lifted it to his mouth, rubbing his lips across her knuckles. "Sure you wouldn't like me to come up and help you?"

"In a word, *no*." She climbed the stairs in silence, and when she rounded the top, he saw her touch the back of her hand to her lips. She was thinking about him.

It was enough for now.

Maria's eyes were closed. Tight. She refused to open them. Refused to look. If she didn't look, maybe it would go away like the other nights when she'd had the dream. *Nightmare.*

There was a spiked band around her head, pressing into her skull. Excruciating anguish forced tears from under her lids that cooled on the journey down her hot face. She was neither asleep nor awake, but somewhere in between, where the past met the present and she was part of both.

A shudder ripped out of her soul as she broke the silence with her sobs. She could hear them, knew they were her own, no matter that the sound seemed to come from a distance.

"Don't dare to move," said the voice that belonged to her past, present and future, for it never went away.

She tried to lie still, but knowing that pain would follow the voice, her skin quivered with tension. She was a bowstring stretched too tight and ready to snap.

The slow sting of cold steel caressed her breast with a lethal kiss.

Her eyes snapped open.

It was dark in her room. Dark as in that other place she wanted to forget. Managed to forget while she was still awake.

The knife glinted as if a breeze had blown moonlight into her room. Blood dripped from its tip onto her breast then it sliced again and completed the sign of the cross.

She screamed and sat up in bed.

Her heart thundered in her chest as she sat up and tried to remember the dream, but as always, when she was fully awake it eluded her.

Maria staggered to the bathroom, her night blindness sending her spinning into the five-drawered chest in the unfamiliar layout.

With her hand clenched on the faucet, she tried to relive the last few moments of the dream. If only she could see his face, she knew she would be safe. Would be able to point the finger and say, "He's the one," for no one had ever been caught, never been sent away and jailed for her abduction.

Cold water sluiced over her wrists as her panic subsided, faded like her memory.

She splashed her face with cold water, jumping when

Franc's voice came from behind her. In her stupor she hadn't heard the door open.

"Maria, are you okay? I thought I heard you call out."

"I had a bad dream." *A nightmare.* Turning off the faucet, she scrabbled blindly for the towel, and one was placed in her hands that bore the scent of her mother's favorite fabric softener. "Thanks."

Though she didn't turn around, she could sense how close he'd come by the warmth that enveloped her from his body. She shivered as she patted her face dry. Not from fear, but from the potent male scents that filled her head and charged her nerves with a different kind of tension.

She realized at that instant Franc didn't worry her that way. It had never occurred to her not to trust him. He'd been up front with what he'd wanted. A sexual encounter only, no ties, no commitment.

Her mother would throw up her hands at the idea, but to Maria it was a hundred times more acceptable than the sort of guy who got his jollies by sneaking around after her.

"Do you want to talk till the memory goes away? I don't mind." His voice came closer as his hands pressed down on her shoulders and squeezed.

"I was hoping not to waken you. That's why I didn't switch on the lights." She bunched the towel and pressed it to her breasts as his palms slid down her arms and transferred their warmth onto her skin where the short sleeves ended.

"No problem. I've been awake since the third time I almost rolled out of bed."

That made her smile, but she didn't turn into his arms, though the temptation was humming through her veins, propelled by the heat of him. "I suppose you're used to bigger and better."

"In beds, certainly. But I prefer my women to come just about here." His chin rested on the top of her head. She looked straight ahead into the mirror. Night blindness was no longer a problem. Though she saw them both through the glass darkly, she saw the truth. They looked good together.

Made for each other. *Too bad.*

Franc touched her collar. "I see you didn't take my advice. At a guess I'd say pajamas…God, I hope it wasn't because you were scared of me."

He stepped back.

Without a second thought, she turned, dropping the towel at their feet as she hurried to reassure him the only way she knew how. His chest was bare, but she didn't hesitate to slide her arms up it, secretly thrilled at the muscles her hands detected. "I've never been frightened of you. I can sense you're not the kind of guy who likes to hurt women."

His arms swept round her back and held her, but not like the night before when he had pressed her close enough to feel every inch of him. "Can I take it from that remark that you know guys who like to hurt women?"

Just like that, between one heartbeat and the next they jumped into the middle of her problem.

Should she tell him? Dare she? What if she was wrong? Franc employed Randy Searle. How would she feel being responsible for him losing his job if she'd got it wrong?

Then she remembered the feeling of eyes boring into the back of her head, and turning just in time to see Searle ducking into a shop doorway. "Randy Searle is stalking me."

It felt as if he stood at the center of a vortex, a false calm holding him steady while everything round him spun. A calm he dared not let loose, or the primitive beast at the back of his mind would let go a howl that would strike fear in the hearts of men. Particularly Randy Searle when he ripped out his throat with his bare hands.

His hands felt rough, huge and barbaric as he pulled her closer, but he couldn't *not* hold her, *not* protect her. He'd never felt this way in his life before, but knew that somehow his instincts had been fine-tuned to work this way, and Maria had it sussed when she sensed he would never harm her. He might break her heart, but he'd protect her body with his life.

Franc breathed through his nose, slow breaths, one after the other, meant to silence the growls still rumbling through his brain. As a child he'd been told one of his ancestors had come from the high mountains beyond Makarska, where civilization had yet to venture and a man's woman was sacrosanct, not to be touched on pain of death. He'd thought his brother Kurt, the climber, had been the only one to inherit that gene, but it seemed it hadn't passed him by.

Maria's body had melded to his. There was only one way to be any closer, and there was no way that would happen tonight after what she had told him.

*After what she had told him.*

"What the hell were you thinking of, gate-crashing the party, looking for Searle? Are you out of your mind? If I hadn't got rid of him, God knows what might have happened."

"You got rid of him? What are you talking about?"

"That's not important." The realization of what he'd told her struck a blow to his vanity. And he thought he'd been so clever. Too clever to brush her off now. "I took one look at you as you entered the restaurant and knew you were too good for him. So I tricked him into leaving."

Maria's breath vented in a long stream. "How could you? If you'd left things alone, this might have been finished. I could have outed him in front of everyone at the party and he wouldn't have dared come near me again."

He rubbed his hand down her back and clunked his knuckles against the basin. "Let's talk this out someplace more comfortable. Your room or mine?"

"Yours has a chair."

"Okay, come with me."


Maria heard his mattress sigh as their combined weight touched down on the bed. She knew how it felt as the sound it made echoed her own sighs.

A burden that for some inexplicable reason had grown lighter when she met Franc was now twice the size it had been before.

That thing they said about a trouble shared was a trouble halved? Was it ever wrong? The chair forgotten, they sat on the bed because he didn't appear to want to let her go.

The way she saw it, what had gone on two days ago had everything to do with Franc's heroic qualities and nothing about justice. That's what she'd gate-crashed the party in search of.

"I take it you didn't go to the police and report him?" Franc was holding her hand in his huge one, yet she didn't have a feeling of being overpowered or swallowed up. For a big man there was gentleness in his touch that he'd probably deny if she mentioned it.

"No, I didn't think they could touch him until he actually did something to me."

His big body jolted as if he'd been struck. "Don't tell me you wanted him to assault you so you could call the cops?"

How could he think she would do that, when all she wanted to do right now was curl up in his arms and go to sleep, a reaction to all the adrenaline that had pumped through her body as she dreamed. "I only wanted to shame him, hoping he would leave me alone."

"I can't figure out why you thought someone was watching you in the first place. Or why you didn't at least tell your parents or your brothers."

"Because I know how it feels. It's like a tap on the shoulder, and then I turn around, hoping someone will truly be standing behind me. But there never is, except those times when I saw Randy."

"Why haven't you told your parents?" The gruffness in his voice underlined how seriously he took the situation, and the vibrations that communicated with her arm through his chest wall urged her to take the plunge.

She took a deep breath as if ready to dive into a bottomless pool she might never find her way out of. Was she ready for this? Was Franc? She'd never told a living soul what she couldn't remember. Until now.

"I didn't want to put them through that again."

His hand tightened, swallowed hers whole. "Again?"

"I was abducted when I was seventeen." His arms tightened around her and she felt the tension in his muscles flow through his palms into her.

For long seconds she sat still, silent. The dark magnified sounds she never noticed in daylight, like inhaling and exhaling. Like Franc's breath softly going in, rushing out in a sigh as he waited for her to speak.

"It made the family very protective of me. Now, Mamma thinks she kept me home too long and ruined my chances of getting married. I'm fine on my own, but you know...she's my mother. We do things to stop them from worrying."

"My mother died before I was two, so I never had to lie to her. No, wipe that! I don't know what I would have done to keep her from fretting."

"I'm sorry, Franc."

"Save your sympathy, hon, it happened a long time ago." The back of his knuckles caressed her cheek and he discovered it was wet. "Hey, hey, baby girl, don't get all wound up. If that guy is bothering you, don't worry, sweetheart, he's dogmeat," he growled in a good gangster imitation and got another hiccup for his reward. A tear-free one this time. Franc didn't think her knowing he meant every word was a good idea. For good or ill, he would keep her close until this was settled.

# *Chapter 5*

Had her tears been for him? A small part of Franc wanted to push her away before he got in too deep. The small impulsive part that wanted to know what the hell she wasn't telling him.

The majority of his instincts won. He pulled her onto his knee and hugged her to his chest, didn't matter that the back of his neck tightened, the hairs on it prickling as if something walked over his grave.

He recognized the honor Maria had done him. Maybe it was something to do with the hour and the darkness, but he felt closer to her than he had to anyone in a long while. At the same time, he wasn't sure he had it in him to bare his soul the way she had done.

He qualified his reluctance with the thought that his situation was different. His father had been the perpetrator of the crime, not the victim.

"Don't you think that what happened before is all the more reason to tell them about the stalker?"

"I thought I could handle the situation myself. This is the

first time I've been home since he began stalking me. And while he was only following me, I thought I could sort it out and move on.''

Make that something pounding on his grave.

''Back up a minute. What exactly do you mean by *only*.''

''I think, I'm not saying I'm positive, but I think he might have been in my room when I went out…yesterday afternoon.''

''Hell, Maria! You need to talk to someone about this. My sister's a cop, I can put you in touch with her.'' Jo would know what to do. She was used to dealing with these situations, diplomatically. Well, some of the time.

''As a detective sergeant with Homicide at Auckland Central, most of the victims she deals with are dead before she gets anywhere near them. Unless you count her husband, Rowan. He took a bullet for her during a hostage situation and saved her life, then two years later he got stabbed saving her a second time from a nutcase who had her staked out as a human sacrifice. I'm pleased to say that since they got married, she seems to have stopped taking so many risks.''

Franc's gut clenched at the thought of what Maria had tried to do. What if he hadn't prevented her from confronting Randy? If Randy *was* the guy watching her, what harm might he have inflicted on her? He shuddered as a list of consequences came to mind.

There was no end to the worst-case scenarios his brain could come up with. As the possibilities presented themselves, he became more and more certain that he had to help her find out one way or the other.

Hell, this was New Zealand; so small a population the possibility of running into a neighbor—or at least their first cousin—a thousand miles from home wasn't unheard of. How hard could it be to keep an eye on Searle?

Very few cases of stalkers were ever reported in the papers. Rapes, murders, yeah, they had their share of those, but stalking was something that happened to celebrities, wasn't it?

He'd have to ask his sister when she came back from her vacation. She would know. Jo had worked as a cop for ten years, a detective for almost seven of them, both in Auckland and down country in Nicks Landing, a little East Coast town. She'd been back in Auckland for a year now, ever since she got married to a Stanhope. That was how he'd gotten his chance to run a Stanhope Holdings company. A chance he'd accepted with open arms. Nepotism? Maybe, but he wasn't too proud. He couldn't afford to be, but that didn't mean he was excused from the need to prove himself. Something he was still working on.

He threaded his fingers through Maria's, and on a rough-honed sigh, said, "I have to say, Randy never struck me as that kind of guy, a loudmouth, maybe. He's always calling the odds on his success with women, but a pervert who stalks them? It just doesn't gel. Not that I'm saying you're wrong, but maybe you got the wrong guy."

"Maybe not, but you didn't see the way he looked at me."

"That's what I mean. The guy is so obvious. He looks at most women that way. Even so, we'll need to make some sort of plan to discover if he actually *is* the one."

"You believe me?"

Until now, Maria hadn't struck him as a woman without much faith in herself. But who knew what fancies played on the mind when you were frightened. Just because he was confident of his abilities to handle anything didn't mean that one day he wouldn't find himself in a situation that scared the heck out of him. "Why wouldn't I believe you?"

"We hardly know each other, how can you be sure I'm telling the truth?"

Amused, he laughed softly under his breath and reached up to touch her face. Her skin felt like satin to his fingertips as he trailed them down her cheek and round to her chin. "Maria, believe me, this close I'd know if you were lying." Franc rubbed the pad of his thumb over her full bottom lip. "Even in the dark your expression gives you away. Your feelings are written on your face for the world to see, so don't ever try fooling anyone."

"I guess it's as well you fooled Searle into going home. He'd have known I was frightened of him."

"You could be right, but only a fool wouldn't have realized the courage it took to come there and spit in his eye. That's what you were going to do, right?"

"Something like that, I thought I'd play it by ear, but I was shaking inside when you went off to fetch him." She laughed, but her humor had the high-pitched quality of a wet fingertip on a crystal glass. The tension in her body increased. It was as if she had to hold herself together or shatter.

"There's a story about that. Do you want to hear it?"

"Is it something bad?"

"Not from where I'm standing. I told you my friend Brent took care of it, but when I asked him to get rid of Searle, he told me he loved me like a brother but he wasn't going to kill for me."

He felt her relax and wished he could do the same.

If Searle was responsible for stalking Maria, he wouldn't put the onus on Brent to take care of him, he'd do it himself.

A feral growl built at the back of his throat as he relived the moment she'd asked for the jerk, but this wasn't *just* about Searle. Mainly it concerned him and Maria. "The thought of Searle laying a hand on you. Like this…"

His hand slid under her silky hair. "Hell, it makes my back teeth ache."

She tilted her head to give him access as he cupped his fingers round her nape. Both movements brought her face closer. Close enough to breathe in the sharp peppermint tang that clung to her breath.

The urge to taste sent his libido into overdrive.

Heart pounding, Maria accepted Franc's embrace, trying to act as if it was the most natural thing in the world. Nothing had prepared her for the emotions this tender caress engendered, for the quivering inside, or the desire to burst into tears again. The experience was all so new, new and wonderful.

It had been one thing to imagine satisfying her curiosity about men, women and sex. But right here, right now, she couldn't conceive of letting anyone other than Franc get this close to her. Close enough to kiss the way they had before.

Franc lifted his thumb higher and traced the whorls of her ear, as the thought of slanting his mouth over hers seemed more and more like the right thing to do. Without conscious guidance, his other hand brushed lightly over her breast.

Her gasp of pleasure filled the silence.

"So, what do you think, are you gonna hit me or kiss me?"

"A kiss would be better," she sighed, wishing she was equipped to handle the longing building inside her.

Such a feeble answer she'd given him, words only words, and none of them capable of explaining the tumult of emotions whirling through her brain.

Her head lifted. Had she come to meet his kiss or had he pulled her closer? She didn't know, didn't care. A rush of sighs tangled in a fine web of anticipation in the bare microsecond it took their mouths to meet.

Ah, God, now she knew her memories of last night weren't an aberration. The sweet, sweet taste of his mouth made her head spin as if a whirlwind had taken hold of her, tossing her so high in the air she never wanted to come down.

Maria struggled in his arms. For one dire moment Franc thought she wanted him to stop, then her hand lifted to hold his head still as their tongues dueled and lips clashed. His overeager libido wanted to sample each sensation, and do it twice, no, three times over.

A startling revelation.

A warning that ought to have made him wonder where this path he was treading led. Too late, he felt hungry as a bear, nose deep in a hive, which had lost its fear of being stung the moment it discovered a feast of honey on the menu.

It was warm under her pajamas. He found the curve of her breasts under the satiny layer. One, then the other swelled to fill his hands with burgeoning female flesh.

He didn't remember turning, moving them onto the bed, but suddenly Maria was under him, arching up as she struggled to fit against his length.

Only his thin cotton boxers, and her summer-weight pajamas, separated them. Franc's heat radiated through the layers into her, and when he swung his leg across hers, she thought she would die from the luxury of having the weight of his body press her down into the soft mattress. A moan tore from her throat as he left his hard male imprint on her belly.

Franc kept the momentum edgy, varying his kisses; *soft,* like a butterfly's caress; *hard,* deep as if to swallow her whole. So much to experience, so much to taste, and only a few days to do it in. He swung from taking mouselike nibbles from her bottom lip to vampire bites on the cord of her neck.

His shoulders bore the kiss of her fingernails as she thrust her hips up under him and into him in a prelude of what was to come.

*Wait.* Savor the moment, the rush, the longing, and let the pitch build until taking her, being inside her, exceeded everything that had gone before.

The room smelled of sex and sweat, and the clean flavor of peppermint had given way to a hot, fierce, hungry flame that consumed them both and soon would fuse them into one.

Thrusting the edges of her pajama jacket aside, Franc basked in her whimpers while his hands, his mouth found her breasts.

"God, I want to see you, I must." His words grazed past her face, edgy like a fight, all bared teeth and bare knuckles for right of possession.

Her breath stuttered as his hand reached for the bedside-light. For an instant her grip tightened on his scalp, demanding his attention, next moment her hands were sliding between them covering the soft flesh he was determined to see. "No, I'd rather it was dark."

Maria's voice crackled out of a throat gone suddenly dry. "You see," she explained, "I've never done this before."

Shaken, his hand froze midair. A hush settled over the room broken only by the sound of Maria's faltering breath close to his ear.

His own caught in his throat as the magnitude of what he'd started hit him like a two-ton truck with a reminder of time and place. Did he dare initiate a virgin in all the delights of sex, with her mother sleeping three doors away?

Magnified a thousand times by the silence blanketing the house, a lock turned and clicked into place. His head swiveled to look over his shoulder as he rolled off Maria, pulling the edges of her top into place as his knees touched the floor and waited for the door to open.

"Santa Claus," Maria whispered as ragged murmurs floated along the hall, followed by footsteps padding in the direction of the stairs.

"What?"

"Someone has gone to put the children's presents out." She didn't want to feel ashamed of what they'd done, or were about to do, but whispering in the dark twisted their encounter into a secret, to be hidden at all cost. She'd hoped for more.

"Your mother?" Another hushed question floated on the silence, as if to speak louder would shatter it.

"No, probably my brothers." They'd protected her for years, and now, albeit unconsciously on their part, they'd blighted her first sexual experience.

Why couldn't she simply have a relationship, a slice out of time where the past didn't count? Hadn't she enough to conceal already: the damaging scars, the worries shrouded in the mystery of what happened during her abduction.

Franc was still kneeling by her bed, not as comfortable as lying beside her but not as dangerous. Keeping his voice low, he asked, "Do you think they heard us?"

"We heard them."

Her reply was simply confirmation of his own line of thought, but she distracted him by scraping a finger over his late-night stubble. "It's no use you thinking to make a dash for it. In case you've forgotten, this is your room."

"So they aren't liable to burst in, is that what you're saying?" Franc sucked in a breath as her finger found the hollow in his throat. No wonder, he couldn't recollect ever being so turned on. He'd heard of men experiencing the pain of unrelieved lust, but never knew it could feel so bad, excruciating, as if he were caught in a vise. It was going to take more than a cold shower to relieve his discomfort.

It would take Maria, but it wasn't going to happen tonight.

Hell, the interruption might have put a damper on his lust, but even dead it wouldn't lie down.

Slipping an arm around her, he rolled Maria, covers and all, into a bundle, then climbed back onto the bed, wrapping the end of the coverlet touching the floor round him. With her settled in his arms, head tucked under his chin, reluctantly, he began to extricate himself. "Hon, I'm thinking we got our timing all wrong. I still want you." *Boy, did he want her.*

"But I can't say I feel comfortable making love to you while your parents are practically sleeping next door."

No point in avoiding the question, Maria had to know. "Is it because I'm a virgin?"

"Hell, no! No, but your first time should be something special. I can't do that for you here with all this tiptoeing around in the dark. It's making me nervous."

"That makes two of us."

*Special,* he'd said. Maria hoped it lived up to its name, though she didn't think anything could thrill her more than being in Franc's arms a few minutes ago.

She squirmed, twisting out of the covers till she and Franc were face-to-face.

Her movements were so arousing, Franc clenched his fists to prevent crying out. Her breath kissed his lips. He closed them tight. All he needed was a taste of her to put his new-found resolve out of kilter.

"You're not just putting me off, are you?" Her hands touched his face. He shuddered. She held him still, kissing him, softly, gently, tracing his lips with the tip of her tongue. His heart began to dance rock 'n' roll on his sternum.

Gripping her wrists, he pushed her away, not caring who heard the moan gouged out of his lungs. She was tearing him apart. And before she was done, it would take a crash course in resuscitation to keep him alive. "Maria, you are killing me."

"Just testing."

"Uh-uh. That kiss definitely came under the heading of teasing. But I'll let you off if you promise me something."

"Anything." The way she purred into his ear, he could tell she meant it. This had to be one of the best and worst nights of his life.

He was holding the most gorgeous woman he'd ever met in his arms, on a bed, and couldn't do a damn thing about it. No, even he couldn't sink that low.

"Day after tomorrow, when we get back to Auckland, you'll let me take you out on a proper date? I'll stay the extra night and drop you home in plenty of time to doll yourself up. Wear that dark plum number that's my favorite."

"You've only seen me in a couple of outfits."

"Don't get picky, and don't interrupt, I'm planning our night out. Round about seven, I'll pick you up in a cab so there's no worry about drinking and driving."

"A limo?"

"You're pushing it, hon." He tweaked her earlobe then began again. "We'll go to one of those restaurants on the waterfront. All you have to do is pop a toothbrush in your bag for after, because you'll spend the rest of the night at my place. That's when we'll finish what we started tonight."

"Mmm, I think I'd enjoy that," she murmured, her breath

warm and damp against his chest, tickling the scattering of hair growing below his throat.

"Great. I'll make the arrangements as soon as I get home. Now that's settled, we ought to try getting some sleep."

"Can we sleep like this, please, with my head on your shoulder? It makes me feel so safe."

"I guess." How could he refuse, when she asked so prettily. But safe? From Searle, maybe? But himself? Why promise something he couldn't guarantee? She burrowed in closer, lying still for a moment before her drowsy response floated up to him.

"Thank you, Franc. You're one of the good guys."

Damn, he didn't feel good, and it wasn't the hunger eating him up inside that sprang to mind, nor knowing sleep would be impossible tonight with Maria lying beside him.

Sure he was intent on having her, just not tonight. But his not giving a damn that it could only last eleven days at most sounded like bad-guy fodder to him. Yet, he was beggared if he would let her go until the end of his holiday break.

Once that was over it would be off with Maria, and on with the work. Same old, same old, just like always. He'd lived with his dream too long to let it go now.

Then again, he couldn't allow her to deal with Searle alone. He felt kind of responsible, since the guy worked for him. Yeah, after the holidays, once he dealt with Searle, he'd let her go.

That's unless they discovered it wasn't his salesman who was watching her. If there really *was* a stalker, then he'd feel obliged to sort the problem out.

His sister could help, though if she'd gone off on their motor yacht for Christmas, it might be well into January till she got back to Auckland.

His brain went on and on until he fell asleep without putting a name to what he'd been doing.

Making excuses to keep seeing Maria.

# *Chapter 6*

Next morning Maria waited on the flagstone-paved patio for Franc. Arching her foot, as she used to as a child, she pointed her toes above the line where two paving stones abutted, arms outstretched to prevent wobbling from side to side. An appropriate game, considering she felt she'd been practicing a high-wire balancing act since the moment she'd gotten out of his bed, and none too steadily at that.

She was still woolgathering when Franc appeared at her elbow and caught her as she finally lost her balance. He didn't look as if he'd spent the night squashed up beside her in a single bed. It was as if shaving had given him a new lease on life. Though she'd rather liked him slightly bristly. "All ready?"

"I am if you are, but what's going to happen when your family finds out we don't have gifts for each other?"

His words brought home to her what a nice guy Franc really was. Although he liked to pretend otherwise, what with his avowal that commitment was the last thing on his mind, and his only goal in life was to become a partner in his brother-in-law's company. "I've thought of that. Though I don't like fooling my parents I think we should say that we'd already exchanged gifts in Auckland before we knew you would come home with me."

"Do you think they'll buy it?"

"Of course they will, they like you. And I'm their daughter, they don't know I have any reason to pretend." Lying to her family was another corruption to blame on Randy Searle. Although, maybe she could cancel it out by remembering if it hadn't been for him, she would never have met Franc.

"Let's turn it into the truth when we get back to Auckland. How 'bout I buy you a pair of earrings that will highlight the graceful curve of your neck."

Color raced into her cheeks as if acknowledging the compliment. She could see from the gleam in his eye that he recognized she wasn't used to receiving them.

Hmmph. Well, two could play that game. "I'll have to think of something to buy that will bring out your best feature." But she didn't have enough experience to compete against Franc and win.

"Better wait a day or two then, because, hon, you haven't seen my best feature yet."

She was still blushing, her mind bedazzled as they walked into the lounge, and the madness that constituted Christmas in the Costello household.

Someone should have warned him.

The Christmas ritual began with small panini rolls, liberally filled with with smoked salmon or ham, and for the sweeter-toothed members—the children and Maria—there were chocolate-filled croissants. Franc had never experienced a Christmas morning like it. No one sat at the table. They piled into the lounge, filling the sofas and chairs, as well as stools and cushions on the floor, and everyone except the children washed down the food with another glass of Falcon Rise's special Italian-style sparkling wine.

Maria had insisted he take the chair while she sat on a pile of cushions at his feet. Every now and then she would look up to catch his reaction to what was happening.

It hadn't taken long to occur to him that, if she had told her family about Searle, the rituals would have gone ahead but only for the children's sakes. And he doubted if even they would have gone about their business so lightheartedly, once the unease permeated down from their parents.

One of the younger children, he'd forgotten his name, said, "Are you guys never going to finish eating? We want to open the presents."

Maria, who was on her third croissant, looked up at Franc, eyes twinkling and a smile on her face as if Searle didn't exist. There was a small streak of chocolate on the side of her mouth. He swiped it off with his thumb then sucked it off. Her pupils blurred as they swallowed up the dark brown in her irises, making him clamp down the urge to pick her up and carry her off to bed.

That was the caveman in him, but he'd checked his club in at the door to the Costello homestead, so he settled for stealing half of the croissant she had left. "Just helping the young guy out," he said before popping it into his mouth.

Without taking her gaze off his mouth, she warned him, "I'll let you off this time, but don't ever come between me and my chocolate if you value your life."

He grinned. Damn, he was actually enjoying himself in this den of domesticity. Who would have believed it? Not his good mate Brent, that's for sure. He narrowed his gaze as it traveled over her. "Looks like I'm going to have to practice asking for mercy."

"If that was an example of what I can expect, me, too."

Within minutes of the second round of drinks being served they were swimming in a sea of Christmas wrapping paper. He didn't ever remember seeing this many presents under a Christmas tree. Not even when his dad was still alive. That must have been in the days before Milo Jellic succumbed to the lure of easy money.

Thoughts of his father managed to take the gloss off a morning that had shone before. Sure, his sister, Jo and her husband, Rowan McQuaid Stanhope, were looking into Milo's past, trying to prove he'd been innocent, set up and maybe even murdered. He didn't know which bothered him most, the fact that there might be nothing to discover, or that he might wake up one morning to be told someone had killed his father by sending him over a cliff, car and all.

The last news he'd heard was that his father had been involved with some woman. "Good on him," he'd said to Jo. Ten years was a long time to go without a woman. But then it had occurred to Franc that maybe she had been the final nudge Milo had needed to turn into a cop on the take, and place *money* before the family who'd needed him. Either way, it couldn't make much difference to Franc; about the only thing he had in common with his father was his surname.

Franc put his hand over the top of his glass to prevent Maria's brother, Andrea, filling it up. He was feeling far too melancholy and no amount of wine was going to cheer him up.

The weight of Maria's arm sat across his knees. He liked the feel of it, the warmth, the subtle ebb and flow of her muscles as she shifted against him and quirked an eyebrow in his direction, as if she'd sensed the change in his mood.

What he needed was some fresh air and Maria, but not necessarily in that order.

He caught her hand in his and tugged gently on her fingers as if to say, "Get up."

"Want to go for that walk you promised me?"

"Sure, give me two minutes and I'll meet you on the patio."

Franc watched her leave the room and edged his way through the piles of wrapping paper the children were collecting as they helped make room for the toys they wanted to play with. Santa had been generous this year.

His mood lifted an inch or too as he realized Santa had already sent him a present. He'd recognized it the moment Maria entered the restaurant. The memory had simply got sidetracked as ineligible alongside all the problems facing Maria that he'd discovered later.

Franc counted the paving stones as he slowly walked to the end of the patio to wait…eight, nine, ten, almost there. His gaze traveled the green, vine-striped horizon where it met up with the sea and sky as he turned to face the house. There were grape leaves as far as the eye could see, a fitting setting for his goddess.

The sound of footsteps drew his glance and he turned to watch his Christmas gift arrive.

"Where are you taking me? I could use some adventure."

Maria blinked up at him as his arm curved around her shoulder. "I thought we'd take in the vines and the view in that order. But, first we have to follow that path to a bridge that crosses the stream at the bottom. Unless you'd prefer to get your feet wet?"

"Maybe later." He grinned, looking down at his soft brown leather loafers. They teamed up with the loose-weave cotton shirt he had on, casual but smart. As for the rest, his tan chinos were the same as those her brothers wore.

They'd only gone a few steps away from the patio when Franc pulled Maria's arm around behind his waist, leaving his on her shoulders. Side by side, they traveled in silence until Franc said, "Sorry if I came across as unsociable toward the end of the gift giving. I started thinking about my family, and before I knew it, I'd dropped out of my comfort zone."

So that was his reason for the change in atmosphere she'd sensed. "Do you miss them?"

"If you'd asked me yesterday, I'd have said no way. But

that was yesterday. I also felt a bit embarrassed about the gifts.''

''Ah, but mothers always cater for the unexpected. You can eat your chocolates and wear your socks with a clear conscience.''

He patted his stomach. ''Do you think I can chance it?''

''If you mean has she poisoned you, you're safe. But if you're asking about putting on weight…'' She let the answer hang a minute while she remembered the feel of his hard body covering hers. Color swept her face, and she tried to hide it by looking around him as she gently pinched his waist. ''No problem there. You can take it.''

''Glad I have your approval,'' he said, lifting her chin till he could look straight into her eyes.

What she saw in them made her heart leap. Suddenly she didn't want to wait another day to discover how making love with Franc felt. The thought of having him inside her brought on an ache that intensified her longing. He leaned over and brushed his lips across hers, gently, sweet as fresh-picked grapes with the warmth of the sun on them, warmth that infused the whole of her body. She'd never in a million years imagined this floaty feeling as if her feet didn't touch the ground.

They walked a few more yards before she dredged a few words out of the knot in her throat. ''Actually, you did me a favor. That's two I owe you now. Instead of mooning sentimentally about this being my last Christmas at Falcon's Rise, I was more concerned you didn't feel left out. Which meant I didn't embarrass myself by coming over all weepy. I guess I did enough of that last night.''

''And with good reason.'' His voice dropped a couple of notches, vibrating through the wall of his chest into her side.

The tips of his fingers drew lazy circles on her shoulder, keeping alive the buzz she'd experienced before. ''You've been through a frightening experience. You know what they say about a trouble shared. I guess we halved it. You ought to feel easier now you've told me.''

''Dumped on you, don't you mean? I guess the tension has been slightly alleviated, but I always feel more relaxed at home. If only I could convince myself I haven't got both of us worked up over a figment of my imagination.''

They were less than three feet from the bridge when he stopped and held her by the shoulders. His hands were warm on the skin left bare by a sleeveless top the color of pale violets. She'd worn it because of a compliment he'd made about her eyes.

His big hands made her feel small, fragile, but with Franc she didn't mind. He probably didn't suspect he had this talent for gentleness, but he'd proved it by not trampling all over her vulnerability.

''I'd wish I could pretend the stalking was all in your mind, but from what you tell me, it's happened too often to be dismissed lightly. When we get back to Auckland, I'm going to give you one of my cell phones. That way you can call me day or night. Anytime you feel you're being watched.''

Franc pushed her away slightly as he gauged her reception of his idea. ''Got that? No matter the hour, you have to call me.''

The area in her brain that wouldn't quit, wouldn't let her cower to Searle, wanted to respond with an irreverent salute, and an ''Aye-aye, sir,'' but she knew he was serious, *deadly* serious. The thought cast up an image to make her shudder.

Her amusement vanished as a somber shadow filled its place.

''Okay, if that's what you want, but I won't feel comfortable waking you up unless it's a matter of…'' She let the rest hang fire. How could she do anything else when they were talking of her life, or maybe death?

''Unless it's too late, you mean. I expect more than that. If you're in the street and feel he's watching, step into a shop or café and give me a call. You don't want to make it too obvious that you're on to him. Then, if Randy is anywhere in sight, we'll know you were correct in your assumption.''

"Or that it's all a horrible coincidence." The corners of her mouth drooped. "Or maybe I'm being paranoid."

"With your history, you have a right. But for the rest of Christmas Day let's try to put it behind us and go for the peace on Earth and all that. There's little chance that anyone is watching you today."

What was it about him apart from a crooked smile that wiped years off his age and sent her heart fluttering, as if she'd swallowed a hundred soft-winged moths.

"I guess I've been acting like a wimp."

"Would a wimp have crashed my party? No way. You are beautiful, so beautiful. I can see why someone would like to spend a lot of time looking at you. But, while they only look, there's little anyone can do."

"You're right. I do feel safe at Falcon's Rise. Safer than in Auckland." She wanted to say "safer because I'm with you," but no matter what he said about calling him if she felt threatened, she knew his presence in her life was strictly temporary. He'd made that perfectly clear yesterday.

Was it wrong to look for more? *Expect more?*

No one could be more suitable than Franc. He was handsome, experienced, the only man to make her feel sex was the natural outcome of their relationship, not something to be feared. Why then, did her insights of the future resemble something from Picasso's Blue Period?

Franc pulled her arm through his as they resumed their walk. A few more steps would take them out of the garden and across the bridge to a north-facing slope ribbed with green-trellised vines. "So, Maria, how does Rosa rate when it comes to cooking turkeys?"

"She makes a pistachio nut stuffing that's to die for."

*Through the telephoto lens Maria appeared close enough to touch. He watched her laugh, eyes crinkling with pleasure as she looked up at the man, Jellic.*

*Moving the camera slightly he cut the guy out of the picture.*

*This new aspect was unforeseen; he'd thought she was afraid of men. It would make things more difficult, yet ultimately more interesting. He smiled at the thought of stealing Maria from under Jellic's nose.*

*The camera clicked, capturing an unguarded moment. As the next frame whirred into place, blood gorged his groin as he imagined the moment the exposed print slid from the chemicals, the pleasure of holding it up for his eyes to feast on. Yes, this enlargement could be nothing less than life size.*

*The smile never left his face. It widened as his teeth clenched, knowing she might never look at him in just that way.*

*Still, he was a man of infinite patience. He could wait.*

"Roses were the last thing I expected to find amongst the vines." Franc stopped to pick a full-blown yellow bloom and handed the fragile flower to Maria.

She held it to her nose and drew in its perfume, her nostrils gently flaring, and her eyes shut, hiding the ecstasy he knew she was feeling. Franc did a mental rundown on the hours until he could get her into his bed, cursing his suggestion that he take her into the city for a meal, when there was a restaurant less than five minutes from his door.

"Its perfume is almost too perfect, my head is spinning. Oh, oh dear," she said, dismayed as the rose fell apart and its petals tumbled from her hands. "Don't you think it's sad, how quickly the roses die in the heat?"

"Tell the truth, it isn't something I've put a lot of thought into, never having much to do with flowers."

"I remember Papa planting these roses when he put in the new vines. They used to be an indicator of any diseases that might attack the grapes, but these days they're more decoration. He ripped out the Muller Thurgau that grew here, and replaced it with red wines. Sangiovese is the newest of the ones he has replaced it with. It's over there.''

Her serious expression amused him, as if she was conducting him round a famous art gallery and desperately trying to pronounce all the artists' names correctly.

''Say that again.''

''Say what again?''

He took a step closer, an invasion of her personal space, and watched her eyelids flicker, their dark lashes twin crescents of sable. Her tongue moistened her lips as his nearness forced her to look up at him. She smelled of rose petals and sunshine. The thought of taking, *owning,* her and the glorious combination made him hard. ''The name of that wine, I want to hear it again.''

''S-s-sangio…''

Before she could finish, his mouth slanted over hers and swallowed the rest of the word. Her eyelids snapped open then sank on a murmur of pleasure.

It was everything he remembered and more. Better. Out here in the open air, just the two of them, as if they were alone in the world, and all their previous stresses counted as nothing.

Slipping his arms round her waist, he began to move as they had when they'd danced, slowly turning to a tune only lovers could hear, on a bed of yellow rose petals.

''Once more, hon, whisper the word for me.''

''Sangiooooooo…''

They kissed again…and again, turning till his head spun with the hot scents of grass, and vines, and roses, the sun, and the sensuality, holding Maria in his arms and never quite letting her finish saying the word.

''I guess we ought to look at the view. I expect they will ask how you liked it,'' she mentioned as they reached the brow at long last.

"My sister, Jo, has a friend with a winery at Pigeon Hill, I think it's quite near, though I've never visited it."

"I know her. Maggie Kovacs she used to be. I believe she married a cop, but he gave up his career and works with her now. Pigeon Hill has a few more hectares in vines than us, but when Gina and my brothers combine their properties, I guess they'll give them a run for their money."

She flashed a rueful smile his way. "That makes me sound very competitive. I'm not really, I'd just like to see my family do well."

"I don't see much wrong with that. Ambition is what lifts you out of the crowd. Without it, my friend Brent and I might be slogging away in dead-end jobs letting other people take credit for our work...our ideas. When I met Stanhope at my sister's wedding, he was impressed by my ideas and gave me this chance. Of course, I couldn't leave Brent behind. We were in the same year at Unitech and have worked together ever since."

"And you don't compete with each other?"

"Only over women." One glance at Maria told him he might have made a hash of his chances by being too clever. "But that was a while ago. Now we're just two old working hacks who know better than to compete over anything."

As he leaned closer, she looked away. Snubbed him. "I always won, but never so well until I met you."

Hands shaping her spine, he felt her shiver as she melted against him. He fought an urge to pull her down to the ground to take her right there on the top of the hill with the smell of the grapevines all about them. Goddess country.

Desire almost won, would have won, if he hadn't seen the flash of sunlight on glass. Seen someone watching them.

Maybe someone innocent.

Maybe not.

He moved so her back was toward the slope where the flash of light had come from. "C'mon, let's go back to the house and offer your mother a hand."

"I always thought you were brave, now I'm sure of it." She winked at him but he couldn't return the gesture. "Okay," she finished. "Next stop the lion's den."

## Chapter 7

Before most members of the household were moving next morning, Franc rolled out of bed with the intention of taking a walk and doing a little on-the-spot investigating. The more he thought about the flash that had made him shepherd Maria back indoors—as he saw it, to safety—the more he needed to be sure he hadn't imagined the diamond-bright light in the midst of the vines.

He wanted confirmation. It made no difference that Maria had confided in him, given him chapter and verse on her reasons for pointing the finger at Searle; witnessing one tiny particle of evidence had opened his eyes to a startling revelation about himself. Hell, if he'd had a daughter who'd been abducted at one time, he'd never let her out of the house without him glued to her side. His stomach churned the way it had for the most of yesterday.

After a whole night of tangling the sheets into one big knot, he'd realized Maria had known the truth of the matter when she'd set out to confront Searle. You couldn't spend the rest of your natural life in fear.

Thanks to his occupation, Franc had an eye for detail; he could look at the big picture without losing sight of the components that made up the whole.

Measuring the angle with his eyes, he stared at the spot on the opposite slope. *The place where he'd almost laid Maria down and made her his own.* The thought of someone spying on them, tainting their moments of intimacy with lewd thoughts, made his skin crawl.

He gauged the distance and took three more paces. If he'd got it correct, the flash had come from right about here.

He studied the ground, looking for clues to something out of the ordinary. Without rushing it, he walked across the curve of the slope, eyes to the ground between the trellises, searching the loose dirt around the roots of the vines and the mown strip of grass bordering them for a sign of someone's presence.

And found it.

He hunkered down. Shoe prints dug more than a quarter of an inch into the soft soil as if someone had stayed in one position for a while. Cross trainers by the look of the pattern on the sole, a full print and one half-size from the toes back, as if the wearer had crouched down and balanced most of his weight on the back of one heel.

He studied the spot intently, knowing a sensible solution would be to take a photo. Too bad he didn't have a camera handy. He lined up his feet with the prints and looked through a small gap that had been cut in the vines. The guy couldn't have got better cover if he'd built himself a duck shooter's hide. From up here he would have had a perfect view of the comings and goings of the Costello household.

What kind of way was this, for anyone without malice, to celebrate Christmas?

Franc pushed to his feet, stood staring for almost two minutes and let his conclusions take shape. Determination changed the thrust of his jaw. He didn't want to see a guy who was innocent take the rap for what was going down around Maria.

If Jo was correct in her assumptions, that's what had happened to his father and the whole of the Jellic family had paid for the injustice.

The way the Costellos had paid. Because, as he'd discovered before he left Maria to seek out his lonely bed, her abductor had never been caught. *Damned* if this guy would get off so easy.

He looked to the horizon. Time to get back to the house. Thunderheads had begun to breach the dark gray rugged peaks of the Barrier Islands and looked ready to charge down on Kawau a few miles' distance across the water. As he headed down the slope, a band of sunlight sliced through the full bellies of the clouds and lit up Little Barrier's crenellated slopes and towering peaks. The impression endured for less than the blink of an eye before the rain front rolled over it.

Funny what a difference a little bit of light made. Yesterday it had taken his life in a different direction. His back teeth ached as he saw his dreams begin to recede, but he was damned if he would let Maria go until he knew she was safe from the Peeping Tom on the hill.

The connecting door to the room Maria had slept in stood open. With a shower in his sights he entered the bathroom and caught her concentrating on her reflection. She stroked a brush through her hair in front of the bathroom mirror, letting the strands curl behind her ears. She had changed into a new apricot crop top that sat almost six inches of skin above white pants. The peachy-pink color brought out sparks of copper in her hair as she tamed its waves with the brush.

He put his hands on her shoulders and stood behind her as he had in the dark that first night. He admired what he saw. No way could he deny it, what with his body reacting like a randy thirteen-year-old's. "Hey, you almost ready to go?"

"Almost. I have to collect a few things from my room once

the kids finish ransacking it. But other than that I'm ready to eat and run.''

As he turned her around into his arms, her hands slid to his neck as if that was their natural position. He drew in her scent, letting it curl around his thought processes to do its worst. *Scramble them.* ''Boy, do you smell good.''

Holding his mouth inches from hers, he moistened his lips. ''You ready for this?''

Eyes wide, she stretched up into his kiss. Her crop top rose with her, and his hands made short work of slipping underneath. She shivered, passing little mewls of pleasure from her mouth to his. He answered with a groan as her skin slipped like satin under his hands. Her mouth flowered under his, welcoming the thrust of his tongue and the scrape of his teeth as he searched for the taste of nectar that haunted like a hunger he couldn't satisfy. He supped and burned with the need to get closer, skin to skin, heart to racing heart.

Her eyelashes fluttered against cheeks, flushed with desire, as he raised his head. She was *his* and absolutely perfect, but the time wasn't. ''I'm sooo looking forward to tonight, Maria.''

She leaned into him, the hard nubs of her breasts left trails of fire down his chest. ''If you keep wanting to jump ahead, you'll never truly enjoy the moment you're in.''

He thought about it for a second as his hand slid between them, cupping her soft female flesh. ''I'm versatile, hon. I can enjoy both. Right now the feel of you is driving me crazy from wanting to be inside you.''

Pressing closer to her, he made his point without words.

''That's what I want, too, but I'm worried that I might disappoint you.''

He flicked his thumb over the sweet hard center of her breast. Her eyes glazed over, and he caught her up against him as her knees caved. ''You couldn't disappoint me if you tried. This is an affair made in heaven…no, Olympus. You know, where goddesses live? First time I saw you, I was absolutely positive that Olympus was your home address.''

Her expression grew serious, her gaze narrowing as she locked on to his. ''Don't put me on a pedestal, Franc, I'm liable to fall off and break your illusions.''

''Don't worry, hon. I'll catch you.''

One glance at her own room and Maria almost threw up her hands in horror. Most of the shoes she'd left behind were scattered on the floor. Boxes she used for storing stuff she hadn't gotten around to throwing away had been opened, her books and photographs piled haphazardly inside.

The windows had been thrown wide and the rising wind flapped at the floral curtains she'd once thought matched so prettily with the sprigged wallpaper. The room lost some of its country-cottage appeal when seen beside Franc's uncompromising maleness.

It definitely wasn't the sort of bedroom you dragged a guy into with sex in mind, she mused, turning her attention to the mess. ''Guess I know what the kids were up to last night.''

''Looks like they've been dressing up or playing hide-and-seek in the closet.'' Franc picked up a book, glimpsed at the couple in a clinch on the cover and set it down on top of an open carton. She waited for a comment, but he didn't ask the obvious— ''Do you like romance novels?'' The big guy was just full of surprises.

''I can't leave my room like this. Mamma has enough work on her hands, so I should tidy up before we take off. But I'm afraid it's going to set back our arrival time in Auckland.''

''How about I help? That should knock a few moments off. You straighten up the piles of shoes,'' he suggested with a raised eyebrow, scanning them as if doing a quick count.

''I like shoes.''

''Hey, I've got nothing against them. They stop wear and tear on the feet.'' He picked up a black sandal with a four-inch heel and examined it. ''Great engineering, but I haven't a clue how women walk in them without falling off. That said, on you they look great. Make your legs look longer than the Homer Tunnel.''

''Well, thanks…I think,'' she said, taking the shoe out of his hands and pairing it with a matching one. ''You stick to closing up the cartons, I'll put the shoes away.''

He bent to straighten a carton, and had it closed and added another to the pile with quick efficient movements.

Warmth welled up in Maria's belly as she sneaked a quick peek at Franc's khaki-clad butt, and before she realized it, she was staring. Spending the next couple of minutes concentrating on the job at hand did nothing to delete the memory. Huh, and he'd said her legs were long.

She could hear Franc working behind her, the sound of cardboard buckling and scraping as he overlapped flaps to hold a box closed, but she wasn't prepared for the ''Damn!'' or the crash that followed.

The box Franc held had emptied its contents, books and old framed photos, onto the floor from underneath. ''Guess this carton was past its use-by date, the bottom just gave way. Do you think Rosa will have any others?''

''Bound to. Are you game enough to interrupt her while I sort out the stuff I want to take back to Auckland? Last time I saw her she was vacuuming.''

''Sure, no problem. Me and Rosa, we're like that.'' He crossed two fingers together and grinned as he started toward the door.

Maria bunched her hands at her waist and cocked her head toward his departing figure. ''Don't get too big-headed. She's a sucker for anyone who compliments her cooking and you were laying it on thick last night.''

He ducked back in for a second. ''I cannot tell a lie. I haven't enjoyed, or eaten so much food, in years.''

This time she waited till he was out of earshot before letting a smile shape her lips as she thought of his fantastic butt. ''It certainly doesn't show, big guy.''

* * *

So much for Franc's boast to Maria that he and her mother were tight. Rosa had insisted on following him back upstairs as if he wasn't to be trusted to repack the contents of the carton.

In the few moments since he'd gone in search of Rosa, the pretty, feminine room had been swamped in the gray gloom of the leaden sky as if it were underwater. Rosa flicked the light switch to on. "It's going to rain," she mentioned as though they were blind to what was happening in the sky outside. "Did you pack raincoats?"

Listening with half an ear, he started to gather the books from the floor. Maria pulled the tag across the last few notches of zipper curving round the small bag of summer clothes she intended to take back to Auckland. "I'm going to be in the car, Mamma. Besides, it might not be raining in Auckland."

He dropped the first pile of paperbacks into the carton and started on another. "Don't worry, I'll take care of her and make sure she doesn't melt. She'll be okay with me."

"Huh, no one can control nature. The storm is going to get a lot worse before it gets better," said Rosa as he dropped the last of the books in the box. The noise caught her attention and she picked a book from the carton. "Why have you kept these? I thought you got rid of them years ago."

"I might want to read them again. In fact…" She took the book Rosa was holding then grabbed a few more. "I think I'll take some back with me."

"I didn't think a man like Franc would leave you much time for reading."

"Mamma…" Maria opened the bag again and pushed the books on top, closing it with an air of finality as Franc picked up some framed photographs, turning them over one by one to examine the glass in case any had cracked in the fall. Most were old photos of the Costello tribe when the kids were young and Rosa and Pietro sprightly.

The last almost startled a gasp out of him, as his breath

backed up behind the lump in his throat. It was of a teenage Maria, a school portrait in black and white. Her face was thinner, her eyes no less huge than when they'd danced together the night he met her. She'd worn her hair long down her back, held back by a bandeau, matching the white regulation blouse with its collar sitting primly over the neckline of a dark-colored uniform. Black, navy, he couldn't tell. And she was absolutely beautiful, so beautiful it twisted his heart simply to look at his goddess in the making.

Embarrassed by the emotions churning in his chest, he laughed, "Hey, Maria. Get a load of this. You look like a little nun, all that black and white. Cute though. You should have this picture on display somewhere."

Rosa took charge. "We have so many photos of Maria the house is full of them."

Funny, he hadn't noticed.

The photo was shoved away out of sight and Rosa piled the others on top. Her mouth was pinched, the lines around it showing her sixty or so years for once. "She's much prettier now. I don't even know why she kept that old photo."

"How old were you then?" he asked, reaching for the question like a drowning man clutching at splinters, unaware of how he'd fallen into a dark bottomless pool he hadn't known existed.

"She was seventeen, an awkward age," murmured Rosa.

Bull's-eye! The answer hit him where it hurt the most. Seventeen. The year she was abducted.

He wanted to say something, anything, to rectify his blunder. Maria looked at him, her eyes wide and dewy as if fighting back emotion—and who could blame her. The next moment he knew he'd been wrong as she shook her head and put an arm round her mother's shoulders and gave her a peck on the cheek. Looking back at him, she shook her head, as if he'd be crass and say more.

As they left the room, Maria was saying, "I don't know about you, Mamma, but I'm starving and I'm sure Franc could eat a horse." He heard a giggle and she continued, "Did you ever see anyone put away so much food?"

The joke was on him, but he deserved it, and it was a relief to hear Rosa reply, "He's a big man, he needs sustenance."

He didn't think he would eat much this morning. After putting his foot in his mouth, he had enough to chew over for a while.

It was an hour before Franc brought the bags down from their rooms to the entrance hall. Rosa had just come through from the kitchen with some food she'd packed for them to take home.

"Thanks," Franc said, "but I already called a restaurant. We have reservations for seven-thirty at a place in the ferry building."

"No problem, eat the food tomorrow. I've wrapped it well. It'll keep, and there is enough to feed both of you."

"Mamma, I'm back at work tomorrow. I don't live in Franc's pocket."

He wanted to open his pocket and tell her to jump right in. It was a pity she had to work between Christmas and New Year's, but then, she hadn't met him before she volunteered to keep the library open in case one of their clients had an emergency.

"Don't refuse, hon, even tomorrow your mother's food will taste better than the pizza I have in the freezer."

Rosa smiled now she'd won. Maria tucked her purse under her arm and took the parcel while he caught up the three bags.

Pietro came out to say his goodbyes urged on by Rosa. "Don't be a stranger now, Franc."

What could he say except, "Thanks," while Maria shooed them back inside from the doorway.

"You don't want to get wet, the rain is blowing straight into the porch."

It was obvious the guy who met them on the way out didn't

mind the rain. It dripped off his hair, off the hem of his anorak and pooled onto the painted wooden floor.

Maria couldn't hide her surprise, "Arthur. What are you doing out in all this rain?" She glanced up and back. "Franc, this is Arthur Collins, a neighbor of ours."

Franc didn't think anything more than a nod of recognition was called for, and it was all he got in return as Arthur swiped the moisture from his rain-darkened hair with a thick palm. The guy was thick all over; his wet sleeves clung to his muscled arms and the anorak was tight round the chest. In a different situation, when Arthur wasn't dripping every which way, he guessed the guy could be attractive to some women.

He wondered what Maria thought.

"Arthur, you're soaked. Don't tell me you walked over."

"Yeah, it's no distance, so I couldn't be bothered getting the car out of the shed."

Maria backed away as Arthur shook the rain off like a big shaggy dog. Deciding it might take a minute or two as the guy began digging inside his raincoat, Franc put the bags down on the floor of the porch and pressed a hand on her shoulder as if to say, "I'm right behind you, hon."

"I brought something for you, Maria." Arthur pulled out a small gift wrapped in red Christmas paper. He handed it to her then sighed as his fingers came away red. He wiped them on his anorak, saying, "Darn rain gets everywhere, sorry about the dye coming off. I just wanted you to have a little something so you wouldn't forget me. They're earrings."

She held the box gingerly. From where Franc stood, her expression looked a little strained as if trying not to show her distaste at her red fingertips. "Arthur, that was kind but you shouldn't have. I haven't got anything for you, sorry."

The chunky guy's shoulders shifted uncomfortably as he blurted out, "That doesn't matter. I just wanted you to know that I get down to Auckland quite often now, to the markets and a few retailers, and I wondered if I could maybe give you

a call sometime. Maybe we could have one of those cappuccinos they love down in the city.''

"That's real nice of you, but I'm seeing someone right now
and I don't think he'd care for me going out with someone
else.''

*If looks could kill.* "This guy here? What'dya call him,
Franc?'' He looked him up and down. "City fella? It won't
last.'' That said, he turned and headed back into the rain. At
the foot of the stairs he looked over his shoulder and got in
a parting remark, "You know where to find me, Maria, I'll
be waiting.''

That, Franc supposed, was meant to cut him down to size.
But he was more interested in the rapidly disappearing prints
the man's trainers left on the stair treads.

"Well, that was interesting.'' Maria turned, but didn't quite
look him in the eye and her chin lifted. "It must be six months
since I last saw him. He helped out at the vintage.''

Franc couldn't get those footprints out of his mind. Seemed
Arthur lived quite close. It would have been easy for him to
slip into the vineyard and spy on them. "Did he cause you
any bother? Annoy you in any way?''

"Who, Arthur? No, he's big but he's a pussycat. This
morning's outing must have taken a lot of courage, because
he's usually quite shy.''

He could tell the moment she realized what he was getting
at. "You don't think Arthur…him? Oh no, that's ridicu-
lous…he wouldn't hurt a fly.''

He could see the wheels turning and almost felt sorry for
planting the suspicion in her mind. Her eyes lost their glow
as she ran her tongue around her teeth then swallowed. "I've
known him most of my life.''

"I didn't want to disillusion you. Hell, you're probably
right about him being an okay guy. But until we know one
way or another, better to believe the best but expect the
worst.''

He pulled out a handkerchief as Maria stripped the paper

from the tiny box. "I hope the dye comes off my fingers as easily," she said, flipping the case open to reveal twin gold hearts. "They're pretty, but I couldn't wear them now."

"Let's do a swap. You take my handkerchief to wipe the worst off your hands and I'll put this gift away someplace safe until we know for sure who is stalking you." He pushed the box and paper in the pocket of his black Gore-Tex jacket. It was one his brother Kurt had given him and the dye wouldn't do much damage to it. "While we're on the subject, you do know whoever is stalking you isn't going to stop at following you? It will escalate."

Her mouth compressed, formed a straight line that looked as if it would never again break into the smile he loved. He wanted to tease her out of her mood by kissing the mole at the corner of her lips but knew not even a kiss would help.

"You mean like him coming into my room and touching my things when I'm not there?"

"Exactly like that. And for that reason, I'll be coming in to check out your house when I drop you off." He picked up the bags. "Have you told your housemates about being stalked?"

She walked beside him to the top of the stairs. The rain was pelting down in sheets but she didn't appear to notice. "No, I haven't told them. I thought I could handle the situation myself. Besides, none of them will be back for at least ten days."

"If we can't sort this problem out by then, you'll have to tell them."

She nodded briefly then squared her shoulders. "Time to make a dash for the car. Christmas is definitely over."

They were on their way back to Auckland, and from the driver's seat of his MX5, Franc asked, "What was all that about the picture?"

"Which one?" She adroitly sidestepped the question by playing dumb. She swallowed, felt her heartbeat pick up speed, faster than when he'd hauled that photo out of the carton and held it carefully with the same large hands that were wrapped firmly around the wheel. But that had been different; she had Mamma to think about. Too busy protecting her mother's feelings to worry about her own.

In a moment Franc would get down to the nitty-gritty, and having already told him she'd been abducted, what use would avoidance of the subject be now? It wasn't that she could elaborate much further. She only remembered in her dreams, her *bad* dreams. And she thanked God they were soon forgotten. She had prayed about the recurring nightmares last night when she went to Mass with her family, and left Franc at home watching television.

Maybe this was her answer. Franc finding the school photo had happened so darn pat. It was his comment about her looking like a little nun that had done it; upset Mamma. But how was he to know of the three scars she bore, silvered through time, but scars nonetheless. Three crosses.

"You know what I'm talking about, hon."

He wasn't really wheedling, but there was an edge of disappointment in his tone. Yeah, she knew what he was talking about, trust.

"You want to know what upset us, is that it?" Her question bounced around the confined space of the car, ricocheting off windows that looked like miniature waterfalls. The rain was so heavy they would be lucky not to run into flooding on the flat ground closer to Warkworth.

"Jeez, was I that obvious?"

She flashed him an annoyed glance and caught him grinning at her. "Keep your eyes on the road, you're making me nervous."

"I will. I'll keep my eyes glued to the road while I listen to your answer."

She eased around, her shoulder leaning against the door. There was a slight draft blowing through it and the damp air chilled her to the bone. To the heart. She'd known Franc for less than five days and from what she'd already confessed, he'd imagined her life had only one direction and that was *down*.

"That photo was taken the week before I was abducted. Mamma got it in the mail the day I disappeared." She twisted the handkerchief Franc had given her between her fingers. The red stains hadn't gone; they lingered like old blood.

"How long were you missing?" He spoke so low she leaned toward him. "How long did he hold you?"

"I'm told it was less than a week. I don't remember. And I don't want to…" She stopped, forgot what she was going to say as the car began to slide into the middle of the road. "My God, what's happening?"

"We're hydroplaning! Hands over your face in case I can't get us out of it."

The tail broke away as Franc steered into the skid, and through the fingers covering her eyes she watched the rain on the windows changed from waterfall to whirlpool as they spun right around and back again. There was a buzzing in her ears as if all the air had been wrung out of the car.

Franc recited curses, some of them she'd never heard of, and just as she thought they'd be sure to land in a ditch or hit a tree, he wrenched the wheel round and the car zoomed up a side road all cylinders firing.

There was a buzzing in her ears. She'd forgotten to breathe. Her first gasp kick-started her burning lungs. The second gave her back her voice. "My God, I thought we were dead for sure."

"You and me both, hon. Hell, am I glad we were wrong."

He pulled the car over into a small slip road in front of a fruit stall and halted. Jerking back the parking brake, he shut down the engine. "It's not true what they say, you know."

"What do they say?"

He turned in his seat and gave her a look that warmed her cold bones, melted them. "That your life flashes in front of your eyes. At least, if it did I was too busy to look."

She stared at him a little longer as she unfastened her seat belt. "I had my eyes covered—most of the time."

But they weren't covered now. She watched him punch the button on his seat belt and met him halfway. Halfway to his arms. Halfway to his mouth. No one had ever kissed her this way before, with such feeling, such passion, not even Franc.

She gave herself up to his embrace, his lips, and kissed him with more heat, more heartfelt emotion than she'd ever kissed anyone before, not even Franc.

In the midst of death, they'd chosen life, chosen each other. For now anyway…

## Chapter 8

The downpour had stopped by the time they drew up in the driveway of the Northcote Point villa Maria shared. They were almost an hour later than they'd calculated, due to the rain and other stuff. Pleasurable stuff. The car windows had been as wet inside as out by the time they resumed their journey, he'd had to wipe the condensation off so they could proceed.

Swinging her legs to exit the car, she let her lips curve into a smile as she stood. Not everything in her life at present had a downside.

On the driver's side, Franc got out. She watched him across the low roof of the sports car as he walked round to open the trunk and remove her bags. He caught her gaze, and her contented expression.

A flash of white teeth broke up the natural tan of his skin, and her grin broadened. They stood gazing at each other down the length of the car like a pair of loons until he looked at his watch and moaned, "Still five hours until I pick you up again."

Too long.

"I'll take a cab tonight. That way I won't have to drink and drive, and since you're the expert on wines, I'm depending on you to choose something special for the occasion."

The thought painted a slash of heat across her cheeks.

*The occasion.* She supposed that was one way to classify her deflowering. If his car hadn't been so small, they might have already accomplished it in the middle of the storm. Now, wouldn't that have been something to tell her grandchildren...oops, if she ever had any, they weren't likely to be Franc's.

"I'll be waiting. Plenty of time left to get ready." She held out her hand for the bags, but he shook his head.

"Uh-uh. Remember, I need to come in and check the place out. I'm not leaving you alone until I'm sure it's safe."

When her parents fussed these days, she wanted to say, "Relax, I'm a big girl now. I can take care of myself." But when Franc did it, her fancy was to cuddle up close to him and enjoy. *Take it while you can get it, hon,* she mused stealing Franc's little endearment. *It won't last forever.* That's for real.

"Okay, I'll go ahead and open the door." With all the dampness in the air, the wood creaked as it opened, after she put her shoulder to it. She picked up on Franc's amusement as he came up the three porch steps behind her. "That door's slightly arthritic with age. It takes a lot to move it. I think its body has shrunk around its bones."

"More likely the door has swelled as a result of the rain front passing through. Probably only needs a little taken off the top and bottom. Remind me to take a look at it sometime."

Sometime in the next ten days? She knew for all he appeared eager to be with her, an underlying part of his mind was chomping at the bit. He wanted to be back at work finishing the project she was researching for him, since it was in the very last stages of development.

He put the bags at her feet. All business again, he told her, "Wait here while I do a quick recon of the house. I'll whistle when it's safe to come in."

She bit her bottom lip to prevent herself from laughing as he came back to pick up the bags. "I could have managed those myself, you know, I have muscles."

"Don't spoil the surprise. That's something I want to discover for myself. But that's not what's tickling you. Come on, cough up, hon, what have I done to amuse you?"

Less than a foot separated them. This close she had to tilt her head back to see his face. His raised eyebrows made another question redundant. She inched closer and his mouth quirked crookedly to one side. She'd remembered the heart-throb he reminded her of, but she wouldn't tell him, he was too darn pleased with himself this afternoon as it was, without making his head any bigger. Another inch and she said, "I was simply imagining what would have happened if one of the other girls had come back early and you'd burst in on them."

She batted her eyelids, testing the newly discovered power of a woman over a man. His eyebrows drew a line above the serious brown depth of his irises as they mirrored his thoughts.

"Correct me if I'm wrong, but they're not due back for another ten days or so, are they?"

"You're right. I told you it was all imagination, and if I had heard screams of outrage I would have come racing to your rescue." She considered for a moment and stretched higher, closer to his mouth. Maria could almost taste him. She moistened her lips anticipating his kiss. Anticipating the sensations his mouth drew from her and the images he would paint in her mind.

The bags hampered his hands and prevented him from pulling her into his arms, or so she thought, as with one palm to steady her on his chest, she brushed his mouth with hers, teasing it with her tongue.

She was wrong. Waiting for his mouth to open set her heart racing and made her brain dizzy with suspense. But she wasn't held in no-man's-land for long. A thump echoed through the hallway as he released the handles. He captured her lips with a determined slant of his mouth, and her body with his freed hands. They splayed across her back pulling her into him, into the magic and mystery he spun with his touch, his kiss. "Mmm."

Her sigh just about covered all she was capable of uttering.

They were standing in the open entranceway where anyone could see them, but that was of no account compared to giving herself up to Franc's embrace and waiting for the world to stand still.

Time twisted and spiraled like two fine wraiths of smoke that became one. Coalescing until a second before the vanishing point, they formed one bright shining moment. The vision was as clear as crystal in her mind. She wondered Franc didn't see it, as well.


He'd anticipated an earlier arrival, knowing Maria's work schedule and how conscientious she was, always hanging her clothes outside the wardrobe ready for the next day. But, she hadn't come alone and he'd barely jumped out the back window in time to watch from the bushes.

*Look at her flaunting her ardor like a slut for anyone to see. For him to see. Did she know he was out here watching? Was this her way of taunting him?*

*The view from where he'd hidden was perfect, almost too perfect, he decided as he predicted Jellic's next move and cursed when he was proved correct.*

*His massive hands closed over her small butt as he lifted her up on him, then the bags were kicked aside as the jerk shouldered the door shut, as if in his face.*

*Pretty Maria. He knew the way to cool Jellic's, or better still, Maria's ardor.*

*With the tip of his knife.*

*Maria knew his skills, his precision work. The weight of the weapon at his hip never bothered him. Comforted more like. He patted it like someone else might spoil a pet.*

*Ha! He'd see who got the last laugh then.*

Instinct drove Franc in the direction of Maria's room.

No time for thought, no time for anything but Maria and the need to finish what they'd started a few hours ago in his car. With the echo of one closing door still ringing in his ears he heeled her bedroom door shut and turned, pressing her back against it to leave his hands free to explore her curves freely.

His heart hammered in his ears as he found her breast and let the perfection of its fit—its weight—in his palm, whip through him like a cyclone.

He was as hard as hell and getting harder as she gathered him to her, hooking her ankles behind him until the steel in his flesh cushioned its ache in the softness that held the only remedy for what ailed him.

Lust; there was no other name for it in his vocabulary. He'd always been a quick study, a good student at school, and from the beginning he'd learned his ABC's and minded his p's and q's, but he'd never learned or wanted to be taught about the L word.

The heat from Maria's mouth threatened to envelope him in a fire that he might not be able to put out, but he'd walked away from worse situations in his life—his family for one—and he could do it again.

Making a slight adjustment to their current position, he scraped his knuckles against the doorframe. The inside of the door had to be as unwieldy as concrete and just as uncomfortable for Maria. This was stupid. Damn straight it was, when there was a bed lying in wait for them on the other side of the room.

"Hang on tight now, I'm going to try to carry you over to the bed without spoiling the good thing we've got going."

He pressed in closer, making sure there was no mistaking the thick, pulsing length on the wrong side of his zipper.

She cocked her head to one side, dragging her passion-weighted lids open to look at him. Her pupils were blurred with a desire that echoed his own, and for the first time in a year he wondered what the hell he'd been thinking, staying celibate all those months when Maria had in actuality been working with him, albeit on the other end of the phone or an e-mail.

Her lips were full and red from the ravishment he'd put them through as she clasped her hands behind his neck. "I'm ready, take me where you will."

"Oh, I will, you can bet the house on it." He took a step backward, then another, taking it easy as if they had all the time in the world, instead of as if he was liable to explode if he didn't get inside her in the next few minutes. But his plan was to land on the bed with Maria on top. Her slight weight against him had brought home the huge differences in their build. Crushing her wasn't a good start for what he had in mind.

Ever helpful, in a voice far more assured than he'd imagined at this moment, she told him, "Two more steps and you'll be lined up with the bed."

"If I end up on the floor, look out, little…" The feel of her stiffening in his arms sent cold shivers through him.

She'd changed her mind.

Unwinding her arms and legs, she cried, "Oh my God, look at that!" In less than a heartbeat she twisted out of his grasp and spun away, grabbing his hand. "Look."

The old disused hearth was filled with pinecones and twigs with dried leaves arranged to fill its empty corners, but on the mantel above, little figurines he hadn't paid much heed to last time he'd been in the room were lying down in pairs. Shepherds lying over shepherdesses and so on, down the width of the wooden mantelpiece. "Is this one of your friend's ideas of a joke?"

"They haven't got it in them to be so crude." She'd begun straightening the ornaments before he could say, "No, leave them as they are."

"But I always keep them just so. I like to look at them from the bed." His head turned in the same direction as hers, though his reason was more about what he'd missed than Maria's view when in bed.

Maria clutched at his wrist, squeezing as if his presence gave her the strength to take in what they saw; the imprint of someone's body pressed into the feather duvet. She whirled into his arms and flung her shuddering body against him, but not with fear, as he soon discovered.

"I'm so angry. Dammit!

"He has almost spoiled everything, being so happy, wanting you more than I wanted the breath to tell you." Her shoulders lifted against his palms as he did his best to quell the anger pulsing through her body. "Thank the Lord we stopped when we did. I'd hate the memory of my first time to be tainted by his presence. It's almost as if he was watching us now."

Franc's back teeth ground down on his anger, filtering the worst of it out so Maria wouldn't know of the murderous force that roared in his head. His inspection had been too cursory. What if he hadn't decided not to wait any longer? What if Maria hadn't teased him into it? Would that pervert have returned the moment his back was turned?

"I can't let you stay here."

As if she hadn't heard, she crossed to the window and pulled up on the handles. The sash slid up without any effort. "I wonder if we have nails anyplace. That would fix him."

"Maria, did you hear what I said? I can't leave you in this house on your own. You have to come home with me."

"I heard." She said it softly, as if something had drained her of the anger that had bubbled over when she'd seen the crude arrangement of the figurines and then Searle's shape on the bed. Who else could it be? Tony? It hadn't been Arthur, for they'd left him behind—he remembered the long hour they'd passed in his car—or had they? He found he much preferred to see her raging, to the fragile silence that encased her now.

Her gaze wandered the room without lighting on anything for more than a second or evincing any reaction until she stood and hurried to the bedside table with its pictures of her family. She picked up a lavish Christmas card. "Look what he's left. Too bad he neglected to sign it."

"That's it," he growled. "I've had enough."

He swung on his heel and practically ripped the door off its hinges as the memory of Maria plastered against its hard surface threw him off balance. Franc was halfway down the hall before he heard her call out, "Where are you going?"

"To call the cops. Something you should have done before this got out of hand."

Later that evening, he told her, "We could have called off the dinner, hon. I don't know if taking you out tonight actually makes sense after getting that kind of shock. And well, hell, this time of year they probably have queues of people waiting for cancellations."

Maria took a sip of her wine. It was exactly what she needed. Not for the shock, to get past Franc's gentle treatment as if she was one of the little ornaments that had been so maligned. She much preferred the Franc who'd pushed her against the door and let her feel his desire in the most explicit way possible. She had nine days left to her—and Franc. She wasn't going to let Randy Searle rub his grubby mind all over what was her best chance of experiencing a once-in-a-lifetime sexual encounter, which, going by Franc's rules, was the safest name for what they had going.

"Franc." He stopped midconcern, catching her impatience on the fly the moment she said his name.

"You are my lover not my mother—"

"Not your lover, either."

"Okay, if you want to be punctilious, my almost lover. As almost as anyone has been." She slipped off her sandal under the table, determined to turn the tone of the evening toward more earthy matters. If being new at this didn't spoil the fun.

So, she'd missed the first time?

Her second attempt was more successful as she wiggled her toes into the space between the cuff of his pants and his leg.

She leaned back in her seat a little and beamed at him, catching a reflective glint in his eye that she hoped to turn into the single-minded gleam of this afternoon.

The next sip of wine went down real well as she inveigled her toes somewhere around calf level, going by the hard muscle they were massaging.

There was a wry twist to Franc's mouth as he asked, "Are you trying to seduce me?"

Letting her eyelids droop, she sent him a burning look that always worked in the movies. "Am I that obvious…? No, I take that back. Am I succeeding?"

In no time flat he turned the tables on her by capturing her foot and pulling it into his lap. His fingers were magic.

Who knew feet could be so erotic? Who knew he could give such a good foot massage? Who knew anything anymore?

As she sighed into her wineglass, it occurred to her that she hadn't grown up until she'd met the big gorgeous guy opposite her four nights ago. And she definitely hadn't known anything so sexy existed. Combined with what Franc was doing, the next sip of wine burned, making her eyes blur as the view from the window out over the harbor took on the shimmering shapes of a mirage.

They had a corner table without too much foot traffic to disturb them. She smiled at her little double entendre. If it hadn't been for that, she doubted she'd have attempted to distract his thoughts that way. On second thought, then she wouldn't have known what she'd been missing.

Her eyes were half-closed and she whimpered softly under

her breath as his thumb pressed a spot in the middle of her sole that took her halfway to heaven. He chose then to reverse his former question. "Am I seducing you?"

"Oh yeah, big-time."

"Are you seducing me?" The wineglass she'd been hiding behind came down onto the table, clenched in her hand for balance as he pulled her forward in her seat and slipped her foot between his thighs. "What do think? Are you succeeding?"

The heat invading her sole was a sure sign that something was happening. She tried an exploratory maneuver, flexing her foot, but all she revealed was her inexperience. Franc gasped aloud.

"Tell me I didn't hurt you." She slid her foot to the floor. When she finally found her sandal, it felt like ice in comparison to the hot steel of his erection. "I guess this is one of those things that should only be practiced by consenting adults in the privacy of their homes."

As he grinned at her, she privately thanked her stars that she hadn't hurt him too badly. "If you're taking votes on that, you've got mine."

"Do you think it will take a lot of practice to get it right?"

He swallowed as if the huskiness in his throat bothered him. "I certainly hope so. In fact, I insist on it."

Maria couldn't help a flush suffusing her face and neck as their server arrived. She was stung by the thought of what would have happened if he'd arrived a few minutes earlier.

He cleared their entrée plates away. "Would you like to see the desserts trolley?"

"What about it, hon, want something sweet?"

The server forgotten, she licked her lips and pouted, watching Franc's eyes darken. Her expression was a touch on the wicked side as she said, "I think I'll wait until we get home."

"Just two coffees, please."

Alone once more, he leaned across the table and grasped

her hand. "And we're never going to be able to go home if you don't cut that out. I didn't wear a jacket."

She giggled, she couldn't help herself. "I never knew seduction could be this much fun."

He picked up her hand, and in front of what seemed like God and the whole world, he kissed her palm and she felt more like crying than laughing, it touched her so deeply.

Touched her to the heart.

Keeping hold of her hand when he'd done, he linked fingers with her. "Fun is good. I want you to be happy. But let's change the subject until we find some of that privacy you were talking about. You start."

"Why were you so angry when the cops wouldn't come out and fingerprint my bedroom?" She'd seen the tight control he'd kept on his exasperation, but after three solid days in his company, the clues to what made him tick—or ticked him off—were more easily recognizable.

She received a brief demonstration of the latent power in his hands as his conjoined fingers tightened on hers. "I wouldn't call it anger, dissatisfaction would be closer to how I felt. In my position, I'm used to getting results, action, when I call for them. For that cop to tell me they had enough cases of breaking and entering on their hands without coming out to one where nothing was taken… Well, let's just say it wasn't conducive to good public relations."

He let go of her hand as their server arrived with two dark and delicious smelling cups of coffee. She looked into Franc's eyes and noted the similarity in color. "I'll take mine black," he said in reply to her silent communication with the cream jug.

For herself she poured a liberal amount of cream into her cup first. "I can't drink it black, too bitter for me."

"Talking about which, you're the one who should be bitter about that cop's laissez-faire attitude."

"But you didn't think to mention Randy to the cop monitoring the phones at the police station."

"How could I, with no proof? When I think of Searle coming into your room, touching your stuff, lying on your bed, the sheer gall of the guy really burns me up."

She took the flames licking at the back of his night-dark eyes as proof that Franc would be as passionate a fighter, as an impassioned defender of weaker mortals, as he was going to be a lover.

With a snort, he tossed back coffee so hot there was no guarantee it would put out the fire in his gut. "You'll be glad to know your plan succeeded. I no longer feel the urge to drag you onto the table and ravish you in front of the other diners. However, I can't give you any guarantee it won't happen again, so let's get the hell out of here while I still can without disgracing us both."

She tilted her cup and drained the last drops of creamy rich coffee. "I'm ready when you are."

He grinned as he stood up and came round to pull her out of her seat. The heat of his body was like a living thing enfolding her. He leaned closer. His breath feathering across her neck, teasing the loose stands that had escaped the complicated knot she'd tied before leaving his apartment.

"I love it when you talk sexy. But I don't need it, hon. A look, one sweet glance from your pansy eyes, is enough to turn me on." The roughened timbre of his voice, a low growl, crashed through her head like thunder, followed by a lightning strike down her spine that spent itself through the soles of her feet.

Not even the brush of his fingers on the skin her dress left bare could earth her in this dimension. With Franc she would never experience plateaus, only heights she'd never dreamed of ascending.

"Whew." Franc shook his fingers as though burned. "If you're going to react like this to everything I say, we'd better get out of here and catch a cab home. That tabletop is looking more and more inviting."

* * *

The restaurant was on the second floor, the first flight of stairs reasonably bright. Once round the corner, it was a different story. Franc noticed the lamp had been smashed, leaving a scattering of glass sparkling in the glow of the street lamps.

"More vandalism." He shook his head, remembering how many times Stanhope Electronics had been the victim of a gang of spray-paint taggers. "Careful where you put your feet, those sandals you're wearing don't give much protection."

"I'm being cautious, but my night vision's not the best."

He positioned himself one step lower than Maria. "Take my hand. You don't want me having to kiss your toes better."

She chuckled. "I don't know. I could live with it."

As soon as he heard her throaty laughter, he swung round. Face-to-face, the big sexy close-up before the kiss. Yeah, he was going to do it, he couldn't wait any longer. With an excess of dark moody lighting, his focal point as he drew near became the luminosity of her eyes. Like black moths on a moonless night, racing to keep ahead of a squall, the dark fringe of her lashes fluttered then gave up and closed as his mouth sought hers. He sighed, finding the still, heartfelt peace before the storm threatening to erupt inside him.

She tasted of coffee, rich, full-bodied, sweetened with need and want, with a sprinkling of yearning to make it uniquely Maria. Forking his fingers through her hair, he held her head still and plundered without undue haste, savoring the moment, the flavor he'd discovered he couldn't get enough of.

Her hands splayed across his back, slipping down to hook in his belt as they swayed against a hurricane of their own making. He lifted his head as a fire engine roared past in the street, filling their dark cave with a cacophony of sound and flashing lights, red, white, red.

With the truck's passing, the quiet deepened, thick as the darkness enveloping them. He knew they ought to be on their way. That there would be no satisfaction to be found here for either of them, but he didn't resist as her arms drew him back in. Didn't resist as she whispered, "More."

"One last kiss," he promised, his mouth seeking hers.

Out of the black unlit corridor leading to the seafront side of the building, glass snapped, splintered under a heavy foot, a sound he might never have noticed while he was enthralled by the sensuality Maria spun around him.

The sound had barely stopped echoing before he lifted her onto the same step as him. In a harsh whisper, he confided, "I don't think we're alone down here. Time to break camp and get out of this spot."

The door shuddered as he slammed it back against the wall, sprang back as he hustled Maria into the street first. The back of his neck prickled as if an unseen hand ruffled his hair, and reminded him how she'd said she'd known she was being watched. He took the edge of the door on his shoulder, swung round and did one last search of the dark maw opening into the corridor. Nothing moved, not even the air, but he knew by the same preternatural instincts Maria had tried to explain that someone was hiding in the passageway, watching.

## Chapter 9

Too impatient to wait for the elevator, Franc had half carried, half chased her to the top floor. Maria wasn't sure if it was the climb to the fourth floor that had winded her. Or whether the excitement, anticipation and inexplicable fear stole her breath.

Laughing, Franc whirled her into his apartment, one hand clasping hers as he spun her out then reeled her back in, catching her against the hard muscles shaping his chest, all while heeling the door shut with a decisive click.

He bent his head to hers, angling it to nuzzle her neck. His breath coated her ear in moist warmth that sent tremors down her spine.

"Mmm, I needed that, hon. Could our cabbie talk or what?"

"I think he was practicing his English on you. And it was sweet of you to let him." She tilted her head sideways, meaning *"try here,"* meaning I love it when you kiss this spot. Her humming senses found a higher note as he played on the cord at her throat until she wanted to scream with delight.

"Sweet be damned. He was lucky it's only a fifteen-minute trip to Birkenhead Point or I would have jumped in the front seat with him to hold his foot to the floor."

Placing one finger over his lips, she murmured, "Hush now, big guy, slow down. Remember what I said about enjoying the moment you're in? Well, this is that moment."

If Franc replied, it was through murmurs of appreciation as he explored a spot that made her beg for more.

Although her focus was becoming blurred by sensation, she bit down hard on her bottom lip before losing all sense of being, and existed only as an extension of Franc.

Should she continue or take it for granted he'd know how she felt? No, she was used to being clear and concise with the technical data she handled. That was the way to go. "You need to know it's a moment I've waited on for a long time. Twenty-seven years to be precise. So, I don't want to be rushed, I want to be taken care of, cherished. If you can't promise me that…maybe I'd better sleep in the room where you shoved my bags before we went out to dinner."

A serious expression cloaked his features and banked his desire to hot coals that shone red in the dark depths of his eyes. "I promised you we'd have this time, promised myself, as well. We've lost four days already, and although your family were nice folks, you're the one I want to share this time with."

Slowly, he brushed her hair back from her face. "I promise not to rush you." Carefully, he cupped her face in his palms and tilted it toward him so there was nothing in her line of vision but him, nothing but Franc. "I promise to take care of you." His forehead rested on hers and he softly rolled it from side to side. "I'll care for you like you've never been cared for before."

Her focus centered on his lips as he spoke, concentrating as much on how he said the words as on what he said. "And you have my promise that for all the days we have left, I will cherish you."

Then he kissed her and she believed him.

* * *

Franc considered himself a man of his word. He'd settled many deals with little more than a handshake and never let his side down. He wouldn't let Maria down, either.

Starting as he meant to go on, he slipped an arm under her knees and lifted her off her feet. Guided by the light from the hall, he left the glare of the overhead light for an occasion when she was less nervous and carried her into his bedroom. There, he laid her on the bed, kept the ambience soft and mellow in the hazy pool of light from his bedside lamp.

While his fingers sought the lamp switch, Maria's worried at the bedcover, rubbing the rough slub-threaded texture that transformed the silky terra-cotta fabric from feminine to masculine. Twenty seconds from the front door to the bed and already she was in way over her head, out of her depth.

She watched Franc loosen his tie. The designer-silk knot slipped over his head and landed on a dark rust tub chair covered in tweed. Her eyes widened as the top buttons of his shirt gave way to hair-roughened skin. Sure she'd seen it—no, felt it before in the dark. It wasn't that. Watching him pull the shirt out of his waistband, a fist of apprehension slammed into her. She was going to have to strip, take off all her clothes and lay her body and all its awful scars open to his perusal.

She couldn't do it, not yet. "I have a nightdress in my bag."

"I know. I saw it before, you brought the lacy chemise."

"I already had it packed."

A wry curl twisted his lips as he undid the last button and let his shirt hang open. Franc felt himself harden; grow harder still as her huge dark eyes surveyed his chest. The one thing he'd never let slide while immersed in his work was his fitness, and Stanhope Electronics had a staff gym he often made use of as his mind pondered weighty questions to do with the project that could make or break his advancement.

"At this juncture, it's not really necessary," he decided, before the promise he'd made Maria shouted in his ears. "But if it makes you more comfortable, I'll go get your bag."

She was standing by the door of the en suite when he returned. Her glance flicked from him to the bag. She held out her hand. "I'll change in here. I should brush my teeth and take down my hair."

What a woman. He held back a grin. "Your hair won't take long, I've managed to demolish most of it, and as for cleaning your teeth? I like how you taste, so don't worry."

He shook his head and let loose the grin as she edged farther back into the en suite. "I like the coffee flavor on you. It reminds me of hot nights and even hotter sex. Mint is more of a morning taste, but with a bit of luck we can make it last until then."

The grin morphed into a full-throated chuckle as her skin flushed, so she shut the door in his face as if to block off the sound. He was still smiling as he tossed his shirt on the chair, undid his waistband, and then remembered the condoms he'd bought in the men's room at the restaurant. Hauling open the drawer, he slipped them in the corner nearest to the bed and pushed the box he'd had for a while to the back of the drawer.

Likely past their use-by date.

By the time Maria reappeared, he was down to his shorts and had thrown back the bedcovers. Backlit, the lace chemise hid nothing from his eyes. He liked how her narrow waistline flared into the silhouette of her hips, could have spent a lifetime looking at her seemingly endless legs. Then she switched off the light, and as if through a network screen, her skin shimmered, pale, alluring and tempting beneath the lace.

Her hair skimmed her shoulders in swaths of polished ebony, smooth and untouchable. He wanted nothing more than to muss it up, as if all that perfection was too good for him, far too good for Franc Jellic, for the son of Milo, the bent cop.

The drug dealer's son.

"You look beautiful. Like a goddess."

Maria swallowed down the temptation to say, "So do you, like a Greek statue, I mean."

Though the light behind him cast most of him in shadow, a glow kissed his shoulders and arms as if he'd been built in homage to an ancient god, so prized they had cast him in gold. How could all of this be for her?

A few days ago the idea would have been inconceivable.

But statues couldn't move closer, as Franc did now, or hold out a hand for her to clasp. It was almost too much. In a rush, she said, "I'll take the other side of the bed."

The panic was all her fault. She should have gone with the flow, let Franc undress her instead of changing in front of the wide en suite mirror, picturing his horror when he saw the view she did. She should have waited until she got him on the bed and asked him to turn out the light. She still could.

It piqued her that his smile was so knowing. That she'd given her nervousness away the second she opened her mouth.

"Uh-uh. That's not how it works. It's not time for bed yet."

"But my—?" She brushed the backs of her fingers down the lace skirt of her chemise that flirted with her knees.

"Looks absolutely stunning. I can't wait to take it off you." She didn't back away as Franc thought she might when he stopped in front of her and lifted the hand she'd used to signal her consternation. He kissed the quivering knuckles, glimpsed uncertainty in her eyes as he looked down. Without her sandals, the top of her head didn't even skim his chin. "I'm going to kiss you. We've kissed before and I know you liked it. It won't be any different than it was then."

Her bottom lip quivered, but he sensed the underlying humor even before she spoke. "We weren't naked before."

His laughter poured over Maria and lifted her courage. "We're not naked now. Just heading in that direction. Don't worry, I said I'd take care of you and I will. We won't advance until you say you're ready to move on."

Franc was as good as his word. Even before he slipped her onto the bed, she was a trembling mass of wants and needs that lived only for his touch. But she hadn't lost all sense of self-preservation.

His mouth was hot and damp on her skin and the lace lying between both added a new element to the experience. Her skin sang in pleasure at the treatment, and at the juncture of her thighs she felt hot and strange as if she were melting.

Her breasts grew tight under his ministrations and she pouted as he moved on from them, lower, swirling his wet tongue into her naval through the lace, sliding her chemise higher, higher, baring her to his mouth.

That's when panic dashed her with cold water and cooled the heat in her blood. She pushed at his hands. "No."

He took his weight on his elbows. His head lifted, revealing the puzzle in his eyes. "I'm not going to hurt you, hon. I just want to make it easier on you, take care of you just like you asked."

"It's not that I dislike what you're doing, but…can we do it with the lights out? I tighten up all over at the thought of you looking at me close up." She was being less than honest. What made her skin creep was the thought of Franc looking at the scar on her belly that ran down from her navel into the dark curls and cross-sectioned the curve of her belly. She imagined disgust on his face when the dimpled scar was revealed. Unlike the others on her breasts, the wound had been deeper, left open too long before needle and thread had drawn the edges together.

Maria nipped at her bottom lip. Had she spoiled the moment? Did he have the patience to cope with her inexperience? It was one thing wanting to be like other women in her age group, who knew how to handle guys like Franc; it was a different proposition entirely, putting it into practice.

To her relief, he simply said, "No sweat, I can fix that for you. There's something I'll need from the drawer soon anyway." He moved away, smoothly extracting a foil packet that

# PLAY

## Lucky 7

### and get 2 FREE BOOKS and a FREE GIFT

**Scratch off the gold area with a coin. Then check below to see the gifts you get!**

## NO COST! NO OBLIGATION TO BUY! NO PURCHASE NECESSARY!

**DETACH AND MAIL CARD TODAY!**

© 2003 HARLEQUIN ENTERPRISES LTD ® and TM are trademarks owned and used by the trademark owner and/or its licensee.

# YES! I have scratched off the gold area. Please send me the **2 FREE BOOKS AND GIFT** for which I qualify. I understand I am under no obligation to purchase any books as explained on the back of this card.

## 345 SDL DZ4Y                    245 SDL DZ5F

| | |
|---|---|
| FIRST NAME | LAST NAME |

ADDRESS

| | |
|---|---|
| APT.# | CITY |

| | |
|---|---|
| STATE/PROV. | ZIP/POSTAL CODE |

(S-IM-04/04)

Worth **2 FREE BOOKS** plus a **FREE GIFT!**

Worth **2 FREE BOOKS!**

Worth **1 FREE BOOK!**

Try Again!

Offer limited to one per household and not valid to current Silhouette Intimate Moments® subscribers. All orders subject to approval. Credit or debit balances in a customer's account(s) may be offset by any other outstanding balance owed by or to the customer.

## The Silhouette Reader Service™ — Here's how it works:

Accepting your 2 free books and gift places you under no obligation to buy anything. You may keep the books and gift and return the shipping statement marked "cancel." If you do not cancel, about a month later we'll send you 6 additional books and bill you just $3.99 each in the U.S., or $4.74 each in Canada, plus 25¢ shipping & handling per book and applicable taxes if any.* That's the complete price and — compared to cover prices of $4.75 each in the U.S. and $5.75 each in Canada — it's quite a bargain! You may cancel at any time, but if you choose to continue, every month we'll send you 6 more books, which you may either purchase at the discount price or return to us and cancel your subscription.

*Terms and prices subject to change without notice. Sales tax applicable in N.Y. Canadian residents will be charged applicable provincial taxes and GST.

If offer card is missing write to: Silhouette Reader Service, 3010 Walden Ave., P.O. Box 1867, Buffalo NY 14240-1867

BUSINESS REPLY MAIL
FIRST-CLASS MAIL    PERMIT NO. 717-003    BUFFALO, NY

POSTAGE WILL BE PAID BY ADDRESSEE

SILHOUETTE READER SERVICE
3010 WALDEN AVE
PO BOX 1867
BUFFALO NY 14240-9952

NO POSTAGE
NECESSARY
IF MAILED
IN THE
UNITED STATES

he held between his teeth as he swamped the room in darkness. Her heart did a little *kerplonk* in her chest as she heard the foil rip.

Life as Maria Costello knew it had suddenly become dead serious.

His hand slid under the silver-gray pillow he'd earlier fanned her hair over, running through the strands with his long fingers. She'd loved the feel of them in her hair, loved knowing her libido was more sensuous than she'd given herself credit for.

With the bedroom in almost total darkness, it took Franc's vision a few moments to adjust. He hadn't drawn the curtains across the large windows, had no need to with his fourth-floor apartment being well above the roofs of his neighbors, but soon became aware of the pale glow of the street lamps melting into the room. They were aided by the lights from Chelsea Sugar Works that lit up the sky to the north of his apartment, and shimmered gold on the waves of the bay from dusk to dawn.

Now was as good a time as any to get rid of his shorts. The soft breeze from the air conditioner brushed over his hot tight flesh, but instead of cooling him down, the weight of his arousal grew. He twisted round on the edge of the bed. He could just make out the black silk of Maria's hair against the pillow, but his ears hadn't picked up the scrape of lace moving against her skin. "Sit up for me, hon."

"Sit up?"

"Yeah, since the dead of night is taking care of your modesty, we might as well remove the little lace number." He felt the mattress give as she pushed up, then he reached for her. "Let me give you a hand. That's it, easy does it. I've got the hem," he said then. "Darn thing's snagged in your hair."

"You weren't calling it a darn thing when you kissed it all over," she whispered as she took over and untangled the lingerie. He heard the chemise land somewhere on the bedcover, soft as a butterfly.

"What if I did? It wasn't because I have a fetish for lace. No way, lady, it was knowing you were inside it."

His forearm brushed against her breast as she started to lie back down. He stopped her with, "No, stay. Come here, come closer to me. That's it, let me feel your breasts against my chest with nothing separating them."

No sooner said, and she knew she wanted it too. Wanted him to feather the soft hair on his pecs across nipples that had beaded into tight whorls as soon as he'd suggested the idea.

The sensation was more than she'd anticipated, more than she'd hoped for. Her basic knowledge of what happened under the sheets when two people wanted each other the way she and Franc did, with both mind and body, took a leap in the dark.

Her breath escaped through a pouted, "Oh."

She wanted this man with every fiber of her being. Dangerous knowledge when he'd only promised her a matter of days.

Her head whirled from a combination of male musk mixed with spicy aftershave. That, and the delightful dance his hands did on her back, round and round, mesmerizing, hypnotizing.

Daring, she leaned closer and licked the skin below the jut of his collarbone. Intrigued by the taste, she tried again, lower this time, her hand fighting to squeeze between two hot bodies melding into one. She moaned her delight as the tip of her finger found the flat round penny of a male nipple. It was no smoother than hers. She swallowed down the excitement of her latest discovery. "I didn't know this happened to men, too."

Leaning back to give her space, Franc shifted his hold from her long smooth back to her breasts. Had it only been two nights since he'd first held their weight in his hands? It felt as if he'd known the shape of her forever. "So now that you know, what are you going to do about it?"

Figuring a little demonstration wouldn't go amiss to get him what he wanted, what he craved, he circled the tight beads puckering her breasts with both thumbs. Gently, carefully, he cherished them with his hands then scraped the beaded skin with the tips of his thumbnails.

She learned quickly.

As she followed his lead, practicing newfound skills on him, Maria's groans of pleasure were too potent to resist. Lowering his mouth, he swallowed the surprised gasps whole, took her breath inside him, made it his again and again, until his head buzzed with carbon dioxide overload.

Maria's head had just begun to cease spinning, when her education moved on to a whole new level. "Just so you know," he said, "I'll let you in on everything that's going to happen. That way, you won't be scared or shocked."

Some of the things she'd done that night had shocked her silly. Had she really suggested Franc carry on where he'd left off at the restaurant?

Franc's voice rippled across her nerve endings. "All you have to keep in mind is what we're doing is normal."

Maria smiled, knowing he couldn't see her for he was kneeling close to the bottom of the bed with one of her feet in his hands, her heel balanced about waist level. His waist.

Her other foot lay close to his hip, and as the pressure of his fingers made her squirm with ecstasy, half pleasure, half pain, she rubbed the edge of her sole over the slim ridge of his hipbone.

Straightening her knee, he stroked her calf and lifted her foot higher. "This is where we find out which little piggy went to market."

A convulsive shudder wracked her spine, and if it wasn't the words themselves that played on her libido, then it was the rough timbre of his voice, like champagne fizzing over ice. She felt the heat of his breath, of his mouth as he nuzzled her instep. Air hissed between her lips as she tried not to shout out loud. But it was impossible to hold back the sound when his tongue flicked across the crease under her big toe.

And when he drew it into his mouth. *Help!*

When she'd suggested they continue where they'd left off at the restaurant, she'd only been teasing, trying to act sophisticated, as if it would be fun. She hadn't known he'd take the idea this far or how much she'd enjoy it.

Her body was as lax as a teddy bear that had been washed and hung out to dry, and her toes still tingled, when he casually slipped in a remark. "It's all downhill from here, hon, the back of your knee, your thigh, so don't get uptight about it. Just lie there and think of the pleasure it's going to bring you."

His outline shimmered where the golden glow from outside slid over his skin the way she wanted to. A telling glimmer of white teeth cut through the darkness, as with a twist of his shoulders he settled lower, his hair brushing her thigh.

Her bones had turned to water, sinking her deeper and deeper into the mattress until she was sure she'd never be able to move from that spot. The feeling lasted just as long as it took to nip the soft skin between his teeth. "Ouch! You nipped me."

"Just making sure you're still awake." Franc soothed the small hurt with his tongue. "Wouldn't want you to get too comfortable and miss out on the good part."

"Promises, promises, tell me when we get there."

"We're there," he replied.

"Where?" she asked as his finger cut a path through the crisp curls between her thighs.

"Virgin territory and I'm getting the first taste."

Maria had no words to describe what was happening. Nothing in the romances she'd read had prepared her for the heat of his mouth, the flicker of his tongue. Her whole body radiated with fire. And Franc was at the core of the conflagration, fueling it with the most intimate of caresses.

No longer the relaxed puddle of flesh and bone he'd created, she was driven higher and higher by his mastery of her senses until she dug her fingers through his hair, gripping his scalp as if it was the only thing anchoring her to the bed.

Not for long. Every muscle tensed as if fear of the unknown held her back, as if nothing would ever be the same if she let go.

Even as she shattered, she knew she was right. Her life had just changed in some indefinable way. But as she floated somewhere around ceiling height, she forgot that Franc wasn't hers for keeps. That she only had him for another few days.

"No, this is the good part. I wouldn't lie to you, so just be patient." Franc wished he could see the look on her face. Sure, he'd brought her to climax, but he didn't want to make her skittish again by turning on the light. Instead, he slowly sheathed himself and nudged her damp folds with the blunt head of his erection, waiting, giving her a few moments to adjust.

Kissing her breasts, he smoothed his palms lightly up and down her arms, setting up a rhythm with both hands and mouth until Maria's hips began to rise in time with his caresses.

Within moments of feeling the tension between her legs build, he sucked one of her dark nipples deep into his mouth while he pressed a short distance inside her. Maria moaned out loud.

She was so tight he didn't know if he'd be able to hold off, but tonight would set the tone for the other nights to come and he didn't want anything to spoil what at the back of his mind he'd named the season of Maria, a summer break to remember.

He slid his hands down and gripped her hips as he established himself an inch farther inside. Distracting her by sliding his mouth higher, he sought out new flavors: her shoulder, the sweet hollow between her collarbone and the base of her throat, the tender skin beneath her jaw.

Then he took her mouth.

It flowered under his, opening like the roses among the vines just for him, her hips rising, writhing in supplication. But he didn't make his final move until her mouth followed his every time he had to lift his head. Searching, demanding, her teeth, tongue and lips impatient, frantic for more, far too involved for her to worry about what else was happening. That's when he pressed home in one smooth surge of his thigh muscles.

This was as new to him as it was to Maria. The urge to draw back and thrust again was fierce. It prowled the back of his mind like a tiger that needed caging, needed whipping into submission.

He turned his thoughts outward, to Maria, to her needs. Slipping his hands under her shoulders, he felt her curves fit against the hard angles of his body as he surrounded her with his warmth, cupping her nape in one palm to massage the back of her head. "How do you feel?"

"Weird. Full, but ple-e-ase, don't stop what you're doing to my scalp. I can take more of that." Her hand pursued a tentative exploration of his jaw, becoming bolder, she traced his mouth with a fingertip. Franc wasn't sure if she was aware of the understated movements inside her, tightening and releasing, holding and letting go, until he wanted to yell uncle and give in to the subtle persuasion before he was certain she was ready for the next step.

"Is that all there is?"

A bark of laughter shook him, rippling from him into her.

"I don't know what's so funny, but do it again," she murmured, her breath brushing his lips.

"Good grief, I think I've created a monster, a precocious monster, but don't let anyone say Franc Jellic doesn't give satisfaction." He drew back, slowly, carefully, until he was barely inside her.

Next moment her legs and arms locked him in a desperate embrace. "No, stop!"

He flexed his hips and thrust. "Stop this?" He eased back and repeated the action.

"No. I can take plenty of that." Her voice sounded deep, throaty, as if it hurt to drag the words out.

She tightened around the next thrust, and he almost lost it. Without volition, his thrusts deepened, sped up, and her hips rose up to meet them. Need and want and hunger turned them into one desperate mass of hands, teeth and tongue, the slap of skin against skin punctuated by gasps and groans as they used their bodies to egg each other on, making their hearts pump faster and blood race like a bushfire through their veins.

The first ripples of her sheath tightening around his thrusting male flesh were like an invitation to Olympus where his goddess lived. He just wanted to be sure she was there to greet him when he came pounding on her gate.

And she was. And it was everything he'd known it would be and more as she gathered him in her soft arms and welcomed the burst of his heat deep inside her.

For the first time in his life Franc understood the full meaning of sated. But in his relaxed contentment he realized the damp on his face wasn't sweat. Instead, Maria's tears flowed freely, dampening his shoulder. "Hell, don't tell me I hurt you, I tried to be careful."

"Shush, it's okay, they're happy tears. I never knew anything could be so beautiful."

He felt almost embarrassed; his arm trembled as he lifted his weight off her. "That's a relief! I wouldn't hurt you for the world, you know that, don't you?" He cupped her face with one hand, swiping at her tears with his thumb. Deep in his chest it hurt when he breathed. "It frightens me that I could make you cry. That anyone might make you cry."

His fist clenched. This wasn't the moment to mention Randy's name, to bring up the pain the guy had caused Maria, but Randy's imprint on Maria's bed had burrowed itself in his memory like a canker he wanted to pluck out.

"I'm okay now. It was emotional overload. I shouldn't have waited so long to discover the delights of the flesh."

He could tell she was teasing him, could feel the shape of her smile against his cheek, but he took no pleasure in the thought of Maria being inducted into—as she put it—the delights of the flesh by someone else. He rolled over with her in his arms until she rested on him instead of taking his weight. "I'm glad you waited for me."

"So am I. I couldn't have had a better teacher, but I don't know if you realized that after a while, you stopped explaining what was going to happen next."

He bussed her chin with his lips. He'd have to watch what he promised Maria. She was the kind of woman who would keep him to his word. "How could I explain what we just experienced? I'm an engineer not a poet."

"That's okay, I was joking, and trying to make you bite. You rose to the bait beautifully. But just think, we get to do it all over again tomorrow night." She wiggled against him as if anticipating the next time they made love.

Boy, did he have a lot to teach Maria. And it was going to be his pleasure. He could feel himself harden, and the way the cushioned softness of her belly accommodated the pressure.

Smiling to himself, Franc asked her, "Who says we have to wait until tomorrow. It's not one of my rules."

Her chest lifted against him in a deep sigh. "Not one of mine, either." Maria tried to close her mind to tomorrow as he began to love her again.

Tomorrow meant going back to Tech-Re-Search, being in the offices alone with the knowledge that outside them Randy Searle might be waiting.

He'd upped the stakes when he'd entered her room, despoiled her possessions. But then, he'd done her the favor of having her transferred bodily to Franc's fourth-floor apartment. Unless he was a mountain climber, he wouldn't be sneaking into this part of her life anytime soon.

"Hon, somehow I don't think I have all your attention."

"Don't worry, Franc, that's one part of my life I can soon remedy." She groaned as he pulled her closer, and gave herself up to the caress of his palms and the heaven of his lips.

Life wasn't all bad.

Tomorrow would have to take care of itself.

# Chapter 10

*Oh, help. It's daylight already.*

Maria jerked up in bed, the covers tucked tight over her bare breasts. Ever mindful of hiding her scars, she'd slept the last couple of hours the same way.

Sighing, she looked down at the crumpled pillow beside her, unable to decide whether to be glad or sad about waking up alone.

Now, where had Franc tossed her chemise after her last attempt to don it during the night? Her eyes searched the room. Spying a pool of lace floating with blatant femininity against the sea of earthy gray carpet, she slipped out of bed, picked it up and caught an endless glimpse of her reflection.

The two large matching mirrors were a grand gesture, one she hadn't expected. They hung opposite each other, one mirror over the bed and the other above a simple, narrow black-granite table.

If it had been her room she'd have flowers on the hard shiny top, so their reflections would bounce back and forth between the two.

She hadn't paid much attention to the carpet previously. Of course, it had been dark, but the only furniture in the room that had any color was the deep rust–colored tub chair that coordinated with the bedspread. That's where Franc had tossed his shirt and pants. It wasn't until after she'd redecorated to her satisfaction in her mind's eye that it occurred to Maria, if the lights had been turned up, it would have been multiple images of her and Franc's skipping from mirror to mirror in a never-ending stream of lovemaking. After what she had done last night, she wouldn't have thought she had a blush left in her, but she was wrong.

The sound of a shower running explained Franc's absence, but at least he had the goodness to leave the bag containing her toiletries on her side of the en suite door.

Covered now, she walked back to the bed and gave the sheets a quick straighten. She smoothed the soft silver percale into place and realized that unlike virgins in the romances she'd read, she hadn't lost a speck of blood. At the back of her mind she'd always carried a worry that more had occurred during her abduction than her parents cared to tell her.

She had been tight though.

But it hadn't hurt too much.

That had to be because Franc had initiated her to lovemaking so gently. The way he had promised. And though she was still tender it was a good feeling, almost as if he was still inside her. Maria straightened, the thought replaced by panic as she saw the time on the bedside clock, a quarter before eight.

She was going to be late for work.

Her clothes were hanging in the room next to Franc's. After he'd rushed her away from the villa, insisting he wouldn't sleep nights knowing she was alone, he'd shown her in there. A gesture to her conscience, as if they hadn't known she'd be sharing his bed. Truth be told, he hadn't slept much in any case, but at least she'd been lying beside him…on him, under him.

Maria opened the closet, a smile curving her lips as she took out a summer-weight navy suit, grabbed clean underwear from a fitted shelf, surprising herself by wondering which set Franc would like best if she ever had enough courage to parade her body in them. As the mirrored door slid back into place, she noticed the flush to her skin.

Not a glow of love, just hours of lovemaking, she had the aches to prove it. That brought on another smile. God, would people take one look at her and know what she'd been doing. Would her mother...

No, she wouldn't be seeing the family for a few weeks.

Pulling down the neck of her chemise she studied the scars on her breasts. With her skin pink from close encounters with the dark stubble on Franc's face, she could almost tell herself they didn't look so bad. She lifted the lace hem but dropped it just as smartly. The thought of missing the eight-thirty bus into the city was enough to change her mind.

Anyway, no need to look if any other patches of skin had retained a glow, she could feel that they did as she made a mad dash down the hall to the main bathroom, knowing the hours between arriving at work and meeting up with Franc in the evening would be the longest in her life.

Franc heard a shower running as he stepped out of his bedroom and solved the mystery of Maria's disappearance from his bed.

When he'd wakened earlier, she'd been lying so still, straight-armed, holding the covers clamped to her side as if she expected him to peek at virtues he'd only felt and imagined last night. Trailing a finger across the top edge of the sheet had only resulted in her pressing her arms closer to her sides. Though he'd laughed to himself at the time, he'd felt an unwelcome twist in his gut to think she didn't trust him. Didn't trust any man, and after what she'd been through in her short life, he couldn't find it in him to blame her.

The coffee was ready before Maria put in an appearance in

the kitchen. She flushed the moment they made eye contact, which brought out the devil in him. "How do you like it in the morning?"

Her eyebrows arched, two dark winged questions above her pansy-colored eyes.

"Coffee, how do you like it in the morning, black or white?"

"White. If I have time to swallow it, I just remembered you live on a different bus route and I've no idea what time the bus arrives or where the bus stop is."

He pushed a mug across the counter in her direction. With her glasses perched on the tip of her nose she looked more of a librarian than he'd first given her credit for. A very sexy librarian. "I've put in lots of cream to cool it down, but don't rush, I'll drive you to work and pick you up again tonight."

She took a quick slurp of coffee and sighed. "Thanks, you've just saved my life twice, first with the coffee and then with the offer of a ride."

"Don't sweat the thanks, hon. I've nothing better to do except shop for basic groceries." *And check on Randy's whereabouts.*

"I'm afraid I can't offer you breakfast. I usually grab something on my way to work. But I can promise you something special tonight. The restaurant where we met is pretty good about sending up meals when I ask."

She flashed him a wicked grin, assuring him she already knew the answer to her question. "And do you do a lot of entertaining?"

He came round the counter and took her empty mug from her hands and replaced it with a cell phone. "You're the first woman apart from my sister. I eat a lot of meals on the run and while I get through work I've brought home. Don't get me wrong, I'm capable of cooking for myself, but this is less hassle and cuts down on burnt offerings and indigestion."

"In that case, I accept with pleasure...and anticipation."

"Yeah, that's all right then. Take this cell phone wherever

you go, as much for my peace of mind as yours. Just access the directory, like this." He showed her. "My number's top of the list. It'll only take seconds to reach me. Here's the ring I've set it to play." The tinkling notes of "Greensleeves" filled the small silence. "Too loud?"

"No, it's swell." She studied his face as he passed her the cell phone. "I never had a guardian angel before."

"Are you lookin' at me?" He pointed a finger at his tough-looking unshaven chin. "Don't get me wrong, but does this look like the face of an angel?"

Her smile said it all: she wasn't taking any excuses.

"Okay, well, maybe on a bad day."

"Thanks for seeing it my way." She slipped the phone inside the purse that matched her suit and lightweight sensible shoes.

He compared how she looked to their first meeting. Okay, still goddess, but a very big businesslike one.

"I'll feel safer knowing you're only a call away," she said and lifted her face to his. He dotted a kiss on the tiny black beauty spot by the corner of her mouth. Maria was learning fast. The only part of their relationship to worry him was that he could see it becoming too darn necessary for his comfort. Good sex will do it every time and he couldn't remember ever having as good sex as he'd had last night.

Suddenly he felt as if life had just taken a gun and shot all his plans in the foot. The thought made him turn his back on her. He wouldn't let it happen, wouldn't let her get under his skin.

He shoved the mugs into the dishwasher and snagged his keys from his pocket. "We'd better get a move on. Wouldn't want you to be late your first day back at work."

"That's no problem. Since I'm in charge while the others are on holiday, I'll just write myself a note."

Marie was glad to lock the glass doors of Tech-Re-Search behind her. When had a day ever dragged out so long? Never.

But then, this was her first day back at work since she'd met Franc.

She looked up and down the street for his car. It was busier than usual, petrol and diesel fumes clogged the air with not even a whisper of a breeze to blow them away. There would be crowds of people in town exchanging gifts that were no use to them, or didn't fit, or were just plain ugly, she realized, remembering the ornament that Luke, her eldest nephew, had bought with his pocket money for Mamma.

Not that Mamma would part with it for love or money. Maria knew her mother of old. Some of her own disastrous purchases still held pride of place at Falcon's Rise.

She stepped closer to the edge of the pavement in case Franc's was part of the large crush of cars cruising the block.

That's when she felt the cold trickle of fear, the icy fingers caressing her spine that stole her breath away. She turned on her heel, wildly looking around, her eyes darting here then there as she groped inside her purse for the cell phone. Darn contraption was so small it must have slid down to the bottom.

In her haste, her shoulder hit something fleshy and human. She could tell from the gasp. Not Randy, thank the Lord!

Then as her gaze lifted past a dark jacket, shiny with wear, past the buttonless black shirt, her eyes latched onto the white dog collar, and she prayed she hadn't uttered her thanks out loud. "Oh, please forgive me, Father."

The unexpected lurch into the priest had thrown her off her stride, but when she received a smile instead of a frown for her almost knocking him over, she calmed down.

An Australian twang shaped his vowels as he pondered the advisability of her remark with an "I'll forgive you, but I'm doubtful if the street is the right place to take confession."

There was a familiar tilt to his head and she'd wondered where they'd met. Maybe he'd been a visiting choirmaster or a priest who'd taken Mass while she was at school, or maybe she glimpsed him in passing and not paid much notice. "Have we met?"

"I shouldn't think so. I've not long arrived in New Zealand from Melbourne to take up the position of chaplain at the hospital. And besides that, I'm not a Catholic priest, so you don't have to call me Father. Reverend or Chaplain will do."

"Oh? You look like someone I knew a long time ago, but I can't remember his name. It will probably come to me when I'm thinking of something else."

"Maybe you've passed me in the street when I've been visiting Saint Andrew's. It's not more than a block away and it's the parish church of some of the poor I have to deal with in my work at the hospital. So many have no money or home to call their own."

"How awful. Bad enough anytime of the year but at Christmas…to be without family. Here, let me give you something to help." She reached into her purse, and as she felt for her wallet, Franc's cell phone slipped into her hand.

"I should think a pretty girl like you would have more urgent things to spend her money on," he said, but as she slid twenty dollars from her wallet, his hand came out to take it.

"Maybe I should be asking how I could help you. You looked distressed before. That's why I came over, to ask if I could help. Then as you turned, you bumped into me."

Maria denied her fears as if they had never been, had never sent panic into overdrive. Why did it seem worse now, as if somehow she had more to lose? Before she came to a conclusion, she heard Franc calling her name.

"Maria."

She spun round, the chaplain forgotten as the moment she'd been waiting all day for began to play out.

"Over here." Franc's voice came closer.

She caught sight of him crossing the last few feet of roadway. "This is who I was waiting for." She threw the chaplain a smile over her shoulder. "I thought he'd gotten lost."

Then he was there, pulling her into his arms, and the scent of him washed over her like a balm, soothing all her worries.

Franc pulled away, as if the chaplain standing next to her had only just pierced his consciousness. "The city is like a madhouse. You wouldn't believe how far away I had to park. I hope you're wearing your walking shoes, hon."

His thick eyebrows rose in a question mark as if waiting for an introduction, a name, but she'd forgotten to ask for one, and before she could correct her mistake, the chaplain tipped his white summer straw hat with its black band, saying, "Thank you for the donation, I can see you're in safe hands now. Goodbye."

"What was that all about? What donation?"

She tried to instill lightness to her tone, but the memory of those anxious moments ran like a dark thread through her words. "I accidentally banged into him. Oh dear, I hit him with my shoulder, it must have hurt. So I gave him a donation for the poor street people he helps to salve my conscience."

"Soooo, how come? It's a wide sidewalk," he said, stating the obvious. Nudging her for an explanation she'd been trying to avoid, knowing it might put a hex on the dinner she'd been looking forward to all day—just her, Franc and candlelight She'd bought a couple of candles for the table.

"All right, you win. I had that feeling I was being watched again, and as I rummaged through my purse for the cell phone and tried to see where Randy was, I shoulder charged the priest. At least I thought he was a priest. But he's only a reverend. Now, have I left anything out? No, I don't think so."

She left the word *satisfied* unsaid. Keeping the childish taunt for another day when Franc was giving off those over-protective vibes. He took the purse from her and looked inside. "Maybe you should throw away some of this stuff, then next time the phone will be easier to find."

After he handed it back, he took her arm, tucking it through his. "The car's this way."

For about ten seconds, she thought of explaining why everything she carried in her purse was not only necessary but also absolutely essential. What was the point? He wouldn't get it, her brothers didn't and they'd been married for years.

"Why can't you take the rest of the break off? I don't like you being alone in that office all day." Franc had been hammering at this argument for all of the ten minutes they'd sat waiting at traffic lights, queuing to get onto the Harbour Bridge.

"Someone has to be at the office in case of an emergency. I can't let my boss down."

He ran his fingers through his hair in frustration. What if something happened when he wasn't on hand to prevent it? His inquiries into Randy's whereabouts had gone nowhere fast. He was out of town, or that was the story he'd been given by the few people Franc thought would know.

The biggest stumbling block came up when he'd asked, "Out of town, where?" No one knew.

He tried a new argument on Maria. "Maybe if you explained to your boss, he'd find someone to take your place."

"Nooo," she gasped, lacing the word with indignation. "Apart from myself, and presumably Randy, you're the only one who knows what's going on." She crossed her arms and went on the defensive. "Instead of rattling on about what might happen, you should be pleased that I've had time to check out that polymer you've had designed to use as a conductive thread. Not a sniff of it anywhere on the Internet."

Though the last bit of information was news he'd been waiting to hear, *that* was the future. He wanted to fix her life now.

He'd made great plans for this evening and he could be shooting them down in flames, but it was as if he couldn't help showing that he was anxious about her. They'd gone all over the stuff about her parents practically hiding her away from anyone but family, as if they suspected everyone who saw her would want to abduct her. An exaggeration? Maybe, but viewed from this distance a slight one to be expected.

At the same time, taking her parents' lead and locking her up in his apartment for the next eight days was starting to sound like the only solution to the problem.

Hell, if Brent could read his thoughts, he'd be telling him his attitude was set on overkill. But, he'd be hard pressed to tell his friend why it felt so necessary to him. Hell, he couldn't explain it to himself, never mind a second party.

They'd barely scraped through the traffic lights, when Maria loosened the knot in her arms and deigned to talk to him again.

"Don't think I haven't thought about broadcasting the trouble I'm having among my friends. But do you know how quickly gossip spreads in this town? With my background, it would only take some journalist to get wind of it, and the whole shebang, including my past abduction, would be front-page news."

She huffed loudly before continuing, a sign that he still wasn't off the hook. "During the holiday season they'll jump on anything more exciting than the latest seaside town to bring in a liquor ban for New Year's."

He got her point only too well. Now that the Santas and the little kids with giant teddies had passed their use-by date, there was a dearth of anything enthralling happening locally.

"I'd forgotten about that."

"Well, that's the difference between us. I can't forget…I mean, I can't remember the abduction, but I can't forget it took place."

The silence between them stretched out as if the past had built a brick wall through the middle of the vehicle. He took his eyes off the traffic ahead of them for less than a second to dart a glance her way. It was long enough to see her fingers twisting in her lap. He realized she was building up to something. The best he could do for the moment was give her time to come out with whatever she had on her mind. He just hadn't expected it to slice through his gut like a ragged-edged blade.

"I dream about what happened, you know? But when I wake, however hard I try, I can't remember the dream."

He couldn't find the words, so he reached over to clasp her hand. The knowledge that this was something he couldn't fix pooled like molten lead in the pit of his stomach.

"Tomorrow, lock yourself in the office and don't let anyone in unless it's someone you know."

"But I know Randy."

He was glad to see the Stafford Road exit coming up, and for the need to concentrate as he changed lanes to slip into another stream. Once again Maria had robbed him of words, but he could think of much better ways to do that. Tonight, he'd keep them so busy Randy wouldn't have a chance to cross either of their minds.

It was dark in the apartment. They'd eaten hours ago then cuddled up on the settee, watching TV. When he'd left her alone a few minutes ago, he'd turned off the lights, teasing, "Wait here in the dark you're so fond of. I've prepared a surprise."

She didn't hear Franc approach as she stood by the window watching the glow from the streetlights, but she sensed him, every hair on her body acted as an antenna when he was around.

A fancy sparked in her imagination as Franc led her through the darkened apartment, that she'd been lost, and he was taking her home. *Home.*

"Welcome to my home," he'd said the first day he'd brought her here. Christmas Eve. Yet her belongings were still in a room that wasn't his. So much for the, *"You can choose any room as long it's mine,"* when he'd asked where she wanted to sleep tonight.

And where was he taking her now? Guiding her past obstacles that loomed in the dark as if they didn't exist. Eyes as yet unused to the black spaces of the interior hallway, she only knew they stood at a doorway when she heard a handle turn and the lock click open.

"Welcome to paradise, hon," he whispered as he pulled her into his room. He'd lit the place with hundreds of candles of all shapes and sizes. Her attempt at adding a romantic ambience to the dinner table appeared halfhearted compared to this, though Franc had been pleased she'd thought of it.

"Great minds think alike," he whispered now, breaking into her thoughts.

Maria culled the figure of hundreds of candles by more than half as her pupils adjusted to the soft wavering brilliance to discover that the reflected glory of the flames danced between both mirrors and glass in the floor-length windows, darkened on the outside by the night sky.

Franc's chest was bare, likewise his feet. No wonder she hadn't heard him cross the living room. She turned to him, finding his features softened by the candlelight and something more, something that whispered between them as tangible as another person in the room. "It's beautiful. How did you manage all this in a few moments?"

"I'm good, hon, but not that good. I set all this up earlier. Why do you think I didn't move your stuff into this room before you went to change? Believe me, It wasn't because I didn't want you sleeping in my arms tonight as I'd promised."

He pulled her into the center of the room. "Look." He turned her to the mirror opposite the foot of his large bed; the long narrow table below it was awash with candles, and their glow was more soft than bright. "Look in the mirror, you're beautiful. And see here."

On the bedside cabinets he'd placed tall columns of pale ivory-scented wax, held by two very modern candelabra either side of the mirror hanging over the bed. "All I've done is put you in the proper setting for romance.

"And look here." Franc turned her this time toward the

tall windows, stretching from floor to ceiling that led onto the balcony. "The whole world dims before your beauty."

Maria saw herself, taller, slimmer, dressed in a mauve dress because he'd said the color made her eyes look like pansies. Her black hair gleamed in untidy curls atop her head, Franc's arms held her. Her narrower shoulders sloped softly in front of Franc. Compared to the width of his chest, she was tiny.

But more, what called to her emotions was his gaze, on her, on her reflection, over and over again. And it was the look in his eyes that made her feel beautiful. Made her heart jolt wildly in her breast, as if it had been missing all the years since she was seventeen and had acknowledged that her life would never be ordinary, never be like other girls', like her peers', and at that moment she found it again.

"Don't move. I'm not too good at this." His hands went to her ears and she felt the cold weight of gold brush her neck. Earrings. "Merry belated Christmas, hon."

She touched the long narrow gold and amethyst drops as she leaned back into his shoulder. Suddenly, wanting more than an image of the man behind her, she turned in his arms. "I'm lost for words, awed that you'd go to all this trouble for me. Thank you, Franc."

The corners of his eyes creased as he sent her a wry smile. "No need for thanks. I did it to seduce you, and I think it worked."

More than a pinch of self-deprecation laced Franc's voice, evoking a questioning lift of her eyebrow. "Okay, you've got me. Sure, I want to seduce you, I'm no fool." His head bent, closing the gap between their mouths. "I want…need to overlay the memories, hidden or not, with romance, with finesse. The initiation is over. This time we're really going to make *love*."

The last word dropped on her lips like an exclamation mark as she exhaled and was left breathless until Franc filled her with his own, kissing her deeply, tongue gliding against tongue, teeth leaving a tattoo on her lips that branded her as his.

"Hone-e-y," he groaned, grazing her temple with the soft slide of stubble. His fingers put a flurry in her nerve endings from wrist to shoulder that spiked in her womb, releasing moist heat inside her panties.

Pressing openmouthed kisses on the curve of her shoulder, he nibbled at the cord of her neck. "I'm glad I didn't mark your skin yesterday. I worried about that."

"Makeup. Concealer," she murmured, sinking back into him, the still-fresh memory lighting a fire inside her, burning strong, burning true, a fitting rival for the heat in Franc's eyes. If he only knew, she would have worn the mark proudly if she hadn't thought it might embarrass him.

Her zipper slid down quicker than his Porsche could go from zero to sixty. Franc nudged her cheek with his chin until she faced straight ahead. "I want you to watch this."

She shivered; more from the way his voice played on her senses than the cooler air striking her breasts as mauve georgette gave way to pale gold skin and black lace. Sliding lower, the curve of her waist, lower, a matching high-cut thong that hid more than one secret. With Franc's guiding hands easing her dress's descent, she watched it fall in a dark puddle at her feet.

As dark as the world she saw outside the window.

Though the lighting was soft, she tensed slightly, worrying about his reaction when her scars were uncovered. Surely, if there was one person she could reveal them to, it was Franc.

Sliding a finger under her bra strap, he ran it up and down. "The black lace can stay on...for a little while."

He cupped her palm in his and placed his lips at its center, making her breath quicken, her body quicken, and her concerns fade away. He sought and found new hollows, the inside of her elbows, the ridge of her collarbone and filled them with kisses.

His bedroom was a place out of time filled with ancient

magic and the dancing light of flickering candles, where his hands held her mesmerized. Touch built on touch. Smooth feminine curves, hers, surrendered to hard hands, his, and she watched it all played out as though it were two other people. Two lovers dancing an erotic ballet choreographed in the land of the Kama Sutra. Honey-colored hands caressed bronzed flanks, and tanned fingers splayed like stars across black lace as if they were both figures carved into the walls of an Indian temple, floating high above a secret jungle.

Her heart bounded as he released her bra, but holding his gaze with hers in the dark-mirrored window provided a reprieve, and soon his hands closed over the pale-silvered remnants of a past she couldn't recall yet wished she could forget.

With a snap, the narrow waist of her thong gave way to his strength, laying her almost completely bare to his eyes, balancing on sandals with straps so fine they looked as if they'd been drawn in henna on her feet.

His hands moved lower, across her belly, below her navel. She held her breath as she sensed his hesitation, like an exclamation in the sensual force he'd built around them.

Her sigh, as his hands moved on, recognized she'd been correct in her perception of the man holding her. He could be trusted, was a much bigger man than the pervert who'd cut her.

Desire weighed heavily on her limbs. Franc became her sole support. Her eyelids drooped as his fingers took up the rhythm of the dance at the heart of her and ripped restless sighs from her throat.

"No, don't close your eyes. I want you to see...look at your reflection in the window."

She wanted to let go, to drift away on a flood of pleasure like nothing she'd known before, but the rough urgent voice in her ear persisted, insisted.

"Look. I want you to see what I see when you shatter."

Franc's long fingers slipped inside her; cold heat in a roaring furnace. His thumb rotated and Maria shattered. Saw what he saw, and didn't recognize the sensual being she'd become under his hands.

# Chapter 11

Some candles burned faster than others while their slow sensual lovemaking played out on the large bed. Eventually, the smell of guttering candlewicks drove a reluctant Franc out of Maria's arms. In the end, he snuffed out every candle but the two branches of aromatic columns beside the bed.

His movements stirred the air, tossing lazy flickers of gold candlelight over the covers to kiss the swell of Maria's breasts as he'd looked down on her. Her eyes were closed, but she wasn't asleep, just avoiding the next hesitant step in their relationship.

Yeah, a relationship. That's what they had going.

When had it morphed from a lighthearted fling for the summer break he'd intended? Become more than an escape from the boredom he'd seen stretching ahead of him. He'd worked nonstop for almost a year on a project on the viability of weaving communications modules into fabric for use on the sleeves or collar of a jacket, but the calls to return to his undertaking grew fainter when he was with Maria.

But right now, as he perused her breasts, thoughts, deep

and unpleasant, gnawed on the explanation Maria had given him for her modesty the first night they'd made love.

Hell, he'd bathed her scars in damp kisses, given the succor of his lips to each scar by turns; though it had been much too late to kiss them better. Too late to wonder if he should have gone about Maria's seduction in some other manner, but in the aftermath of pleasure, there was no way he could go on ignoring his discovery.

The sooner the questions were asked and done with, the better.

In an ironic twist, sharing a trouble might half it, but a secret kept too long increased exponentially. The idea crossed his mind that some of his own secrets might benefit from an airing now that his sister had begun her crusade to discover the truth of Milo Jellic's life, and death.

What had happened, only three weeks after he turned thirteen, had shaped the rest of his life. How could he expect Maria to bare her soul, her hurts, while he left his own skeletons moldering in the closet as if he was ashamed of all he stood for?

He grabbed a couple of pillows that had taken a nosedive off the bed and plunked them under the headboard. "C'mon, Maria, I know you're not asleep, you can't fool me."

She opened one eye. "Brute. I'd like to be asleep."

"Too bad." He slipped the other two pillows from under her neck and piled them on top of the others, then pulled back the covers and slid in beside her, resting his shoulders on the stack of silky cushioned percale.

Tapping her on the tip of her cute nose, he said, "Come up here beside me. It's time we got naked with something other than our skin." Her eyes snapped open, the pretense of being sleepy over and done with. "I'm talking about the truth."

Maria sat up, the covers collapsing in a ruche of silver-gray and terra-cotta that skimmed her lower hips and left most of her belly and its scar available to his gaze.

Her stare challenged his right to know the truth. A challenge that the image of pert breasts with tight, crested nipples negated.

Laying an arm along the top of the stack of pillows, his voice soft, satiny, persuasive, threaded with a kindness he hadn't known existed inside him, he whispered, "C'mon, hon, I want you up here next to me so we can hug. It won't be all that bad, we just need to get this over with and move on. Kinda like, you show me your scars and I'll show you mine."

Her nose and chin lifted a fraction as if she wanted him to understand she was giving in under protest. "All right, if you insist."

A moment later, she snuggled against his side and let him wrap his arm around her, let him hug her against his ribs. But for all that, the tension in her muscles didn't subside, it grew stronger.

"Mmm," she sighed, lying. "I feel better already."

"Good try, hon, but not good enough. Though, if it makes it easier on you, I'll start." The suggestion was all she needed to relax more, and she rested her head on his shoulder so that fine strands of black hair waved like seaweed caught in the ebb and flow of his breath.

"My father, Milo Jellic, was a cop. When I was thirteen he drove his car over the edge of the cliffs at Torbay and took his own life. Suicide. Later it came out, courtesy of his best friend and partner, that my father had been dealing in drugs, and when he thought his superiors were on to him, he'd taken the easy way out.

"So, not only was he a crooked cop who committed suicide, he didn't have the guts to face the music for his sins and left his family behind to face the shame in his place."

"Oh, Franc, I'm sorry. You must…" He laid a finger over her lips; he didn't want her sympathy, just her.

"Shh, don't stop me, I'm on a roll. It's not a pretty story, but that's the legacy my father left the five of us, my three brothers, my sister, Jo, and me. Out of us all, Jo, the youngest, never believed it. 'All lies' she'd say, and no one could convince her otherwise, not even our grandmother, Grandma Glamuzina, who was left to finish dragging us up the best way she knew how. Strictly, the way they had in the old country where she was born. What else could she do with four teenage boys and a half-grown girl who challenged her at every turn? In the end, Jo went to Saint Margaret's to be taught by the nuns. That's where she and Maggie Kovacs, or should I say, Strachan, from Pigeon Hill Winery, met.''

He felt Maria's lips touch where his neck met his shoulder. ''Your grandmother did a great job with you. I never thought I'd meet a guy who wouldn't turn away in disgust at my disfigurement.''

Tightening his arm, he pulled her closer into a bear hug, then forking his fingers through her hair, gently massaged her scalp, the way he knew she liked it. He reassured her, ''I think the passage of time since you were seventeen has made you believe the scars are worse than they are. Tell me, would you feel differently about me if I'd had surgical scars?''

''Of course not. But the last ten years have been weird. For most of those years my family have treated me like spun glass, as if I'd break if a guy even looked at me.''

She picked up his hand lying on the covers, lifted it over her breast, pressing it against her nipple. The point stabbed the center of his palm like a burning lance, yet as his hand contracted around her firm flesh, it was the rush of her heartbeat that said it all. How could he applaud her family's stance without her telling him once more that he was her lover not her mother?

He compromised. ''Doesn't feel like you'd break to me, not even if I squeezed harder, like this.''

Air hissed between her teeth as he suited action to words. ''I'll give you a million dollars not to stop what you're doing. I love the feel of your hands on me,'' she told him, and he marveled silently at the difference a day made.

She would never have expressed her need to be touched in

*Shadows of the Past*

a certain way when they first met, although, there had been the continuing episodes with her feet. He smiled at the memory and drawled a silent "Oh, yeah." What had started as piece of fun had gotten away from them.

He didn't know what brought his brother-in-law to mind, but he realized telling her about Rowan and Jo might not help, but it couldn't hurt. "Did I tell you that my boss, Rowan McQuaid Stanhope, saved my sister's life? He took a bullet from a rifle in the thigh as he pushed Jo out of the way. But in the way that no good deed ever goes unpunished, it cost Rowan his career and left horrific scars where the shot cost him muscle, as well as bone." He traced the shape of the cross on one of her breasts and Maria stilled as if she hardly dared breathe. "If Jo could live with that, there's no way a little-bitty mark like this is going to stop me being with you."

"You have a way with words, Franc Jellic, and I'm thankful for it. Suddenly my angst over the marks on my body seems almost too precious."

"God, I didn't mean it like that, hon. The scars are real, they're war wounds. I just don't want you to be too ashamed to reveal a part of your history that wasn't of your own making. Hell, you didn't ask for this. You were seventeen. I looked at the photo of you at that age and saw nothing but innocence shining out of it. The fault was his, not yours."

He'd be lying if he said he expected the next question she came out with. "Could you tell if I was truly a virgin the first time we made love?"

Stunned, he floundered, scrabbling for the right words. "You were extremely tight, but did I deflower you? I wouldn't know. In my life there has been a shortage of virgins. How many before you? None that I can recall. So how's a guy to get the hang of what exactly makes a difference…"

The meaning of her question finally sank into his thick skull. And he cursed beneath his breath. Damn Rosa Costello for not setting her straight. He knew Maria had no memory of the trauma, but her mother, her sister, someone in her family should be the one to clear up her suspicions, to reassure her.

"Maria, I'm sure your mother would have told you if you'd been…" He cleared his throat to help him spit out the word.

"Raped." He ground it out, hating the image that sprang to life by saying her name and that *damn* word in the same sentence.

"Don't torture yourself over it. I was so caught up in making sure I didn't spoil your first experience, I don't remember anything except the pleasure of being inside you. And I have to tell you, hon, the satisfaction gets better every time."

He tilted her head up from his shoulder and pressed a kiss on her forehead. "Promise you'll put the idea out of your mind and not let it spoil the rest of our time together, or, the rest of your life." *After he was gone.* "It's not important to me."

*Coward!*

His fingers contracted against her scalp, an automatic reflex from sinews desperate to form a fist to shake in anger.

Maria winced.

He pasted an apologetic smile on his lips, hoping she couldn't read the thoughts behind his eyes. Hoping she couldn't see his imagination squeeze its hands round the throat of the bastard who had done this to her.

Maria turned in his arms, pressed her breasts against his chest, and the image disappeared as fast as the notion had jumped into his mind. The sway she had over his libido erased everything from his mind but her and the way she made him feel.

She traced the shape of his ear with a fingertip, blowing into the whorls and hollows with a husky purring sound.

He was being softened up for something. It might not be something he'd care for, but while the fingers of her other hand explored his chest, he didn't let her effort and attention to detail go unanswered and did some hands-on research of his own.

"It occurred...to me." She drew the words out with breathless hesitations. "That since you think being inside me...just gets better each time...maybe we should try breaking the record and find out just...how...good it can get."

The last came out in a warm damp rush against his ear, making his gut contract on a spasm of lust. He'd been hard since the moment he hit the sheets again and pulled her, soft and warm and smelling of sex, against his side. Now he was a dead ringer for the title Man of Steel.

"You're on, hon" was forced past his strangled larynx.

Relief came to his rescue as Maria actually giggled, a delightful sound that he'd felt in danger of never hearing again.

With her hands on his shoulders, she forced him back against the pillows. "Darn straight, I'm on, big guy. This time, I get to be on top."

Maria couldn't understand why she wasn't tired. After the night she and Franc had put in, she ought to be glad to be at work. Glad to have a whole day to daydream of Franc.

Yet all she could think of as—per his orders—she locked the glass entrance doors to Tech-Re-Search with her inside, was how soon could she do it all over again.

At least the assignment she was working on was for Stanhope Electronics and through them, indirectly for Franc. His brilliant idea of weaving two-way transmitters into the fabric of a jacket was ahead of its time, and soon he'd informed her, she'd have to begin research on visuals that would be as good, if not better, than the latest cell phones. She couldn't wait to start on another project that would stretch her mind.

She was up to her elbows in research printouts off the World Wide Web, when the doorbell rang. Someone had followed the instructions she'd taped to the inside of the glass door.

She looked around her untidy desk, searching for her glasses. They were nowhere to be seen. Probably hiding under the masses of paper her research had generated. That was the trouble with being short-sighted, she had to keep taking them off. No matter, she wouldn't need them simply to answer the door.

Yet, her spine tensed as she pulled open one of the doors on the office side of the lobby, wishing her boss had installed some kind of security camera she could check, *without* revealing her presence to the person on the other end of the bell push.

Her internal alarm stopped ringing when she recognized the chaplain six feet away, waving a piece of paper at her through the plate glass.

She hadn't realized he knew where she worked, but then he'd probably seen her leaving yesterday evening, the way she'd caught glimpses of him around the area without taking any particular notice until she bumped into him.

The stiffness in her spine eased as he smiled. "I've brought you a receipt for the donation you gave me. If you'd rather, I can slip it through this gap between the doors."

She had the key in the lock as she spoke, "That's okay. I would have left the doors open, but Franc—you met him yesterday—insisted I lock myself inside."

The chaplain nodded in understanding as she swung one side of the doors ajar. "I gather you're working alone at the moment." He kept nodding, taking her confirmation for granted. "Well, I don't blame him, a young girl like you, so...so pretty, you can't be too careful."

He raised his hat, holding it above his fair, receding hair in a courtly gesture. Old-fashioned manners, no doubt learned as part of his seminary training.

Someone ought to tell him he looked younger with his hat on. Maria smiled up at him; his eyes were an unusual light gray that looked out at her as if they'd seen sights that had aged them. Maybe working with the poor had done that. And it was an effect that made the dark rings circling his irises appear black against the whites. The deep lines in the corners of his eyes made her wonder if he'd worked as a missionary, maybe in a hot climate where the glare of the sun made it impossible not to squint through your eyelashes.

Her smile deepened as she realized she was imbuing him with one of the fantasies from her childhood. "Thanks for the compliment. I must tell Franc he has your support. He worries about me. Now, what's this about a receipt?"

"I thought you might like one for the twenty dollars. Some people claim their charitable donations against their taxes."

"It hardly seems that charitable. In fact, now that I think of it, maybe I should have given you more. I can't leave the office unattended, but if you'd like to come in for a coffee, my wallet is inside."

She stepped aside as he said, "That would be…" Only to be interrupted by someone calling her name.

Now she wished she'd taken the time to wear her glasses.

"Maria." Her name came again, closer this time. Close enough to recognize Arthur Collins.

He lumbered up to the door, his muscles packed tightly inside the checked shirt and jeans he was wearing, work gear for the Collinses, both father and son, who grew produce for the Auckland market. "Sheesh." He wiped sweat off his forehead with the back of his hand. "Sorry, that's what I get for rushing in this heat. Thought I might miss you."

He gave the chaplain the once-over and visibly relaxed. "D'you pray around here, Father?"

"This is Chaplain…" Embarrassed, Maria suddenly remembered she'd forgotten to get his name.

She turned in the reverend's direction. His hat shaded his expression as she played tag with the attention of both men.

The chaplain spoke first. "That's all right. I can see you're going to be busy. Maybe another day?"

"You know where to find me."

Once more, the chaplain raised his hat to her. "That's right, my dear, I do." He dismissed Arthur with a nod, including him in his "Goodbye."

Watching the chaplain turn the corner in the direction of

Saint Andrew's Church, she inquired, "What brings you this distance, Arthur? It's a good few blocks from the market."

"Your brother told me you worked here, so I thought I'd drop by while I was in the neighborhood. Then I saw you talking to the priest."

"He's not Catholic. Presbyterian, I think. He's chaplain at Auckland Hospital." She wondered which brother she had to thank for setting Arthur on to her. As soon as she found out, she'd pay him back in spades.

"Makes no difference to me, never go to church." Arthur swiped his forehead again. He might have muscles but he didn't look fit after walking up the hill Wellesley Street was built on.

"Bet you've got air-conditioning in there."

"Sorry, Arthur. I can't invite you in. Company policy." She could imagine Franc condoning a quiet chat and a cup of coffee with the chaplain, but she well remembered his take on Arthur. No way was she going to rock the boat for the few days between now and when Franc returned to work.

Her thoughts floated her off on a scenario where Franc personally brought her assignments into Tech-Re-Search because he couldn't stand not having her in his life anymore. Had she been mad to agree to his deadline?

Her dream balloon popped when Arthur leaned closer, one hand opening and closing on the doorjamb so that his muscles flexed. "How about one of those cappuccinos then? On me."

If she hadn't been alone, she might have found it laughable the way Arthur was coming on to her. Why now, for heaven's sake, after all these years he'd lived with his parents across the road and never said as much as boo in her direction?

Even as she began to decline his invitation, "I would have—" a lightbulb moment hit her in the middle of her refusal. Of course, Arthur had heard about her parents retiring and splitting up Falcon's Rise "—but I'm alone in the office and somebody has to answer the phones. Maybe another time when you're in town, now that you know where I work." She gave him her best smile and shot his aspirations down gently. ''In fact, call me next time. I'm sure Franc would love to join us. He didn't get much chance to know you last time you met. And I'm sure he'll be accompanying me home in future. He just loved his visit to Falcon's Rise.''

Locked inside once more, knowing Arthur didn't have her number, Maria grinned. Speaking into the empty office in a gruff voice not unlike Arthur's, she said, ''It's a dirty job, but somebody had to do it.''

Wait till she told Franc that Arthur was after her for her share of the vineyard. Maybe the thought of her being an heiress would make him keep her on when their time was up.

Wishful thinking, Franc didn't need her money. It was his own success that drove him, not the thought of living off someone else's efforts.

She shook her head as she frowned at the receipt that recorded, received from Maria Costello, the sum of twenty dollars. She couldn't quite make out the name of the charity.

Never mind she knew she wouldn't claim it off her tax anyway. The reminder that by April the first, when her tax forms would have to be filled out, she wouldn't be caring if she saved a few cents or not. She would be on her own again, with nothing left but the memories she and Franc were making together.

Her thoughts shifted to Randy Searle.

Would he be out of her life by then, or would Franc's departure signal open season on Maria?

# Chapter 12

By lunchtime Saturday, Maria felt she'd earned her keep by doing a share of Franc's housework. Being typically male, he would have left it until his cleaner returned after the holidays, but Maria had insisted that was a cop-out, and refused to let him get away with the excuse.

She joined him in the kitchen when she finished, and was in the process of teasing him about the cleaning equipment, or lack thereof, she'd found in the apartment. "I can't believe that someone used to your level of technology has such a ratty vacuum cleaner. Doesn't your cleaner complain?"

"She brings her own. Besides, there's nothing wrong with that one. It was my grandmother's. Grandma Glamuzina used it every day for years and I inherited the machine." His voice echoed back at her from the pantry.

"It shows."

He looked around the white pantry door and slanted an eyebrow in her direction as if waiting for the punch line.

"That she used it every day."

As in most of the other rooms in the apartment, the decor

was in shades of black, white and gray, the white kitchen with black granite counters looked clean and bright. Yet Maria wished she could lay her hands on a fern or two or maybe a red geranium to cheer the kitchen up and turn it into a place with a bit of life instead of second cousin to a mortuary.

A little voice in her head cautioned her, "That would be one way to lose him quick, to start taking over his living space with feminine froufrou."

Maria wasn't stupid; she'd seen the movie.

Though he'd showered her with fancy aromatic candles, Franc didn't have a history that urged him to get his fingers dirty with rich brown soil, to make things grow, as her father and brothers did. No, it was the technical aspect of electronics and software that rang Franc's bell. He'd fixed the little problem with her laptop last night in no time flat. A guy like Franc was handy to have around even without the great sex.

He'd been staring at her while her mind went on a journey of its own. It took her a second to realign her thoughts and say, "I only meant that it must have sentimental value. No one would give it houseroom otherwise."

Franc closed the pantry. "I think I must have created a monster when I took you in off the streets." He advanced toward her with a look in his eyes that made her shiver with anticipation and sent an excited giggle up the back of her throat to spill over just before he reached her.

"What with you criticizing my equipment." He tried a theatrical leer, and when that didn't work, pretended to twirl a mustache. "And the sexual demands you make in the bedroom, your mother wouldn't recognize you as the meek-and-mild daughter I took home on Christmas Eve."

Joining in the game, she grabbed the front of his T-shirt, pulling him closer. "Kiss me," she demanded, lifting her mouth to his, and when he obliged, hooked a leg round the back of his knee until he fitted against the tingling between her legs and helped ease its intensity.

Her head was spinning, dazzled by the glorious combination of his taste and hers as their tongues stroked in a coup de grâce that nobody suffered or lost. They both won. "Take me to bed," she moaned, impatient to finish what she'd started.

Franc lifted his head, a dazed, clouded look in his eyes. She didn't need to feel the hard, thick ridge rubbing against her belly to know how aroused he felt. "I've created a monster, an insatiable one. But why go to bed? What's wrong with the counter?"

"I just cleaned them."

A chuckle tumbled out of his mouth. She felt its journey as it bubbled up in his chest then poured over her.

*She could love this man.*

He kept on laughing as he told her, "God, I just heard Mamma Costello speaking. When you get older, you're going to be just like her." As he finished speaking, both pairs of eyes widened as his stomach rumbled.

"You need to be fed."

"Guess what? We need to shop. There's nothing in there that would go even halfway to making a decent lunch, unless you can work some magic with stuffed olives and pickled gherkins."

She shook her head. "Not even Mamma could work magic with that combination."

"Then we need to eat out, and then we need to grocery-shop."

"I can do the groceries," she offered, knowing her father's aversion to trailing round the supermarket after her mother.

"Oh, no, I'm not letting you out of my sight. Look what happened yesterday while I wasn't there. Not one, but two men, came calling on you at work. I can just see some lothario cornering you in the produce section." He bent toward her as he spoke, his hands tickling and his mouth inches from the side of her neck.

She lifted her chin to give him better access.

"He'll cover you with grapes and cherries and eat you all

up.'' He showed her how, in the curve where her shoulder met her neck. The wide, low neck of the turquoise T-shirt she'd chosen for its coolness gave him the freedom to choose the most tender spot.

Franc was heading lower, his chin grazing the curve of her breast. ''And if you escape, he'll come after you. He won't stop till he has you, even if it means chasing you round the checkout counter...'' His voice faded away as she shuddered. No sex involved. ''Oh, God, I'm sorry, hon. I'd forgotten about Randy.''

She placed a finger over his lips to still his apology. ''So had I, big guy. That's one good thing about you and me together, you make me forget.''

Franc opened his mouth to reply, but the doorbell got in first. They both turned together, but only Franc voiced his thoughts. ''Who the hell can that be?''

If thoughts of Randy had made Franc's arousal subside, the sight of what looked like the whole Costello tribe on the other side of the peephole in his front door was a dash of ice-cold water.

''Wow—'' he finger-combed his hair then smoothed it back with the flat of his palm as he opened the door and was swamped with a mixture of men, women and children ''—this is a surprise.''

*How did they find us?*

''Maria,'' he called over the buzz of greetings, kissed cheeks and the feel of small sticky hands wiping past his knees, Ricky most likely. He counted heads.

''Your family has arrived.''

*Come and rescue me.*

A suspicion lurked at the back of his mind that Maria's mother was a witch. How else had she known he was hungry? Or that the formidable smell of coriander, basil and oregano, combined with tomato and a sprinkling of Parmesan cheese, would make him forgive her anything? Including invading his apartment without warning.

Since meeting Maria, Franc had discovered two new weaknesses: Italian cooking the way Rosa Costello did it, and Italian women, namely, Maria. That her mother had a hand in both those weaknesses no longer came as a surprise.

"You've saved our lives, Mrs. Costello." He was still wary enough not to call her Mamma or Rosa to her face. "We were about to go out to eat and then call in at the supermarket."

Her mother had followed them into the kitchen, taken some casserole dishes and tinfoil trays from Maria's sister, Giovanna, and her two sisters-in-law, Sarah and Carol, and then shooed them back into the sitting room. A room that had shrunk from the large open space he'd always considered it to be. But between children running round his black leather lounge suite, and men sprawling at their ease on top of the soft-cushioned seats, he could tell he needed twice as much room to house all the Costellos comfortably.

Strangely, it didn't bother him as it might have a few days ago, and that laid-back, take-life-as-it-comes attitude should have given him something else to worry about.

He was a planner, and the situation with Maria and her family had never been part of any plan he'd concocted. Not even a glimmer of light on his laptop where he'd once had the foresight to list all his goals. And until he'd met Maria, he'd never veered from that set path.

Never considered it, until Maria.

The woman in question was busying herself switching on the oven and pushing a deep dish of pasta into the microwave. She wasn't quite as laid-back. "How did you know where Franc lives, Mamma?"

Maria peeled back tinfoil from a tray, looked inside, took a deep satisfied sniff and covered a huge dish of what looked like lasagna back up again.

"It's listed in the phone directory. You'd given me Franc's number, so it was easy to check."

The lasagna went into the oven. Maria closed the door on the foil tray. "I wonder you didn't think to give us some warning."

"It was a surprise." Rosa turned to him, her dark, wide-eyed stare asking for confirmation that she'd done the right thing. Over the top of her mother's head, Maria's almost identical eyes rolled as if to say her mother was full of surprises lately.

"Doesn't matter to me, I'm easy."

Maria's eyes spoke volumes, and the glint in them confirmed what he'd told her earlier. He'd created a monster, one that wasn't above sharing a laugh with him over his discomfort at the double entendre. But it was true; where Maria was concerned he was *easy*.

"At least you brought plenty of food, Mamma. Franc has a large appetite." She qualified the words by saying, "You know, he eats enough for two men."

"Good, I like that in a man. Maria, I noticed Franc has a large dining table. Why don't you show your sister where he keeps the tablecloths and silverware, while Franc shows me round his apartment."

Tablecloths were something they hadn't bothered with before. When on his own, he either ate in the kitchen or on the run, and the night he'd ordered dinner for them both, the Point restaurant that had catered the meal had supplied everything.

"Top drawer, left-hand side of the black-lacquer credenza, take whatever you can find," he said. And when they both appeared puzzled, he explained, "The tablecloths. I inherited them along with the vacuum cleaner, so they don't come with guarantees."

"If they were your grandmother's, as well, I'm sure they'll be perfect." Maria poked him in the ribs as she went past. "Don't let the food burn while I'm gone."

"Here, before you go, take the men some beer." That was one thing he hadn't run out of.

With Maria gone, that left just him and Rosa in the kitchen, as she'd no doubt intended. He'd yet to experience having the hard word put on him by the mother of someone he was dating. But he was sure the unenviable task was uppermost in Rosa's mind.

"She really likes you, my Maria."

"I hope so."

"No, she really does. I've never seen her so relaxed, except with family. Yes, she likes you."

He was feeling his way here, not exactly sure what was coming next but determined to run with it. "Well, I really like her." Flattening his palm against the second door in the kitchen that would take him through to the hallway, he said, "If you follow me, I'll show you the rest of the apartment."

Rosa followed. But he had to wonder why she thought it necessary to bring her purse along.

There was a certain amount of relief in the knowledge that they'd tidied up earlier and there were no messed-up beds or nightdresses hanging off the chair in his bedroom. Maria had given up wearing one. "What was the point," she'd said, "when you're going to take it off anyway."

"The main bathroom is in here." He flung open the door. "It's just your basic white. I haven't done much more to the place yet than move my stuff in. I bought it mostly furnished, apart from the beds."

Maria's toiletries were arranged on the counter of the vanity, a splash of color in a sea of white. He didn't know why the sameness bothered him now, when at the time he'd bought the apartment he'd simply agreed with the Realtor that all the rooms with hard surfaces looked clean.

"My office is on the south side, as well, since it doesn't need much sun, and this is Maria's room facing north."

Her mother looked in the door and nodded. Sunshine dazzled on the blue quilt and pillow set Jo had given him as a housewarming gift. The bed looked as though it had never been slept in, and it hadn't. During his short stay in the apartment, less than four months, Maria was the first woman—first anybody—he hadn't been pleased to see the back of, as they left him to get on with his work in peace. Hell, he'd hardly thought of work from the moment he and Maria met. He knew that would change though, it always had in the past.

She was the only woman to sleep, actually sleep, in his bed. He'd bought the king-size bed a few years ago when he got sick of his feet dangling over the end of a normal mattress, and she was the only one of maybe three women he'd taken to it that he hadn't wanted to send away when the sex was over.

Sleeping together as opposed to making love had seemed to carry a ring of permanence and needed to be avoided at all cost.

"So, Maria hasn't moved in with you?"

"She's only living in the apartment until after the holiday break. When the women she shares with come back to the villa, Maria will go home, too."

"It's not permanent then."

Franc pulled the door closed. "No, it's not a permanent arrangement. Down here at the end is my bedroom. It runs the full width of the building and has its own terrace and en suite."

She followed him into the bedroom and walked across the carpet Maria had raced around with the vacuum cleaner. "Nice view."

View? He hoped she couldn't see what he did when he looked in the room. Couldn't remember the smell of Maria on his skin.

"That's Chelsea Sugar Works where the boat is docked. Behind it, covered in native bush, is Kauri Point reserve. It was the most expensive extra in the apartment." He said the words as he had many times before, but this time he didn't laugh when he mentioned the cost of the view.

He had a feeling in his bones that the most expensive extra was now the one he kept catching flashes of in his mind's eye. Of Maria, her head on his shoulder, her reflection boneless and pliant, succumbing to the pleasure of his hands as he brought her to completion.

Of her sitting astride him the first time she'd demanded to be on top, and the fearless way she'd ridden him, how her being much smaller made it easy to clasp her breasts as she slid up and down on his shaft.

Oh, yeah. No doubt about it, the little fling he'd embarked on so readily was bound to cost him dearly, one way or another.

"I brought you something."

Franc blinked into the moment, shook the erotic images from his mind as Rosa handed him a small parcel, saying "Open it here, now, while we're alone."

He could feel the smooth ridge of a frame under the plain gold paper as he slid his finger beneath the tape holding it closed. He forced himself to say, "I hope this isn't some sort of gag present that's going explode."

The upward flash of her eyes said, "As if I would."

It was the photo of Maria at seventeen, a smaller version. He stared down at it, his throat working, wondering how her mother had been able to bring herself to parcel up the picture and frame after it had upset her so badly, when he'd unearthed a similar one from the box in Maria's closet.

"My daughter, my Maria's told you, hasn't she?"

"About what happened, just after this? Yeah, she told me."

"You're a good man, Franc Jellic. You should keep the photo. I don't think it can hurt any of us anymore."

The urge to tell Rosa why Maria was really staying with him tangled with both the relief and dismay that she trusted him with her daughter. Before the words could bubble to the surface and he betrayed Maria, her mother abandoned the emotion she'd showed earlier and asked briskly, "What's through here?"

He showed her. "It's nothing fancy."

It seemed she agreed. Nodding, she said, "More white."

"I was thinking of buying a few ferns."

"That might help," she agreed, but without enthusiasm. Then she spied the bath. "Oh, is this a spa bath?"

"I don't use it much."

Her expression was innocent, but her words caught him on the hop, as she picked up a pair of white lace panties drying on the heated towel rail. "Maybe you'll make more use of it when you marry my daughter."

"Oh, Mamma! How could you?"

Maria had gone looking for Franc and her mother to tell them lunch was ready. She heard the voices and followed them to the en suite. The last thing she'd expected to overhear was Mamma's blatant coercion. And for once in her life Maria intended setting her mother straight. "This is the twenty-first century, Mamma. Just because a couple sleep together, it doesn't necessarily lead to marriage."

Two more steps into the crowded en suite aligned Maria with Franc. She laid her hand on his arm, wanting to emphasize the two-against-one odds on her mother winning this round. His skin was warm under her palm, but though she'd expected his muscles to be tense, his arm felt quite relaxed.

"Don't get upset, hon. I don't blame your mother for doing her job. I expect it comes with the territory." He reached for the panties her mother was holding. "These feel dry now, better put them away."

Suddenly, Franc was in control, taking charge of the situation. He ushered her out of the en suite. "Take a look at what your mother gave me."

Mamma, who had been remarkably silent up till now, followed them into the bedroom as Franc placed her old school picture in her hands. "You don't mind, do you, darling? I'm sorry about the fuss I made over the photo when you were home at Christmas."

"Of course I don't mind." To show her mother all was forgiven, Maria went over and pulled her mother into an exuberant hug. She couldn't help looking at the photo she still held. Had she really ever looked that angelic? She swung round but kept one arm about her mother's shoulders. "Take a look, Franc." She held the photo next to her face. "What do think? Doesn't look much like me now, does it?"

"You've grown up," he said. His voice was rough. It skittered over her nerve endings like a runaway train jumping the track, and though he was more than two yards away and her arm was still round her mother, she wanted him.

Franc was right, she had grown up, but it had only happened in the last week when he had treated her like a woman. A sensual being with wants and needs that only he could fill.

It was a shame their relationship had a stopwatch counting down the days, the minutes, the seconds. They could have had something good together, but it hurt too much to put a name to it yet. A shame that the answering glow, the smolder she recognized in his eyes, would never really be fulfilled.

Ambition and success didn't come without sacrifices.

"Let me take another look at that picture," her mother said, holding out her hand, impatient as always.

She passed it over, and her mother stared down at it for long seconds, as if she'd never seen it until that moment. "He was a brilliant photographer, he caught everything that was good and decent about you, except for your sense of humor. He forgot your smile."

"Let me see?"

"Oh, don't you start, too, Franc. The photo's a fraud. I was every bit as mischievous as anyone else in my class." She poked her mother in the ribs. "We got up to pranks even you never knew about, Mamma. Do you want to know what we did with Sister Constance's bloomers? Now, *there* was a big lady."

"I don't want to know, so don't soil my ears with such nonsense. Besides, I thought your man was hungry and needed to be fed?"

"That's what I came to tell you. Lunch is ready."

Her mother went first and Maria followed her to the door

as Franc put the frame down on the black marble table, among the candles he'd lit the night he'd really treated her like the goddess he kept comparing her to. When she thought about it, they had probably been Mamma's first clue.

"Oh, don't put it there, big guy. It makes the table look like an altar."

His hand was on her shoulder, ready to leave the bedroom, when he looked back at the photograph then down at her. "Your mamma was right, he was a brilliant photographer, an artist. The photograph is perfect, but it's a still life and doesn't capture what I see when I look at you."

She leaned up against him, careless of whether her mother saw them in the doorway or not. After the panties, nothing was going to shock her mother. "Just for that," she whispered, stretching up to his ear as if she was going to say something sexy she didn't want anyone else to hear, "you can have two helpings of lasagna."

"Uh-uh, my choice…" His voice tailed away and she wasn't absolutely positive she'd heard correctly, but she thought he said, "I choose you."

# *Chapter 13*

Hands linked and arms swinging as they walked, Franc escorted Maria across Takapuna esplanade on Sunday after lunch. He carted an old cabin bag stuffed with towels and drinks and lotions, while Maria carried an old plaid car rug he'd had forever.

Brilliant sunshine slanted up off the golden sands, almost blinding him, yet he kept his sunglasses pushed on top of his hair as he glanced down at Maria hurrying beside him with two steps to his one.

It was stupid, he knew that, but somehow he shrank from darkening her image through his Polaroid lenses. She'd started it with this fancy she had about someone's shadow coming over her and the thought had become contagious. From the moment he'd slipped on his shades to leave the apartment, he'd sensed a shift in perspective that dissolved the promise of a brilliant summer's day into something darker that hid beyond his peripheral vision.

Maria caught his glance, her eyes reflecting the tinge of

apprehension his gaze held. "What's wrong, big guy, too much sunblock on my nose?"

"Nothing like that. I can't remember the last time I spent a day at the beach, and here we are all togged out like a couple of teenagers about to hit the sands." His family had taken an aversion to the North Shore beaches after his father's car, with him in it, had done a nosedive onto the rocks at Torbay about fifteen kilometers up the coast.

She flung back her head and laughed so that her hair kissed the tops of her shoulders. "A teenager? God, don't remind me, it was Agonyville. My days at the beach were over before I had a chance to enjoy that age. But being with you makes me feel I could cope with anything."

He looked down at the one-piece swimsuit she had on. "Not confident enough to buy that bikini I liked."

"I should hope not, but don't you like knowing that I keep some things labeled for your eyes only."

"Now, *that* I can go along with." He scanned the strip of beach bordering the Pacific for a less crowded spot than the area next to Takapuna boat ramp. He should have figured on the last Sunday of the year bringing the local sun worshipers out in droves.

"You weren't saying that when I couldn't make up my mind which one to buy. And now I see why. One-thirty in the afternoon and everyone got here before us. We should have bought a take-away lunch to eat on the beach."

He untwisted his fingers from hers and changed the subject as they reached the steps to the beach. "Lift up the hem of your sarong, hon. I wouldn't want you to trip."

Her sarong, thin opaque cotton in a mix of oranges and yellows over red, had come in a set with the red one-piece, and tied around the waist. They'd bought the outfit in a Takapuna store less than an hour ago. "And don't worry about being a little late, what man is going to say no to his own personal swimsuit parade? To go in and grab one off the rack wouldn't have been as much fun, just faster. And as for eating lunch, I hate sand between my teeth.''

His fingers petted the satiny skin above her waist as she walked with him down the steps. Maria was beautifully shaped, graceful; he loved to watch her move around his apartment, loved the way her hips swung when she walked, loved everything about her. Especially the way she'd laughed when he complimented her figure, saying, ''It's all the pasta Mamma fed me.''

On the sands, Maria leaned into his side, their arms crossing as he felt her thumb hook over the waistband of his cargo shorts. She looked up at him, her eyes brimming with mischief as she moistened her lips with the tip of her tongue.

That was all it took, a look, a lick. Blood flooded his groin. And to complicate matters, she said, ''And we both know you don't *do* fast.''

Her voice had a compelling huskiness that usually signaled she wanted to make love.

''I *do* thorough, and take pride in my work as you well know.''

She rubbed her hip against the top of his thigh, reminding him of how much shorter she was. Over the last few days he'd learned she was his equal in all the ways that counted. But if he wanted to be able to walk across the sand without everyone knowing how horny she made him, he had to keep his mind off sex.

Great sex. Fantastic sex. The best sex anyone ever had, any place, anytime. Oh, man, was he ever in trouble.

''Do you want me to get arrested? If so, carry on. I'll be the happiest guy in Takapuna lockup.''

''They'd have to lock me up with you, big guy. You promised me until the end of the summer break and after today, I have another three days outstanding.''

Her reminder was something he could have done without. *Dammit all to hell!* He'd begun to wish he'd never put a time limit on their association. It showed in the urge he obeyed to slip his sunglasses down over his eyes. Maria had learned to read him too well. No sooner than he felt a shadow racing toward him. One he couldn't stop or duck away from, since it belonged to Old Man Time.

Contrary to what he'd told himself earlier, his sunglasses had made it easier to search out a spot on the sand that wasn't already occupied. "C'mon, hon. I've found us an opening."

Two minutes later, the plaid rug was spread out, the cooler within reach and the suntan lotion in Franc's hand.

A quick glance around him showed that maybe he hadn't been so lucky after all, too many buff young guys with great bods in the vicinity, most of them staring at Maria unwrapping her sarong as if she were peeling the paper off a belated Christmas present. The sight of a couple of volleyballs didn't imbue him with much hope that they would take themselves off closer to the water, to play on the hard-packed wet sand.

He'd allow them two accidental throws in Maria's direction, any more and he'd show them how to make points the hard way.

Franc stripped off his navy polo shirt as Maria sank to her knees on the rug. The high-cut legs of her suit made her thighs look long and sleekly muscled. As he unzipped his cargo shorts, quickly stepping out of them, he had a flashback of her legs locked around his waist. Too many flashbacks and his black swim shorts wouldn't leave much to the imagination.

He dropped to the rug beside her and placed the bottle of suntan lotion in her hand. "You promised to rub this on my back."

She unscrewed the top and poured some into her palm. "And I always keep my promises."

He lay down and let her hands move across his back, firmly massaging the lotion into his skin, and thought about promises. Only three more days after today, and the time he'd promised her was up. What would it take to get an extended deadline?

* * *

As she sat on her own, Maria decided Takapuna beach was becoming more and more crowded and the jerks outnumbered the good guys like Franc about six to one.

At least that's how it felt when she heard a voice call, "Hey, Maria, I didn't know you came down here."

She looked up. The sun was behind him, throwing a completely misplaced shimmer of gold around his silhouette, like a picture of Saint Peter her grandmother in Italy had once sent her. Tony Cahill, trolling for chicks, she supposed.

"Hi, Tony." To be polite, she gave him a meager wave, wishing she had the courage to give him an Italian salute she'd seen one of her brothers use. He deserved it after copping a feel of her breast the day her car wouldn't start.

"Wheeew." The long sigh didn't help. Didn't change things. Franc had gone to buy ice creams and until he returned she was on her own. Or had been, until Tony turned up.

What would happen when Franc came back? She'd seen him bristle, a low growl rumbling at the back of his throat every time the guys playing volleyball made some ham-fisted shot that landed beside her.

Though, if she was being honest with herself, it hadn't been nearly as exciting as watching Franc's muscles ripple as he leaped for a high shot and punched the ball back at them. He'd looked tough, and dangerous, a combination that made her heart flip over as the sight took her breath away.

Digging her toes into the sand under the rug, she hugged her arms around her knees so Tony had no chance to look down her cleavage. *Where was Franc with that ice cream?*

Her desire for something cold evaporated.

The moment Franc had left the rug and trudged across the soft sand to the truck on the esplanade, shivers had iced her spine.

Automatically, her gaze had spun round, as it had the first time the sensation had crept up on her as she walked down Wellesley Street to catch the bus home. That day, she'd felt the first tentative fingers of fear stroke the back of her neck, like an elongated shadow from the past she couldn't remember, stretching out to pull her into its embrace.

And now in the full glare of a sun so harsh, where the only place for specters should be straight down, six feet under the sand, it had touched her again. Stroked her again.

It had to be Randy, but in a crowd this big how could she pick out one face when so many sun-bleached male heads surrounded her? Before Tony had turned up, she'd been fighting an urge to run, to blend into the crowd and disappear, hide, until Franc returned, which only went to show how she was beginning to depend on him.

The thought that she might be playing into Randy's hands had stopped her flight. That might be exactly what he wanted, to fluster her into running somewhere Franc couldn't protect her.

Then Tony had arrived.

With the flight-or-fight urge still winging through her veins, she reached for the sarong that matched her swimsuit. Though cut low at the back and high at the legs, the swimsuit Franc had helped her pick was sexy but not see-through. It hid her scars. Yet, from the way Tony stared, it appeared there was every chance of him having been born with X-ray vision.

"I noticed how your car isn't back in the carport. If you want to catch a ride home from the beach, just say the word."

She knew which word she'd like to use but it wasn't ladylike. Although…if the situation ever called for it…?

"Thanks," she lied. "But I have transport. You remember Franc? He'll be back any second now with ice cream."

"Yeah, remember the guy."

Fed up with staring at his knees, Maria shaded her eyes with her hand. From Tony's expression, it wasn't one of his favorite memories.

"Saw him take off. Was hoping he'd gone home. Noticed he couldn't fix your car, either. Saw it getting towed."

"I guess you see most things from your house, it's on one of the highest sections of the street."

"Yeah, usually see you trotting off to work and walking home from the bus. To see you in your prissy work suits, no one would guess you could look like a babe."

She shivered as Tony's shadow fell across her, blocking the sun. She must be the only icicle on the beach. She signaled with her hand. "Do you mind? You're shading me."

Big mistake. He obviously took it as an invitation to sit down and plunked his towel next to the plaid rug. "Ought to wear that color more often, red suits you."

He didn't touch her physically; he didn't need to, with his eyes doing an imitation of a slug crawling over her shoulders.

Desperate, she looked behind her and heaved a sigh as she caught a glimpse of Franc. He was literally hotfooting it across the sand to her, dodging between groups of sun lovers.

At last she was able to breathe easy.

She knew Tony and his friends in the corner house were university students, sharing the rent the way she did with her friends, but he was younger and should have his sights fixed on someone closer to his own age.

What was it about her lately that attracted all the wrong men?

She listed them in her head, as if counting down the seconds till Franc reached her. Randy, Tony, Arthur, the guys tossing the volleyball in her direction, deliberately trying to rile Franc—they'd all focused in on her like heat-seeking missiles.

Aargh. Not a good metaphor.

She wondered if there was a sign on her forehead, like a party hat. Only it didn't say Kiss-Me-Quick; it read, Frighten the Pants Off Me.

Funny how much braver she was when Franc was around.

He took one look at Tony and his nostrils flared on a huge breath that inflated his chest. Although she admitted, his expression might have been more effective if he wasn't holding two ice-cream cones.

"You lose your way?" asked Franc.

His meaning had to be obvious, even to someone as full of his self-worth as Tony. "No, I'm not lost."

Testosterone was having a field day.

Franc sounded remarkably calm as he handed her a waffle cone that should have melted simply from the heat in his eyes. She moved over and he sat down between her and Tony.

Although, from his patient "Then I suggest you give it a try starting now" sounded as if he could chew butter and swallow it whole, Tony got the message.

"Know when I'm not wanted." The younger guy jumped up and grabbed his towel.

Franc didn't bother to acknowledge the reply. Just stared, all jutting chin and aggressive slant to his shoulders. Too stupid to live, Tony took a parting shot, "See you around, Maria."

"Not if I see him first," she muttered, snuggling close to Franc, her ice cream at a safe distance so it wouldn't drip. "My hero to the rescue again."

Male hormones sparked at the back of his dark eyes, making her skin feel all goosey. She leaned into his arm, then noticed the other ice cream. "Uh-oh, Tony got sand everywhere."

She held her waffle cone closer to Franc's mouth. "We'll have to share. One lick for you, one lick for me."

Franc laughed. Afternoon reprieved. "Hon, you *know* what I like." His warm laughter spilled over her, washing away her fears and drowning the shadows.

"As soon as we finish the ice cream, let's go home."

"Sure, hon." He took a large mouthful of strawberry ice cream, at least half. There was a gleam in his eye as he told her, "You really *do* know what I like."

*She attracted men like flies. Sooner than later he was going to have to swat some of them, particularly Jellic. The bastard treated her like a tawdry sexual object.*

*Jellic couldn't see the qualities that he'd found in Maria. The angelic goodness that shone out of her.*

*Jellic had sullied her glow with his grubby fingers and it would be up to him to erase the tarnish and make her shine again the way he knew she would for him.*

*Only for him.*

It was New Year's Eve. Franc was planning something special.

He'd called Maria at work, saying he might not be there when she arrived home but he was taking her out. "Dress casual but elegant."

Casual? Elegant? What exactly did that mean?

And he wanted to make sure of her shoe size. "You shall go to the ball, Cinderella," she sang to herself as she picked up her purse. There had been no calls for hours. Most of the work she'd done that day had been for Stanhope Electronics and she was sure they, or rather Franc, could wait a few more hours until she collated the last of her findings.

He was going to be over the moon with what she'd discovered today. And no one was going to know or care if she left work early. Tomorrow was the first day of a brand-new year, and after Franc's call she'd stopped thinking of the two days until the end of the summer break as a bridge between her earth-shattering love affair and the drab return of normality.

He couldn't simply make love to her as he had last night then shut her out of his life forever. Once Randy was no longer looming on her personal horizon, maybe they wouldn't live together, but surely he'd call her sometimes as he had today and say, *"Wear something casual but elegant"* again.

But, unless she got to the shops before they closed, she'd have nothing that fitted the description.

She locked the interior doors behind her, but her mind was focused on color. Which should she wear? And should it be something her mother would like or something that Franc would want to rip off as soon as he got her home?

The white envelope lying on the floor inside the plate-glass doors looked like something that could wait until next year, and then she noticed her name hand-written on the front.

No time now. She pushed the envelope inside her purse then locked the door and beeped the alarm system with her remote control.

Leaving everything behind her locked up tight, she hurried down the hill to Queen Street and a boutique that she thought might just have what Franc had in mind.

The sweater she chose was a pale, silvery lilac with fine white stripes. Sleek and silky, it had a wide rolled neck that drooped off one shoulder or could be pushed down off both.

Maria smiled as she glimpsed her workaday reflection in one of the large mirrors as she entered the bedroom. The wide neckline meant no bra was possible, but she couldn't imagine Franc objecting.

The pants were silky too, plain white with lilac binding on the pockets that slanted across the curve from waist to hip. She flung her parcels and purse down on the bed as the door-bell rang. Had Franc locked himself out?

A woman holding a bouquet of dark red roses, that's what Maria saw when she squinted through the peephole.

She opened the door. "Maria Costello?"

"For me? How lovely." She opened her arms and took the bouquet, with no doubt of who had sent them. Something special was going to happen and she was glad she'd spent a small fortune at Perdito's Queen Street boutique.

Her hand rifled through paper, cellophane and roses in search of the card. Then the deliverywoman spoke up, "Oh, there's no card. They said it had been sent separately."

Maria covered her mouth with her hand, "Oops, I pushed it into my purse and forgot about it. I'll go read it now. Bye."

She closed the door behind the deliverywoman. Rushed

through to the bedroom, laying the roses on the kitchen counter on the way past. Now, where had she seen a vase? Did Franc even have one?

She took out her wallet. The card was underneath.

With impatient fingers she ripped the envelope. Was this all part of the surprise for tonight?

The card was white, expensive, embossed with silver writing. The words on the front read, *In Deepest Sympathy*.

It tumbled from her hands onto the bed she shared with Franc.

What kind of sick joke was this?

The card couldn't have come from Franc.

Her heart pounded so hard she could hear its echo in her ears. Gingerly she picked up the card with the tips of her fingers. She could hardly bear to touch it, but she had to find out what it said inside. Find out who had played this cruel trick on her.

Suddenly, she remembered the roses. Remembered burying her nose in their scent as she'd carried them into the kitchen. She felt sick inside, their perfume was on her hands, and as she shuddered, a couple of photographs fell out of the card onto the bed. The first was of her, taken yesterday at the beach in her red swimsuit. Someone had cut tiny crosses through the photographic paper. One on each breast, the other from navel to the apex of her thighs. She threw it away in disgust.

Who knew about her scars? Randy? How had he found out?

The situation was worse than even she had imagined. Tears ran down her cheeks. She let them. Anything that blurred her vision from something she dreaded seeing couldn't be that bad.

The second photo wrenched a sob from her lips. It was of a headstone. On it, in black ink, someone had printed:

Franc Jellic
Born March 14, 1970, Died January 1, 2005.

Tomorrow!

And underneath written much larger, the letters RIP.

The threat contained in the photo was blatant, but this time it wasn't aimed at her. It was meant for Franc. Her thoughts railed at the devilish nature of the fiend who'd sent the threat, and a moment's sanity only just prevented her fingers ripping the photo in two.

If she had ever thought it could be a joke, she didn't now.

But who had sent it? Randy? Was he that mad? That devious?

To threaten his boss…

She opened the card carefully, as the thought of preserving forensic evidence jumped to the forefront of her mind.

Leave him today, Maria.

Only you can save Franc Jellic's life.

Of course, the coward hadn't dared to sign the threat.

It was weird how he knew what would motivate her to leave Franc. Were her feelings so obvious that he knew how to exploit them, how to rob her of the last few hours of her once-in-a-lifetime fling?

She felt numb, dead inside. Knuckling the tears from her eyes, she left Franc's bedroom to go pack.

Once more the rose perfume on her hands made her feel sick.

Sick with anger.

She shook from the intensity of it as she walked back to the kitchen. Before she packed, she had one urgent task to deal with, some roses to kill.

# Chapter 14

Franc put the shoebox he was carrying down on the counter and stared around his kitchen.

It took a lot to amaze him these days. From the instant Maria gate-crashed into his life she had dazzled him, turned his world upside down and made him see his future from a different perspective.

*And again, the unexpected.*

He drew a deep breath. The room held the same lush smell of roses that he'd caught the moment as he walked through his apartment door.

Deep red roses like the petals scattered all over the floor, like the few thrusting their bruised heads above the lid of his garbage bin.

What'n all hell had Maria been up to while he was out making arrangements for their New Year's Eve entertainment?

Leaving the floral disaster scene behind, he waded through the petals into the hallway. "Maria!"

The word echoed back at him with an emptiness that took

him by the throat, as through the gaping door of the second bedroom he saw the bed strewn with Maria's bags and clothes, some neither in nor out, like a shattered rainbow of all the colors that suited her best.

She was leaving him.

*"Maria."*

Her name bounced off the walls, off the closed doors that shut him out of the other rooms. Picking up speed, he dashed into the room they'd shared every night since, at his impulsive insistence, she'd moved in to share his apartment.

The best impulse he'd ever had.

Pink shopping bags brightened the grayness of his bedcover in a splash of optimism that typified Maria. Hadn't she done the same to his dull workbound life?

His heart rate eased from a racing trip-trap to the slow heavy thud of the largest Billy Goat Gruff of troll-killing fame. She'd been shopping at Perdito's.

He wondered what she'd forgotten that she'd had to dash out in a hurry to buy. Well, he'd surprise her by cleaning up the mess.

She might have won the game of hide-and-seek, if a low, keening sob hadn't stalled him at the bedroom door and sent him charging into the en suite.

Fear hit him fair and square in the middle of the chest and the heart stopped, missed one beat then another. He let out a curse as her grip on the curved edge of the white-faux marble basin tightened as if she'd collapse without its support.

She was sick. Had to be to pretend she hadn't noticed him. Her head bowed, hair a tumble of black waves hiding her face, shutting out his reflection as if she couldn't bear to look at the two of them together. He came up behind and gripped her shoulders.

"God almighty, what happened?"

Her breath rattled, a harsh, dry sound torn from her throat that unmanned him. He loosened her grip on the basin, turned her in his arms and pushed her hair back from her face. Her eyes were dry too, hot, burning with a light he'd never seen before.

Hoped never to see again.

"Speak to me, hon, what happened? Who did this to you?"

She pushed his hands away, slapped at them when he resisted. Her laugh reminded him of dry ice, cruel and cutting, as she said, "I did. I did it to myself. Dumb, huh?"

Her hair swung as she tossed her head back, defiant, daring him. "I thought I'd be gone before you got back, but you caught me and now I have to tell you to your face instead of writing a note. How cowardly was that?"

"You're leaving, why? We still have..."

"Oh...yeah, what is it, two days three nights of your precious time left." Her hand formed a fist to clutch against her breasts as he reached out. "No, don't! Don't touch me. Don't lay one finger on me."

Maria shuddered, hating herself for the part she'd decided to play once she'd discovered she was trapped in the apartment with her bags half packed. No way out and no way back. If it hadn't been for those damn roses she would have made it. Even now their perfume hung about her like a miasma of evil thoughts.

She had to keep up the act, play the part and make him hate her. She had to smile and hide her broken heart.

"I don't get it, what's changed?"

"My mind. I've changed my mind." She turned her shoulder to him and turned on the faucet. It took guts to hurt someone she...she cared for. Even to herself she couldn't say the word.

She thrust her wrists under the cold water, but it didn't quench the painful burn in her blood, in her belly. The urge to spill her guts and lay it all out and let Franc take the responsibility for his life.

*Or death.*

The water shushed over her wrists, swirled round the basin, gurgled down the drain as she waited for him to say something, anything. She glanced into the mirror. His face was carved in stone. Not a good memory to carry away with her.

She grasped the faucet hard, tight so it cut into her palm. "I've discovered that I couldn't play happy family any longer and pretend that you weren't going to toss me away like yesterday's newspaper as soon as Stanhope Electronics reopened its doors."

"It doesn't have to end then."

She sensed the words were forced, puzzled. It made it worse knowing he might have caved, might have taken a chance. That they could have made this affair work, could have turned it into something that didn't have a use-by date.

"But it would end someday. And I find myself getting too used to seeing your face in the morning. Better to cut the cord now and give myself a shot at looking round for a guy who's interested in something more permanent."

"So, you want someone else?"

Anger at last. Leashed anger, but maybe she could set it free. She grabbed the guest towel off the ring and looked away from the mirror as she dried her hands, unable to face the results of her handiwork.

"Well, duh? You must have noticed how I enjoyed the sex. I don't want to give that up. I just need to find someone I care less for, so I don't get hurt again."

"You think I would hurt you?"

His voice crowded her, rippled across the nerve endings at her nape the way it did when he spooned with her in bed and talked close to her ear.

"Hell!" She could imagine the lift of his eyebrows, for she never swore. "You couldn't help yourself. My fault, I walked into our deal with my eyes wide shut, but I already know how to do victim, and I refuse to play the role again, so just let me go and forget me."

She didn't say "the way I'll forget you." That was one lie she couldn't bring herself to mouth.

"And if I don't want to forget you? If I don't want to give up the sex, the great sex, what then?"

She wouldn't look, didn't need to. She could sense how close he was. The heat of his body invaded the taut muscles of her back as she breathed in his scent.

Why had she imagined she could pull this off? Burying her face in the towel to hide the emotions, twisting her expression, she stepped away and hit the wall. A real wall.

Trapped, by her feelings for him.

Trapped between his arms as he flattened his palms either side of her head against the cold sheen of white painted wall. His breath was hot on her neck, on her ear. "How about something to remember you by before you leave."

Indignant heat suffused her face. Franc was playing his part too well, had his lines off *too* pat.

His mouth traced the line of her neck and muttered temptation in her ear. "I liked the sex, as well, the great sex. How about now? Right here, right now against the wall. No one knows what you like the way I do, hon. No one knows which buttons to push, what turns you on."

The thick hard ridge of his arousal pressed against her bottom, flattening her against the cold wall. Her nipples froze, hardened into beads of ice while flames licked at her neck.

If she was going to make an end to this, she knew it had to be now. Before her wants, her needs, led her astray.

She let her body go lax, let it sag against the wall, using his triumph at her imagined capitulation against him. Twisting, bumping him out of the way, she turned, hand held high to wipe the satisfaction off his face.

She hesitated a second too long.

Long enough to look in his eyes. Long enough for him to press her palm to his hair-roughened jaw, to feel him swallow convulsively instead of humoring her futile resistance with laughter. When he carried her palm to his lips and placed a kiss at its heart, she allowed him unconditional surrender.

Wanting Franc was killing her.

Wanting her might kill him.

Franc was past taking anything concerning Maria for granted, or blaming the maelstrom they'd come through with anything as crass as PMS. One emotional storm was over and another in the making as Maria stretched up on her toes to close in on his mouth.

He took her mouth gently, carefully, wary of tipping the teetering balance of their relationship past the point where nothing could be retrieved.

It was Maria who forced the issue, forced the pace with her succulent mouth; questing tongue and torturous sweet bites that made his bottom lip throb from her attentions.

She arched against him, fumbling at his shirt buttons and ripping them off when they failed to yield to her gentler persuasion. He'd thought to persuade her with slow seduction, to get to the truth. She'd said so much yet left everything important unsaid. But if he weren't to fall behind in the race she'd started, seduction would have to give way to unadulterated lust. The only L word he dared use.

Her hands were on his belt buckle. "I want you now."

It took her forever to reach for his zipper. Her blouse parted in his grip like it had been made of tissue paper, and her bra gave way before he resorted to nipping it off, its straps sliding down her arms to bare her breasts.

He didn't see the scars, simply recognized she was beautiful, and made to fit him, and to tremble at his caress, as she did now. One-handed, he bunched her skirt round her waist and cupped her, feeling the damp warmth of arousal flow through her panties onto his fingers. He removed the last barrier with a simple twist of his fingers and slid one inside.

She moaned, reaching for him, nearly setting him off from the pleasure of her talented caress as she measured the weight of him, sliding her thumb, back and forth, again and again. He had taught her that, taught her too well.

Cold sweat beaded his forehead and top lip. He fought for control, groaning, "No more, hon. No more. When I explode,

I want to be inside you, driving you crazy the way you're doing to me.''

She backed off, but only with her hands. The magic she worked with her mouth on his nipples made his chest feel as if it had been pierced with hot nails. ''Better?'' she asked as he gasped his needs out loud.

There was only one thing for it. He rid himself of his pants and boxers. Stepped out and left them huddled on the floor as he lifted Maria onto the vanity and set her purse spinning onto the floor.

''Ouch! It's cold.''

''It'll get warmer.''

He pulled her skirt down, sliding her bottom closer as he opened her thighs and stepped between them till they were touching but not joined.

Her eyelids hid what he needed to see. Needed to know.

''Look at me.''

No butterfly flutter of lashes answered his demand; her lids were heavy with the weight of desire. They opened slowly, grazing across deep violet irises blurred with need.

''Now look down.'' He kissed his fingertips and touched them to the scar that had been gouged across her belly. ''That is past history. Long gone. There are only two of us in this room. You and me.''

He leaned into her as her gaze lowered. Slid his aching length up over her moist folds, simulating the act that nature had shaped them to perform when she stirred their pheromones and called them to the dance. He pulled back, felt her shiver as the blunt tip she'd caressed dragged over the hot button hiding at her center. ''Do you want this?''

''I want you.''

''It's all part of the same deal. Take it or leave it. I'll stop now and let you go if that's what you want. No more cater-wauling or threats, just goodbye.''

He bent his head and took her lips, filled her with all the tenderness he could muster. ''What's it to be?''

"Heaven forgive me, I can't leave. I just pray we never rue the day we met. Two weeks isn't long enough to know if our relationship has staying power. But I want to find out."

"Same goes." He pulled back and cupped her hips in his large palms.

"Before we go any further there's something you should know."

"Tell me later, just don't try to stop me now," he growled, spreading his legs until his long-suffering flesh was angled for the perfect entry and he slid into her waiting heat with one impatient thrust of his hips.

The noise of their mating bounced off the hard surfaces around them in echoes both erotic and tender, skin slapping against skin, and murmured endearments entwined them in a melody played to a rhythm written by Mother Nature.

Maria dazzled him with her touch and raised the hair on the back of his neck with her dangerous enthusiasm, her willingness to put everything on the line to please him. And he gave back measure for measure till he thought his heart would burst with the emotions swelling it.

He'd known this was no casual fling, known from the first time he'd made love to her that his feelings were a banner twisting in the wind that only Maria could unravel. He'd hidden the knowledge, shoved it to the back of his mind and pulled a dark curtain across to render it invisible.

Maria had cut a swath through the curtain, but with his family history he knew better than to hope he could have it all. *Maria and his ambitions.*

But he was running out of road, taking off into a space where nothing mattered but being with Maria, rocking her in the cradle of his hips as her climax rippled over him and blew him apart in a starburst pleasure he'd never found with anyone else.

It took a long time for Maria to come down from the place Franc had taken her. Had she ever been so high before? Ever soared amongst the galaxy?

Then Franc brought her down to earth with a bang, fluttering in freefall with no notion of making a safe landing. "What was it you wanted to tell me? Before…"

"Before we half killed each other?" Help, where had that come from? It was too close to the truth to take her impulsive outburst lightly. No matter what she did, made love, stayed, left, the threat wasn't going to disappear. "Untangle me and help me down, then I'll tell you."

He winced as he stepped back and accidentally heeled something into the shower door as he moved away and they were no longer as one. "I think my left leg went to sleep. Wait till I pick up your purse, you might need something."

What did he think this occasion called for—lipstick? The occasion. It dawned on her shell-shocked synapses that as Franc pulled away he hadn't worn a condom. As if life wasn't terrifying enough, she could be pregnant.

From the frown on his face as he straightened, Maria guessed that he had received the same jolt to his memory at almost the same moment it hit her. They both spoke together.

She said, "We didn't use a condom."

He said, "Where the hell did this crap come from?"

Then he said, "Dammit. I hope you're not pregnant, because according to this I'll be dead by tomorrow."

# Chapter 15

So this had been the surprise Franc had planned. Pleasant though it was, Maria was certain he would confirm that the bombshell she'd dropped on him had topped this. But then, having someone predict the day of your death wasn't an everyday occurrence.

Maria looked around the saloon of the motor yacht *Stanhope's Fancy II*. Feeling dwarfed was not exactly new to her, not when she spent so much time around Franc, but his sister, Jo McQuaid Stanhope, measured in at six feet without high heels—a fact that had to intimidate some of the killers Franc said she had a knack for catching. But this wasn't Auckland Central, the detective sergeant was off duty and Maria had no intention of killing anyone. Though she did have motive.

Maria gave the thought a mental raspberry. She was doing her best to see the funny side of life without much success.

But no wonder Franc had thought Jo could help. The confident way Jo held herself showed she knew her own worth, not only as someone married to a millionaire but as a cop.

The mere fact that Franc had planned on introducing her to

a member of his family *before* the threat, showed a departure from his original plans for a brief fling. Familywise, until now, all she'd been sure of was that Franc had spent his life trying to live down his father's reputation.

Jo's husband, Rowan, stood a shade taller than Franc, but it didn't show as they pored over the death-threat card and mutilated photographs. Rowan had come down to join them from the flying wheelhouse of the motor yacht as soon as they anchored in Waitamata Harbour.

"So tell me again," Jo asked, her eyes twinkling as if this was the fun, girl-talk part of the deal. "How did he manage to smuggle you out of his apartment?"

"It does sound like something from a movie. We went down in the elevator to the basement garage, and he had me stay in the elevator until he looked around to make sure there was no one in sight, and then he hid me in the back seat with a traveling rug over me. You have no idea the twists and turns he took to make sure we weren't being followed. I thought I might be seasick by the time he finished." She looked out at the harbor from the window of the yacht as it rocked on the wash of a passing boat, wondering if she might still be seasick.

Maria looked down at the white boat shoes she was wearing. They had been part of Franc's surprise; a short boat trip on the *Stanhope's Fancy* had been the rest, only now the term *safe haven* seemed more appropriate than a short holiday cruise.

Jo got up from the custom-built sofa they were sharing, covered in a mixture of blue-grays and peaches; it toned well with the apricot suede and natural-wood walls. Maria watched her skirt the dining table the men leaned on, to open a freezer in the galley, and then quickly and efficiently she slid the contents of a plastic bag into an ice bucket.

"I know it's too early to toast in the new year," she said, opening a cabinet next to the dining saloon. "But I'm sure after all your hassles, a small reviving glass with a little kick to it might be just the thing to settle your nerves."

"Wine for me if you have any," Maria answered before remembering that one of those hassles could be she was pregnant.

Had Franc mentioned that to his sister when he told her about the death threat? It seemed so *minute* a problem when looked at alongside the fact that someone wanted to kill Franc; she had refused to take the possibility seriously. It had struck her as funny that *he* should take an opposing stance.

Jo turned her attention to the men. "Now that you've studied the evidence, Rowan, what do you think?" Though she was a card-carrying member of the New Zealand police and Rowan a member of the hugely rich Stanhope family and Franc's immediate boss, they both worked as a team and it showed.

"Here's what I reckon, Peaches." Neither Franc nor Jo seemed to perceive anything peculiar in the diminutive Rowan used for his wife who was actually a very feminine version of Franc. "I think the threat needs to be taken seriously. But whether Randy Searle has the kind of psychological profile to carry the threat out, I couldn't say. Human Resources should have his work history, check it out when you go back to work on Thursday."

"But surely you won't let him go back to work until this guy's been found," Maria blurted out. So what if Rowan was his boss? He should be Jo's husband first.

Rowan threw her a quizzical look from under his tawny eyebrows, his green eyes glinting, emphasizing the contrast between him and his wife. "That's up to Franc, but I can assure you, I'll be putting extra security on at Stanhope Electronics, if that makes you feel any better."

It didn't. The more she thought about the situation, the more she was sure she should have moved out of Franc's apartment with a view to never seeing him again. How would she feel if anything happened to him? Could she ever live with herself again?

"I'll be going to work on Thursday, and so will you," Franc said. "As I told you earlier, if we completely change our lives around because of this guy, Randy—if that's who it is—then he's won.''

Had she ever truly taken notice of the stubborn jut to Franc's chin until today? No, if she had, it might have warned her of the downside to having a fling... Some fling! Look how it had turned out, with Franc's life in danger.

Jo was messing around in the drinks cabinet, setting out bottles and glasses as if nothing had rocked her world the way it had Maria's. This must be what it was like to be a cop who lived with the constant threat of danger. She was glad Franc had taken up electronics rather than following in his father's footsteps.

Maria stood up and went to help her hostess, needing to do something, anything rather than speculate about the subject of Franc's death.

Rowan was holding the photograph of her up to the light. A surge of color slashed Maria's cheekbones; she could feel the burn as she tensed, waiting for him to speak.

''Jo, have you worked out what these crosses cut in the photo of Maria are in aid of?''

Rowan's stare went straight over Maria's head as she placed four wineglasses on the table. She could imagine Jo, behind her, mouthing, ''Tell you later'' but Maria kept her eyes forward, kept them on Franc as if he were her lifeline.

Maria had gone down to their cabin to change. Franc could tell she felt uncomfortable next to his sister, who looked tall and elegant in a designer outfit she'd probably let Rowan talk her into. Franc liked that Rowan didn't mind showing how much he loved Jo. They were a couple in a million, and he didn't mean because of the Stanhope money.

He wondered if it could have been like that for him and Maria, if they'd had a chance without this stalking business blowing up in their faces. Then again, if it hadn't been for Randy, what were the chances that he and Maria would even have met?

"Now that Maria's gone downstairs, and there are only the three of us, I have something to tell you guys," said Jo.

"Something you couldn't tell Maria?" Franc said.

"I didn't want to embarrass her any more than Rowan did when he made the comment on how her photograph had been cut. I thought her name was familiar when you introduced us, but one look at that picture and I remembered. It was one of the first big cases I worked on. You'll remember it, Rowan."

"Costello?"

Jo pointedly looked over her shoulder to the stairs, then back at Rowan, until he said, "Oh, hell yes! I remember. They found her wandering around naked and bleeding from all these sliced wounds, poor little sod. Hadn't she been abducted from some girls' boarding school?"

"Shh, keep your voice down, sound travels on here." Jo gave Rowan the look. Franc had often been on the receiving end of it when they were young. He might have become the recipient of Grandma Glamuzina's vacuum cleaner and table-cloths, but what Jo had inherited was a lot more potent.

"Here's the plan," she said, including both guys. "I'll send the cards and photographs for forensics to go over. Rowan, you look after the security for these two. And Rowan, you should see what you can find out about Randy Searle. Find out where he's been in the ten years since Maria was abducted and I'll look up the old files on her case, see which suspects we were looking at back then."

"Look," Franc said to his sister. "Maria hasn't any memory of what happened to her at that time. Post-traumatic stress amnesia."

"Has her family ever thought of using hypnosis?" Rowan wondered out loud.

"No, not that Maria's ever mentioned. I think they were quite happy for her to forget the whole abduction ever happened. She never could though. She has dreams about it, but can't remember them afterward. They terrify her. Scared the living daylights out of me, I'll tell you, the first time I heard her. All she's told me is that the dreams have gotten more frequent since this business with Randy."

Franc took a swallow of his drink, and for a few minutes they all kept their own council as if the answer could be found in the liquor swirling inside their glasses. At last Franc broke the silence. "So what is brother Scott up to these days, Rowan. He hasn't been in my neck of the woods for a while."

"He's looking at some properties that might come up for sale soon in Australia. He's heard a rumor and thought it would be worthwhile checking it out. A pretty mixed bag from what I hear. From electronics to pastoral land."

"Electronics? Let me know if he needs an opinion."

Rowan grinned. "Scott doesn't much care for asking anyone's opinion these days, not even mine. He's been pretty restless."

Jo caught Rowan's smile and passed it back. "He needs to find himself a wife. I keep telling him, 'Find a nice woman and settle down,' but he doesn't want to hear it."

Franc looked up. "Talking about nice women, here comes mine now." Maria looked fantastic, and about as far removed as possible from the woman in his en suite this afternoon who had tried to dump him. "Come and sit by me, hon. I've missed you, but the wait was worth it. Is that the outfit you bought from Perdito's?"

She nodded and did a twirl for him. "What do you think?"

The wide neckline left one shoulder bare. He could tell straight off she wasn't wearing a bra and he had a sudden desire to stand in front of her, or cover Rowan's eyes. Either way, she looked beautiful. The lilac top brought out the deep pansy-brown in her eyes. And he couldn't wait to strip it off her.

"Franc's awfully protective of you."

Maria felt the cords at the back of her neck tighten. This was the first time she'd been alone with Franc's sister. Was this the moment when Jo gave her flack for putting her brother's life in danger?

Jo halted her preparations for midnight and the beginning of the new year and did little more than cast a glance over her shoulder. "It suits him. I can't remember the last time he thought of anything but work," she said, turning back to her task of picking out four matching champagne flutes. But she wasn't done. "Don't get me wrong, I'm not implying Franc is selfish, just driven."

Would Jo be as pleased if she knew everything? Maria let out a sigh that scraped the soles of her new boat shoes and left a dent in her lungs as it wrenched loose. "Don't get your hopes up. Chances are it won't last. I come with an awful lot of baggage."

"You couldn't come with any more baggage than the Jellic family. Has Franc told you about our father?"

"He did, I'm sorry. I bet you adored him." Maria thought about her father. If her abduction had been hard on Mamma, it had been much worse on Papa, but being the man, the head of an Italian household, he hadn't been able to let it show. "Little girls always favor their fathers, I did mine. He took it hard when they never caught the guy who abducted me. He aged overnight."

Maria cocked her head to one side as she told Jo, "I couldn't help noticing you realized who I was."

"Cops never forget their first big case. I wish we could have put the bastard away for what he did to you."

"So does my family. That's why I never reported Randy to the cops. Apart from the fact I didn't have any real proof, just a feeling, I didn't want my parents having to relive it all again. But it could still happen, if the newspapers get hold of the story...you know, and connect the two. My name is probably on file."

"As a cop I can't help wishing you had reported the stalking. You're a strong woman, Maria, but don't try to take on too much by yourself."

Maria shrugged off the compliment. "I try to be strong, it only works sometimes." It didn't always work. As she'd proven that afternoon, when it came to Franc she was putty.

"But don't let your strength isolate you. You're exactly what my brother needs. You make a good team."

"You think he needed all this hassle? I don't think this is what you meant when you told him to have a quiet Christmas. It certainly hasn't worked out that way."

"It's early days yet. So far he's only had his life threatened once. I almost got Rowan killed twice." Jo halted midbreath to hand Maria two champagne flutes. "As I said, early days. Now we'd better join the guys or New Year's will get there before us. You go up first," she urged, gathering up the bottle of French champagne plus two other flutes.

Maria went ahead. The steps led to the upper saloon, which was part of the boat's flying bridge. Rowan and Franc had busied themselves planning where they should spend the next couple of days while Jo organized the wine for the midnight toast.

Franc stood up from the curved, blue-gray leather lounger, one of two built into the window-lined bridge. "I'll take them," he said of the glasses, as if she wasn't capable of carrying them another two feet. But the smile that accompanied the words made up for them. For once Maria wasn't going to argue that she could do it herself. Jo was right. Franc was concerned for her, and this was his way of showing it. Maria no longer looked on it as the kind of concern her parents had displayed when she was younger when she'd felt locked inside a glass case, away from life. Away from the good things life brought, as well as the bad.

Rowan occupied the twin-size driver's seat that had been turned around to face the saloon. "We've decided to sail out to Waiheke Island tomorrow. It's one of the most beautiful spots in the Hauraki Gulf. Maria, wait till you visit our favorite cove."

Jo placed the champagne bottle and the rest of the glasses on the table beside the two that Franc had taken from Maria. "Almost ready. There's still a champagne bucket filled with ice in the galley."

Rowan stretched and stood up. "No problem."

Jo raised her eyebrows at Franc, laughing. "Such gallantry. And we've only been married a year."

Rowan grinned with the easy humor of a big man who knew how to roll with the punches. "It's all these late nights. This woman is insatiable."

Maria had been under the impression that being a homicide detective at Auckland Central, Jo wouldn't have a blush left in her, but her husband could do it for her. Stepping round the table to stand next to Jo, Rowan took the opportunity to steal a quick kiss. "Getting in training for midnight. Ten minutes to go."

Franc laughed, "Yeah, go for it, boss. I'm sure you need all the practice you can get."

When you saw them together, Jo and Rowan took up a massive amount of space. Yet, from the minute she'd been introduced, Maria had thought them a perfect match. Tall, Jo might be, but Rowan stood five inches taller than his wife.

In less than a few minutes they were all comfortably ensconced in the soft island of light the upper saloon made on the dark harbor. Through the windows they had a three-hundred-and-sixty-degree view of the lights on the North Shore, the Harbour Bridge and Auckland City, where the Sky Tower above the casino was putting on a laser-light display. Rowan sat with his arm circling his wife's shoulders, the champagne in front of them ready for midnight and the fireworks display to strike.

"What's the news on the investigation you're doing on Dad?"

"My goodness, Franc, I thought you were just like Kel."

Maria felt Jo's gaze switch to her. "Kel is one of our twin brothers. When he was last in Auckland, he acted as if he'd been conceived in a test-tube and never had a father. He flew into a rage when I tried to tell him how our investigation was going. But he's had a change of heart since he fell in love."

Franc couldn't hide his surprise. "Where did you hear that?"

"I had a call from him today. He wanted to bring me up

to speed on the case he'd been working on. Remember, I told you he'd been here in November?'' Franc nodded. ''Well, right about now he should be flying from Singapore to San Francisco to propose marriage to the woman he was tailing back then. Kel's a drug enforcement agent, some sort of squirrelly organization.''

Rowan gave Jo a nudge as if to watch what she said in front of Maria. ''Don't be like that,'' his wife complained. ''Maria's almost family.''

It was Maria's turn to blush. She hoped Franc didn't think she'd been spinning Jo a line when they were in the galley.

''But, as I was saying, since Kel was in the country, we've discovered the name of the woman Dad was seeing, and it doesn't look good. Her husband was someone Dad had put behind bars. The trouble is, just over a year ago, Rowan and I had a sniff of the same guy when we were down in Nicks Landing, and there was a definite connection to Dad's old partner, Rocky Skelton. But since Rocky managed to get himself murdered by his wife…''

Jo raised her eyebrows at Maria. ''That was one of those incidents I told you about where Rowan nearly lost his life because of me.''

Rowan's foot kicked the coffee table as his wife grabbed him and gave him a kiss. Those two didn't care who knew they were in love. ''My hero,'' Jo chuckled as Rowan pulled her onto his knee. ''Now, what was I saying? Yes, I'm afraid that line of inquiry might have died with Rocky, but I'm still hopeful.''

A minute before midnight, the champagne flutes were filled ready for the toast, and as the seconds ticked down Franc gazed into her eyes. She wondered what he saw. Did he see that she didn't know how she could let him go? That she was sure that once he reached Stanhope Electronics in two days' time he'd forget all about her, plus the problems and threats she'd brought into his life? As Jo said, Franc was driven. She hadn't said why, but just as her past had pushed her into trying

to confront Randy Searle, Franc's family history reflected his
need to succeed, to be a better man than his father.

Suddenly the eyes that looked into hers were filled with
stars and it took her a second to realize the fireworks display
had begun. "Happy New Year, honey."

He bent his head to kiss her, but didn't have to strain as
Maria was already stretching up to meet him, needing to discover if the magic between them still existed.

It did.

Lifting his mouth from hers, he whispered, "When we go
down to our stateroom, let's make a fireworks display of our
own."

She felt in complete accord and murmured, "Yes, let's."

Their extra two days together passed in a flash, and soon
Maria was being dropped off at the old villa at Northcote
Point in a taxi. She knew her friends, Tess and Linda, had
already arrived—their car was already in the carport—and as
promised, the mechanic had delivered Maria's car.

A dreadful ache invaded her heart. Seeing everything so
normal made it feel as if the last couple of weeks had never
been. As if it was all a dream.

It was a dream she awoke from when the cell phone Franc
had loaned her rang, breaking into her discussion with Tess
and Linda about families and what gifts they'd been given
and what they'd done during the break.

She slipped into the hallway to speak to him, knowing it
would be him, as no one else had this number. "Hi, how you
doin', hon?"

"Good, it feels funny being back, as if I'd never been
away."

"Don't say that. I thought I'd made a big impression on
you."

She could hear him chuckling. The sound rippled through
her and plucked at her funny bone. In her heart of hearts,
Maria knew she was going to miss Franc so much. She missed

him now, and hearing his voice spelled out what she had lost in huge letters.

He'd become a friend as well as a lover, and their association had grown to the stage where she didn't get into a flap over teasing him. "Well, it was definitely *big,* some might say huge. I'll let you know when I've had more experience."

"Ouch, you know how to hit where it hurts, hon, but no more funning, let's get serious. Rowan has organized a team of security guys to keep an eye on you round the clock—don't worry, you won't notice them," he told her as she made a sound of protest. "These guys are the best, count on it."

"I'm trying to decide whether to tell Tess and Linda. Do you think they're in any danger?"

"I don't think so, hon, *if* this is Randy, and I've no reason to suspect otherwise, his eyes seem firmly fixed on you. Though if he knows me at all, he'd have realized his threat wouldn't work…" He paused as if considering his words. "I called to tell you, when I got home there was a message on the answering machine from the mechanic who fixed your car. The motor had been deliberately disabled by removing the motor from the distributor; presumably to prevent you leaving Auckland. Seems even back then Randy was prepared to go further than we imagined."

When she reentered the sitting room, Tess said, "I take it *that* wasn't another of those hang-up calls. We've had four since we got back. I thought a heavy breather had latched onto us."

Had the stalking progressed to this, or was Randy checking on her whereabouts? As she sat down, Maria made up her mind to tell her friends what had really been happening in her life. And finished by saying, "But if Mamma or any of the family call, don't say a word. I don't want them insisting I go back to Falcon's Rise to live. They have their own plans and I refuse to let them put them on hold because of me. Papa needs to retire."

It wasn't until the next afternoon when she returned to her office at Tech-Re-Search that she got *the* phone call. This time it wasn't a hang-up and it wasn't Randy. But she recognized Kathy Gilbertson from the experimental lab; she'd dealt with her before. But why would she call, instead of Franc, when he'd assured her she would only have to deal with him from now on.

Her first reaction was to get hold of Franc.

"Kathy instructed me to pack up all my research notes and take them to the Mile-a-Minute agency on the next corner to be delivered to Stanhope Electronics," she told Franc over the phone. "She said the agency was expecting me and would deliver the notes straightaway.

"I agreed, I didn't know what else to do."

"You did well, hon. Randy has obviously conned Kathy into helping him."

Maria's shoulders sagged as she let out a sigh. "I was certain the call wasn't legitimate, certain that if you'd wanted the research notes, you would have collected them yourself."

"You know me too well, Maria. I wouldn't have been able to resist collecting a little sugar at the same time."

"What now, Franc? Do you want me to follow her instructions?"

It didn't matter if it was a setup, or that she was sure Randy would be waiting for her...if Franc asked, she would do it. She would screw up the courage she'd used to gate-crash the party, especially if it meant ridding her life of Randy Searle, and the nightmares he'd brought back, once and for all.

## Chapter 16

His mate Brent had been in Franc's office when he received the call from Maria. The moment she mentioned Kathy's name, the memory of the technician playing tongue tag with Searle meant it didn't take a leap of faith to be certain she was in collusion with the guy.

"What did Maria want?"

Franc told him before he made for the door. For now, he had to rely on Brent to take care of Kathy Gilbertson, plus do what he could to discover her part in Searle's scheme.

After all he'd done to make interpersonal relationships congenial, and Stanhope Electronics a place where employees enjoyed working, it burned to think he had not one but two traitors on his staff.

Stopping briefly on the way out, he checked with the receptionist and discovered that, as he'd thought, Searle hadn't turned up for work.

Did the guy suspect they were onto him? Was that why he'd conned Kathy into doing his dirty work? And had the news that Maria had come looking for Searle at the party somehow gotten to the guy's ears? Hell, why didn't it make sense?

If Searle had threatened him by sending those photos to Maria, then yes, he definitely knew of the connection. There had to be more to it. Were the research papers simply to get Maria out of the office or did he have an interest in them as well?

Damn, he didn't have time to work it all out. His mind was going round in circles, one thought chasing another without coming to a conclusion that made any sense. He would take it to the experts and call Rowan.

That done, he thanked God he'd told Maria not to leave Tech-Re-Search until she knew he was close at hand. Sure, Rowan was going to alert the security team member keeping watch over her. That didn't mean Franc was going to sit back and leave her safety to the professionals.

But his mind wouldn't leave it alone; he wished he could figure out what Randy was up to. Was this a way of getting back at him? Instead of killing him, he thought he could kill his career? Yeah, sure, he *must* know the research was replaceable. That there would be copies. It just didn't gel.

Franc flashed a quick glance at the clock on the dash. Less than five minutes and he'd be in the vicinity, provided of course he could get parking within a few blocks of Tech-Re-Search.

He picked up his cell phone to give Rowan a progress report; and make sure his brother-in-law had given his security team the heads up, the one who should be tailing his car, as well as the one watching Maria. Hell, wouldn't you know it? The damn situation was turning into a game of follow the leader.

"I'm almost there," he said when Rowan answered.

"Jo's beaten you to it. She's across the street from Maria's office and I'm a couple of blocks away, walking. It's no distance for Jo. Auckland Central is practically on Maria's doorstep."

"No excuse necessary, but you might have told me this was turning into a family affair.'' He ought to be reassured, yet Franc couldn't stop a wry twist shaping his lips. This whole stalker business looked to be turning into a slapstick farce.

No way was Searle going to get away with his plans. Franc tightened his one-handed grip on the wheel the way he'd imagined gripping the scruff of Searle's neck, wishing he knew what the bastard had up his sleeve.

Rowan was breathing hard when he answered. Franc could imagine him hurrying uphill from the Viaduct where the yacht was berthed. "You didn't really think I would let you go after Searle alone? I have a stake in the outcome, as well. Bottom line, the guy works for me, and the research that's been asked for is Stanhope property. But if we cut away the crap, Jo would kill me if I let anything happen to you.''

"Nice to know someone cares, even if it's for a secondhand reason.'' The words were hardly out of Franc's mouth when he caught sight of a parking spot opening up. "Gotta go, I'm on Hobson Street. Catch you soon.''

When Tech-Re-Search was in sight, Franc called Maria from a shop doorway, downhill and on the other side of Wellesley Street.

It took three minutes for her to appear, minutes he sweated, knowing he was asking a lot of her. Hell, she could have downright refused and he wouldn't have blamed her. Maria had a lot of guts for a woman who'd been to hell and back again. If she didn't remember the nightmares she had in the night, he couldn't get them out of his mind, or forget the feel of her in his arms as he hushed her back to sleep.

If anything happened to her because of him, the Costello family couldn't lay any more blame his way than he would himself. The agony of prospective loss surged through him. Was she carrying his cell phone? Should he call her to urge her to turn around and go back to her office?

As if to steer him back on track, Searle stepped out of the

doorway no more than fifteen meters from Maria. Though if he hadn't been focused on the guy he might not have recognized him out of his salesman's uniform of dark suit and tie. Today Searle had pulled on black jeans and sweatshirt and topped the outfit off with a cap, pulled low over his eyes, but his walk gave him away. Franc would recognize that swagger anywhere. All he could do now was keep Maria safe, as he'd been trying to do since she'd first told him about Searle stalking her.

So far so good. Franc began shortening the gap between him and the other two by striding up the sidewalk as soon as he saw Searle quicken his pace. Damn, what had made him think being on this side of the street was a good idea? He would have to get across to the other side as soon as possible; even from this distance the expression on Searle's face said "take no prisoners."

The lights at the intersection below him turned red and the traffic slowed as he cut between two parked cars, his eyes on Searle. He watched him close the distance, ten meters, five, time to make a move.

But Franc hadn't noticed the bus careering down the hill. He jumped back into the protection afforded by the other cars as it slowed down in a squeal of air brakes, blocking his view.

Wasn't it always the damn way? What the hell was happening across the street? He dodged behind the bus, praying as he ran that the next lane was clear. It wasn't. He let two cars grind up the slope, slowed by lack of momentum.

The moment he saw Searle's hands reach for Maria, he went for it, arm outstretched, palm raised to the car coming at him and a look on his face that said don't mess with me.

Maria found it hard keeping her eyes forward, when all her senses screamed to look around for Randy, yet she didn't dare in case it meant giving the game away. With each step she took, the foot hitting the sidewalk felt heavier than the last.

What was it about her life that it became cataclysmic without the least little push from her?

For all that her goal for the last few months had centered on being like everyone else, like Tess and Linda, a normal woman, with normal relationships, look where she'd landed.

And for all she'd summoned the courage to gate-crash a party so she could confront Randy Searle, the moment the back of her began prickling again, Maria knew she wasn't really cut out for this cops-and-robbers lark.

Tires squealed and horns blared. The acrid smell made her feel queasy; at least it was something to blame for her stomach churning. As she looked into the roadway to see which car was tearing up the pavement, she caught a quick glimpse of Franc dodging between a delivery truck and a car in the middle of the road.

She froze on the spot, stumbling forward as someone bumped into her behind and the parcel went flying from her hands.

"Oops, sorry. Here, let me get that for you" came an apology and a young guy in black bent forward to retrieve her parcel just as the crush of people from the Walk Now signal surged uphill toward her.

"That's okay I could have managed," she stumbled, one eye keeping a lookout for Randy as she reached out to take the courier pack.

Although a cap shaded his eyes as the guy stood up, something about the jut of his chin and the determination etched on his lips shouted Randy, and she froze for an instant, shouting "Give that back" as she recovered her wits.

For her trouble she received a push with the flat of his hand on her chest that sent her reeling. Unfortunately, there was no one behind her to soften her fall.

Her momentum sent her hurtling back to land on the sidewalk. Elbow first she hit the paving. Pain, hot and blinding ricocheted up her arm and into her shoulder. She thought she'd pass out, or be sick as her stomach rushed up to meet her throat.

Incensed, she kicked out, aiming a shoe at his ankle in an effort to trip him, but he was too wily. Dancing back from a princess heel that wasn't nearly as lethal as she'd like, he darted into the traffic in a clash of shouts and curses not a yard away from Franc.

People passing, gawping, made no more impression than a blur of color in her peripheral vision. Inside her space, time stood still. The rest of the world spun around her as Randy dodged into the other pedestrians, but his unhindered passing didn't go unnoticed. Somewhere in her mind rang the word, *cowards!*

God, why had she put all her work in the pack when plain copy paper would have done as well?

Stupid! Stupid!

She shouldn't have gone along with this harebrained scheme. The plot had been hatched in far too much haste.

Suddenly, Maria realized for all her anxieties, the stalking hadn't been about her, but her research.

Footsteps thundered down the sidewalk toward her.

"Out of the way!" She recognized the voice, Rowan. Randy was gone. Didn't he realize he hadn't a chance? Franc must have crossed the street by now.

Four-inch stilettos would have done the trick, she decided, and closed her eyes against the pain and the knowledge that there were people standing around looking at her. Would it have hurt them to help her up?

Franc and Rowan reached her before her pity party could get up steam. For a second, they both looked down from miles above her, then Franc knelt. "Are you okay, hon? Where does it hurt."

She'd barely time to gasp a breath, never mind answer, when Rowan told Franc, "You look after Maria. Jo's still on Searle's tail and I'm damned if I'm going to let the bastard get away with this." He took another look at Maria as Franc helped her sit up. "Don't worry, he'll pay for what he did to you."

Rowan raced off as Franc ran his hands over her. "Where does it hurt worst? Do you think anything is broken?"

She sucked up the pain. "My dignity, then my elbow, but I don't think either of them are permanently damaged." Her effort lasted until Franc rubbed her elbow, then she winced. Her moan escaped as she began to take her bearings and discovered that the crowd still hadn't moved away. "Get me out of here, big guy, and I'll be your slave for life."

She watched him frown, knew he was worried about her, and that gave her the courage to laugh. "It's okay, my dignity took the worst beating and it won't get better until I'm outta here."

Franc stared at a dozen or so openly curious eyes and whispered, "Ghouls…bet they're disappointed there's no blood."

He helped her to her feet, but once there, it was as if he didn't give a damn about who was watching. He pulled her into his embrace. "God, I'm sorry, hon, I didn't mean you to get hurt. I'll take you back to work, or would you rather go home?"

"Work. I may be smaller than you but I'm no delicate flower."

He cupped her face between his huge palms and kissed her hard, putting his heart into it as if in defiance of the stares and titters. "I hope they catch up with Searle soon and give him more than a few bruises."

"I tried…but he dodged my feet." His kiss had left her breathless, yet hopeful because of the feelings Franc had poured into it. She didn't want to give this up. How could he?

"You're a goddamn heroine, Maria Costello." Franc took her uninjured arm to keep her steady, but as he looked over his shoulder in the direction Rowan had taken, she realized he was still feeling antsy over Randy's escape. She supposed it was a man thing, wanting to be in on the kill.

"Go after him, I'll be all right."

For the first time since they'd met, she caught a hint of indecision in his expression. Lifting her hand to push him away hurt more than the pain in her elbow. She'd been wrong it had been the relief that she'd tasted on his lips. Relief that now Randy would be caught, their brief fling was over.

She *was* losing him.

Grasping at any straw to fend off her somber thoughts, she was relieved to hear someone calling her name, "Maria. Whatever happened, my dear?"

She looked up the hill as the chaplain squeezed down past the gawpers to reach her side. "Someone knocked me down and stole the courier pack I was carrying. I'm a little shaken, but not really badly hurt."

"Thank goodness for that."

The moment the idea popped into her head, she turned to the chaplain. "Would you mind walking me to my office? I know Franc is dying to go deal with the guy who hurt me, but he doesn't want to leave me alone."

"Of course, it's not a problem. I was going in your direction anyway. Here, take my arm."

She gave Franc a push. "Go on, Franc, go. You know you want to. I'll be fine with the chaplain."

He hesitated, looked from one to the other until the chaplain assured him, "She's in good hands, my son. Don't worry, I'll take excellent care of Maria."

"Thanks, Chaplain."

He turned to Maria and bent over to give her a peck on the forehead. A peck this time, for goodness' sake, as if she was his little sister. He'd never been content with anything less than a full-blown, mouth-to-mouth, tongue-wrestling kiss since the first night she'd met him. Romance had gone out the window when business was at stake.

"Maria, I'll call soon, hopefully with news that we've got the bastard locked up." Franc raised his eyebrows to the chaplain as if in apology for the curse word. A second later, he took off after his brother-in-law.

The chaplain reached between the two people he'd brushed aside earlier and made room for Maria to pass, saying benignly, "It's all over now, people. God bless. You can safely go on your way knowing no one got hurt."

Doing the *polite* thing was the furthest from Maria's needs, but when they reached Tech-Re-Search, she asked the chaplain inside for coffee. Guilt scored a hit square on her solar plexus as he excused himself, "Another time, my dear. I've a lot of work ahead of me today."

What right had she to feel so relieved. The chaplain had shown her nothing but kindness. Driven by that thought, she pushed open the plate-glass door and gave him an open invitation, "Well, I insist that you make it soon. You've been so kind, and I want to repay all your goodness."

"I'll look forward to the coffee, the ministry runs on it. That and tea," he joked. "I'm sure we'll meet again soon, considering the way we seem to keep bumping into each other."

Inside, Maria closed the door to her office without mentioning what had happened to a soul at Tech-Re-Search.

Sighing, she leaned her back against the door as if barricading it to give herself time to reflect, time to put her life in perspective now that Randy was surely on his way to Auckland Central lockup. Not for a minute did she doubt that Rowan and Jo had caught him before he'd run too far.

She felt more troubled and less sure about her and Franc. Had time caught up with them at last? With Randy locked up, he had no need to feel concerned that a guy employed by him was stalking her. She ought to feel relief that Randy Searle was taken care of at last. With him out of her life, surely the shadows of the past that kept sneaking up on her in her dreams would gradually fade away again, only to bother in times of stress. Maria willed herself to shrug off the feelings of melancholia. So, it would take her a while to get over Franc?

She'd gone into the game knowing it had a stopwatch counting down the seconds. And even though she'd never forget him, he *had* given her something she'd never had before, confidence in herself as a woman.

Oh, he would call, and maybe he would chat about what had happened, and then he would take her research and bury himself in work. She could see it coming, heading toward her like a runaway train, but she wouldn't step in front of it and send her life into limbo as her parents had done last time.

She was a big girl now. Franc had warned her from the very beginning that work was what he lived for. The sex had just been an opportunity to while away a couple of weeks. To play.

She squeezed her eyes shut and her fists into tight balls. The pain in her elbow as she pressed hard against the door was as nothing to the pain in her heart. Laughter escaped her lips; a harsh dry sound that tore from her lungs and sliced her throat with its sharp edges, for she knew the laugh was on her.

Maria Costello had found love in the wrong place and with the wrong guy, and didn't have enough experience to know what to do to mend her problem.

*Nor bars a prison make, he thought, looking round him at the standard-issue green paint that gave Auckland Central lockup a malevolent hue. A drab dreary place, he'd no intention staying in it any longer than he had to.*

*Another saying—Needs must when the Devil drives—almost had him laughing out loud at its appropriateness. He forced it back, to save it for later when he would have the last laugh. No need to make the cop leading him to the cells suspicious.*

*A feeling of exhilaration filled him at the realization it would all be over soon. The patience he'd shown during months he'd spent stalking Maria was about to reap its re-*

*ward. There was only one more thing in his way. One more man who'd thought he could lay hands on what belonged to him. But he was wrong!*

*Even in death, Maria would always be his.*

*Undecided was the best* word to describe Maria's mood. Yes, Franc had called, and yes, Randy Searle was locked up...*locked up for now* was her knee-jerk reaction.

A detective had arrived at the Northcote Point villa over two hours ago to interview her, which made four hours since Franc had called her to say he would come round.

"I need to have a word with you."

Maria had a feeling that the word would be *goodbye*.

The later it got, the higher the humidity climbed. Now it was in the nineties, and the air, heavy with moisture, wrapped everyone in a thick blanket too heavy to scramble out from under. Unlike Maria, who perched on the edge of a rattan chair so very little skin touched, Tess and Linda sprawled over the mismatched sofa and chair in front of the fan.

They'd all succumbed to T-shirts and shorts the minute they'd gotten home from work, and after a light salad that Maria had found hard to swallow, they couldn't summon up enough energy to do more than switch on the TV.

Linda controlled the remote and flicked to a comedy the moment the news turned to sports, no need to wait for the weather forecast, it would be more of the same.

"Well, at least you didn't make the local news," yawned Tess. "So you can stop worrying about hordes of reporters eager to make a slim connection between today's incident and the past."

"Yeah," agreed Linda. "Maybe you can stop jumping like a scalded cat every time a car drives along the street."

"It's not that," Maria said. "I'm over worrying about reporters. My future doesn't depend on them. Franc said he'd come over tonight and I'm sure he's going to dump me."

"That's easily fixed, dump him first." Tess shifted positions to the other corner of her chair and hung her leg over the opposite arm in search of a cool place. "That's what I'd do."

Linda disagreed. "But Maria's not you. Sure, she might have wanted to be like us, out on dates two or three nights a week, but no one can teach you how to get over rejection. It's something you have to tough out by yourself."

"It's not as if I didn't know it was coming. I just didn't think I'd fall in love with him so soon." Maria got up and started to pace. "How do I get over love?"

"Chocolate, lots of chocolate," Tess said. "They say there's something in it that helps mend broken hearts."

Linda never thought along the same lines as Tess, but Maria was used to their lighthearted wrangling.

"No chocolate, no way," Linda barked. "All that does is make you so fat it's impossible to get another date when you get over your broken heart. And you will, Maria. The pain will eventually go away."

"From where my life stands at the moment, I can't see that ever happening. Now I know why those blighted lovers in historical romances went into a decline."

"Phooey. You've only just started to live, don't throw in the towel already—" Linda broke off as the doorbell rang.

"I'll get it," sang Maria and started to dash to the door.

"Wait!" hollered Tess. "Turn around, let me look at you. Okay, not bad, fluff up your hair and lick your lips."

Maria pulled down on the creased legs of her shorts, after she did as instructed, though she felt stupid standing there like a storefront dummy.

"Yeah, like that. Now go out there with your head high and your chest out."

As she left the room, she heard her friends laugh. "Sex on legs. He doesn't stand a chance."

Her breaths came thick and fast and her heart thumped a tattoo in her ears as she opened the door. "Oh, it's you," she said, hoping her words weren't laced with the disappointment she felt as her heart dropped and landed at her feet. "I was expecting Franc."

She heard him sigh and even before he spoke, Maria knew something was wrong. "That's why I'm here. There's been a car accident and Franc's asking for you."

The news hit her like a kick to the stomach. Her vision blurred and the messenger's face melted away in the tears welling in her eyes. "Where is he?"

"Auckland Hospital. I'll take you, but we'd better hurry."

A dead feeling washed over her, numbing her brain as she said, "Start the car. I'll go get my purse."

The only thing she comprehended was if Franc died, her life would be empty. Oh, she'd survive; she'd done it before. God, she'd become a card-carrying member of the survivors' union. But without Franc there would be a gap in her life no one else could fill.

Her jaw firmed as she lightly jumped down the porch steps and ran to the car waiting to take her to Franc. If it took all that was in her, she'd make sure he would become a survivor, too.

## Chapter 17

$F$ranc knew he should have called Maria again before turning up on her doorstep, but what could he have said?

This evening had opened his eyes to the consequences of threatening someone's life. Of course, it had been all heat and words, but try telling the cops that. He had to admit; finding himself a suspect in a murder case had given his confidence a knock. And of course, being his sister, Jo had to go away and leave him to get on with the interview.

It was the darnedest thing Randy Searle dying that way. Seems he had more enemies than you could poke a stick at, for *he* definitely hadn't poisoned the guy.

Searle might have been a rat of the lowest order, putting Maria through all that stalking business just to get his hands on the research she'd been doing for Stanhope Electronics, but the man wasn't worth a life sentence. Franc had an inkling of the guy who might be behind the theft, but with Searle dead, they'd never be able to prove it, unless Kathy Gilbertson knew.

He'd first taken over at Stanhope Electronics in an attempt

to bring the place into the twenty-first century. The previous CEO, Bradbury Fyfe had been given a golden handshake worth six figures, to leave, and as a consequence hated his guts. Fyfe hated Brent's guts, too, but that had its roots in a competition over a woman, not his job as general manager, though that could be placed under the heading of putting the boot in.

Searle had worked for Fyfe; in fact, the guy had brought Searle into the company from England. He must remember to inform Jo about the connection between the two.

All thought of Searle and Fyfe's possible collusion melted away as Franc turned his car into Maria's driveway. A spark of hope brightened his day. Since her car still resided in the carport, chances were she hadn't gone off in a fit of pique because he'd been later than intended.

Franc took the porch steps two at a time. Tension added its two cents' worth to what had been one of the worst days of his life. That's if he discounted his mother dying practically before he'd taken his first step, and his father playing stunt driver on the cliffs at Torbay.

Doubt had just spritzed a dash of cold water on his plans.

What if Maria said no?

He pressed his thumb on the doorbell and clinked the car keys to the rhythm of his impatient heart. As the ringing faded, silence prevailed. No one, it seemed, was in a rush to open the door, and when it did, a pair of blue eyes peeped at him through the gap left by the safety chain. It wasn't Maria.

"Can I speak to Maria?"

"Who wants to see her?"

He admired her caution, but she should have known by now Searle was locked up, even if she hadn't yet heard he was dead. No doubt that piece of information would hit the late-news headlines. "Tell Maria that it's Franc Jellic, and I really need to talk to her."

"Pull the other one, mate, Franc Jellic is in hospital, all

smashed up from a car accident, and Maria's with him, so buzz off.''

He put his shoulder to the door just as she was about to close it in his face. "Wait a minute, Tess, Linda, whichever one you are, what the hell are you talking about? I'm Franc Jellic and I can prove it.'' He shoved his fist into his back pocket and pulled out his wallet.

''Just because you've done your homework and have our names down pat, you don't fool me.'' Then she started to shout, ''Linda! Come and help me shut the door.''

''Here, take this.'' He pushed his wallet at her and let it fall through the gap onto the floor at her feet. ''Close the door if you must, but when you've looked at my ID, open it again. We need to talk. Randy Searle was killed tonight and Maria could be in danger. Check it out. I'm alive and kicking.'' He stepped back and let her close the door, though he felt like taking his toe to the door to prove the kicking part.

Where was a boot when you needed it? He looked down at the loafers he'd put on after ducking home to change and wash the stink of Auckland Central from him. He'd visited there before, to see Jo, and he'd been interested in everything she'd shown him, but it took on a different ambience from the wrong side of an interview table.

He could hear a buzz of conversation on the other side of frosted-glass door panels that had survived intact from the early 1900s. A minute later the door opened again, this time without the chain. ''We're two to one and we've got your wallet.''

''Hang on to it if you like, it isn't much of a weapon though. Are you going to tell me where Maria's gone and what's all this nonsense about me being in the hospital?''

''Someone came for her, a man. We peeped through the window, thinking it was you because we wanted to see who'd been leading Maria on a merry dance since we left for the summer break.''

She stopped for a breath and the other one chipped in, ''Oh

my God! We didn't get a good look. Before we'd time to pull the curtain back, Maria rushed in and grabbed her purse. She said you'd been seriously injured in a car smash and you were asking for her.''

"From your hospital bed.''

Linda flung the door wide. "The phone's down the hall. Do you want us to call the cops or will you do it?''

He followed them into the hallway and took the wallet that Linda handed him. "Thanks, I know where it is but I'll use my cell phone,'' he said, his mind frantically dragging up umpteen scenarios as he punched in Jo's number. "Did you see the car she left in?''

"We were too busy talking about you, wondering what could have happened. We actually thought of driving across the bridge to Auckland Hospital after her. You know, in case she needed a hug.''

Damn, they didn't even have the make of the car to go on. Where to start...where to start? The words went around his mind in circles but he didn't dare show his panic to Maria's friends.

"Put those hugs on hold, I'm sure she's going to need them before we get her out of this one. Now, has anyone else been hanging round the villa, apart from Randy Searle and Tony who lives on the corner? I want to give the cops every smidgen of information I can, so they can get the ball rolling.''

And what was he going to say to Jo? That the guy who'd sent Maria the threat was still around and about to do his worst because he knew they'd tried to put one over on him.

Maria's brain felt as if it had been cleaved in two and neither left nor right side was controlling her thinking processes. Where on earth was she and how had she gotten there?

She raised her head slowly, very slowly. She'd never been drunk in her life, but she imagined this was how a hangover would feel. Her left arm must have gone to sleep; she couldn't feel it. Instead, a sharp pain streaked up to her shoulder each time she tried moving her fingers. It was cold. Oh, so cold, and damp. Her bones ached as she pushed up on her other elbow. "Ooow." That was the one she'd landed on when Randy let go and she hit the pavement.

Breathe slowly, deeply, till the pain goes away.

If only it was that easy.

She shivered; and grew goose pimples. Why was it so cold? She shook her aching head. Her brain sloshed from side to side as she tried making sense of things. If it was winter, why in all that was holy had she worn shorts and a T-shirt?

She gave it a minute and tried again, gritting her teeth against the pain. It took her longer than that to focus, to adjust her cockeyed vision to the dim light. A yellow light, it came from over her right shoulder and barely made the distance to where she was tied up.

Tied up! She stared above her shoulder where her left hand dangled from a manacle fastened to the wall with a short chain. No wonder she'd lost all feeling in it. She started shivering for real, great wracking shudders that hyphenated the sobs coursing up her throat. Gradually, she forced her breathing back to normal. She had to calm down, look around and scope the landscape of her prison.

First thing she had to do was push far enough up the wall to try to restore her circulation, then see how hard it was going to be to remove the manacle.

The wall at her back was damp, but she leaned on it, needing support, as the least bit of movement made her head spin and deep breathing was all that countered the sensation.

Uncomfortable, she pulled down on a leg of her shorts. It had bunched up and was cutting into her thigh. The action brought with it a flash of memory. Her posing in front of Tess and Linda, licking her lips and fluffing her hair before she went out to meet Franc.

Franc! The accident…then it all came flooding back. The hand over her mouth, the chloroform just like the last time…

Exactly like last time.

She looked around, knowing she had been in this place before.

If ever there was a memory to make her flesh crawl...

At Franc's behest, Tess and Linda went over anyone who might have taken a fancy to Maria. In one way he was glad there were so few others apart from Tony Cahill and Arthur Collins, and though he couldn't see her being naive enough to go off with either of them, they would have to be checked out.

Jo and Rowan were on their way and put out an all points bulletin with Maria's description, and much as he wanted to batter down Tony's door and ask where Maria was, he had overstepped the mark once that day and it wouldn't do Maria any good for him to be pulled in for questioning again.

He'd only to let his mind drift back to Maria for his nerves to start jumping. God, he prayed she wasn't too frightened.

The moment he found her he would lift her in his arms and never let her go. He tried to imagine what she must be going through, but that brought up pictures of her scars gained from her last encounter with an abductor. There wasn't a doubt in his frazzled mind that it had happened again.

Dread bathed his skin with cold sweat. Last time what happened to her was so horrific she'd shut the memory away. Now her dreams were haunted by the shadows of her past. What if they got her back and she'd forgotten him, forgotten the fun they'd had and the nights of splendor in each other's arms?

His ambitions faded to nothing in comparison.

Maria congratulated herself on having found a hairpin caught up in the ends of her hair. It had turned up like manna from heaven, but could she make it work?

Hope blossomed in her chest, yet like a desert oasis there was still a chance her escape could be a mirage.

Terrified she would drop the hairpin on the dank floor, she

held it between her teeth, straightening it into a slightly wavy strip of metal. Tess and Linda used to laugh at her, saying hairpins were old-fashioned contraptions. Now it could be her way out of here. Thank heavens she hadn't chosen the butterflies she'd worn to gate-crash Franc's party…

"Oh, Franc." Her lip quivered. Was he out there searching for her? God help her if he'd changed his mind about calling at the villa. She took the hairpin out of her mouth and concentrated on bending the metal tip in a crack in the mortar between the stone blocks.

"God helps them who help themselves."

Would her abductor appreciate that thought? A few moments ago she'd discovered an alcove above her head. And now that her eyes had become accustomed to the gloom, she could see there were more, darker shadows where the absence of light hung like a gray curtain. She was in a crypt, but she wouldn't let her imagination dwell on it. Not if she wanted to get out.

She briskly rubbed the tip of the hairpin against the wall, hoping a little friction would bend it into an L shape. Yes!

Now all she had to do was twist around to reach the lock on her manacle. How much jiggling around it would take to unlock it was another story.

Tess and Linda had wanted to go with Franc, but there had been no point. Better they stayed where they were and minded the phone in case Maria called.

Jo and Rowan had arrived and they'd tried Tony, who hadn't been home. From there, they'd all gone into Auckland's Central Business District where the suspect worked nights as a busboy. He'd been there since 5:00 p.m. And his boss backed up his story, which meant they were *back* where they'd started.

Franc had been forced to call Andrea, Maria's brother, knew he should have done it sooner, but he'd hoped for better news before the Costellos descended en masse. The moment they found Maria, Rosa would be over her like a blanket, smothering her with care and attention until her daughter lost herself again.

And he was positive that was the last thing Maria wanted.

He huffed down his nose, what the hell, he'd be the same. That's how it went when you loved someone—there, at last he'd admitted it. But when you cared for a person, and that person was your life, then you had to look to the future, not hide them away from the past. Oh, he'd no doubt that the shadows would come creeping out again, but if he had his way, he would be sharing her nights and doing his damnedest to diminish the power of her dreams. All they had to do was find her.

Franc looked at his watch, four hours since she'd been taken.

He went back to watching the phone.

"Staring at it won't make it ring." Jo pushed a cup of coffee in his hands and sat down opposite. "Rowan's on his cell phone rounding up a search party."

"If only we knew where to send them."

"Don't worry, something will come up soon, brother, I'm sure of it. Let's brainstorm."

"Where do we start?" A thought zapped him, an image of Searle being led away by uniformed cops. "Do you believe in coincidence?"

Franc went on without giving Jo a chance to reply. "If we leave out Searle stealing the research papers, two tragic events have happened within hours of one another. Searle died of poisoning and Maria was abducted. You're not going to tell me there is no connection, for I won't believe it."

Jo leaned forward. "You knew both of them, Franc. I only came into Maria's life three days ago, and I never met Randy Searle until I cuffed him and read him his rights. If there is a connection, you're going to have to help me figure it out."

The leather chair squeaked as she leaned forward to put down her coffee. In a blinding flash, the truth struck him. If

Jo hadn't fallen in love with Rowan—never mind that she still worked as a cop—she wouldn't be living the high life she did now, with expensive designer furniture in the penultimate apartment of the Quay West building, and he would still be fighting his way up the career ladder.

There was always a connection.

"The obvious place to start is Searle and who killed him, or rather, who had a chance to kill him, for believe me, he wasn't the type to carry cyanide in a hollow tooth. If he'd had visitors, the police would have checked them, but what about visitors to other prisoners?"

"Hang on a sec, I grabbed a copy of the duty cop's sheet."

She went to her purse. His eyes widened as she pulled out a Glock .9mm, laying it on the table as she dug deeper. He supposed, intellectually, he'd realized that Jo would carry a gun. But seeing it lying there out in the open, then being pushed back into his *little* sister's purse was like a hard slap of reality. He wondered how many times she'd used the weapon, and hoped she wouldn't have to use it anywhere near Maria.

"Okay." She plunked herself down in her chair. The heavy furniture didn't give an inch, and neither would Jo. "What have we here? A quiet day by all accounts, three lawyers visiting clients and a priest picked up a vagrant, charged with being drunk and disorderly in public, and took him to the homeless shelter."

Something clicked. "A priest you say, you got a name?"

"The writing's bad, it's a foreign name."

"More foreign than Jellic?"

"Yeah, yeah, I get your drift. Here, you take a look."

Franc scanned the sheet. Its being a photocopy didn't help. Somebody needed to replace the toner. Then he yelped, "Judas priest, what's the IQ level of the cop on duty? This says Father Iscariot. Get it? Judas Iscariot?"

Jo came round the table to his side and snatched the paper from his hands. "You're spot on, it does say Iscariot. Dumb ass not picking up on that. But just as folks are inclined to trust cops, same goes with priests. You don't expect them to lie.''

"Or kill.'' Then dawn broke over his head, flooding his brain with a cruel, cold light. "Shit, the chaplain!"

"What chaplain?"

"Said he worked at Auckland Hospital but had a lot to do with the street people that hung around the CBD. Damn, it all fits. Maria would have had no suspicion if he told her I'd been in an accident. She would have trusted him. She sees him around all the time. She even gave him a donation for the poor the other day.''

A sick guilty feeling invaded the pit of his stomach. "Hell, I trusted him myself, so much so, I practically pushed her into his arms after Searle knocked her down. I so wanted to get my hands on Searle for what he did to her.''

"I noticed that when you hit him, but you're sure it wasn't because he stole your research?'' Jo wrinkled her forehead at him.

He was shocked she had to ask. "Uh-uh, Maria comes way ahead of the research. I can redo the research, I can't replace Maria.''

Jo strode over to the door and called out to her husband. She came back, saying, "We need to get Rowan in on this now. I have to tell you, it was close by church grounds where we found Maria last time, but it's so long ago I can't remember the name. Did the chaplain tell her which church he was affiliated with?''

"I think Maria said Saint Andrew's.''

Jo did a high-five sign in the air. "That's the one. Brother, this case is starting to gel.''

Rowan entered the room, and Franc sought assurance, asking, "Do villains really return to the scene of a crime?''

But Jo refused to let his doubts blur the vision in her mind's eye. The wheels were ticking in her brain and she was on a roll. "I'll lay you a thousand to one odds that this villain has.

To him, replaying the past is all part of the thrill.'' Glancing at Franc, she saw feelings he didn't even try to hide. ''Sorry, brother, I forgot it was personal.''

Damn straight it was personal.

No way could Franc blank out the knowledge that it would be the woman he loved on the other end of the priest's knife.

*Someone was coming.*

Maria froze in her attempt to open the lock. She slumped down and pretended to be unconscious the way he'd left her. The way the chaplain had left her. How could the fuzz in her brain have concealed that from her? Or maybe she just hadn't wanted to believe that a man she'd put her trust in could abuse her this way.

She knew there was more, more information filed away at the back of her mind that she was too scared to extract. Her past had caught up with her, morphed into one with her future until she had no way of telling them apart.

Until her future was her past.

From the regular judder of shoes against stone, she could tell he was walking down steps. The way out had to be on the far right-hand corner of the crypt. As he turned up the lamp, pale gold light spilled over an old table that blocked Maria's path to the stairs and safety.

She wanted to cringe as stone grit scraped underfoot, and he drew closer, holding an oil lamp. Hoisted high, the lamp, unlike Aladdin's, wasn't likely to make her dreams come true. Only one man could do that and his name was Franc Jellic.

Had he deliberately set the lamp at an angle that turned his features into a Halloween mask? Grotesque, but that wasn't what drew her eyes. Wasn't what shocked Maria. Staring back from the wall were a hundred images and all of them of Maria Costello.

One glimpse at the photos and everything became clear. Mamma had said she looked beautiful. Franc had said she looked like a little nun, angelic. Well, she didn't feel angelic as she looked at the photographs and the man who had taken them. All she saw was the innocence he had robbed her of. "I remember you now."

He smiled, actually smiled as if it was a great joke. "Took you long enough. I walked past you in the street a dozen times before I spoke and never once saw a flash of recognition. That's when I knew it would be safe to finish what I'd started."

Ten years ago, she'd struggled against the shackle as she did now. Her brief rally halted as she felt a slight give in the metal. She had done it, but she didn't dare let *him* know.

"Come back to rape me again, did you? Once wasn't enough?"

"Sorry to spoil your illusion that I'm a monster, I never raped you."

"I don't believe you."

"That's your prerogative. But that's not why you're here. Look at yourself, at your pictures. The first time I saw you through the lens of my camera, I knew you were perfect, too good for this world. That's when I captured your innocence and took it for my own."

A black rage flooded her, filled her with hatred for this man who'd shattered her very existence. Done it once and had come back to do it again just as her life had become real and meaningful, made her *feel* real. Franc had done that, done it through love, not with cruelty like the monster before her.

With the rage came strength, came the will to diminish his power over her until it shriveled up and disappeared. "Perfect, was it? Well, I'm not perfect now." She put her hand to her breast. "You saw to that."

"It served its purpose to show whom you were meant for."

"You're mad, absolutely mad. Do you know I'm no longer intact, no longer perfect in that way? Franc Jellic saw to that. I walked into his arms and begged him to turn me into a real woman. How does that turn you on? You couldn't imagine the things we did together, Franc and me." She raised her voice, hoping it would carry. She knew where she was now. Knew the way to safety and Franc. She'd escaped this dungeon once. She could do it again. She had the power; she felt it rush through her veins.

The gleam in his eyes was evangelic, the maniacal sort. Convinced he would be her salvation. "Not enough to avert your death. He'll understand, he'll forgive you."

Her jaw clenched as her lips twisted in a sneer she had no control over. "But will he forgive you?"

"I'm not important, merely an instrument in a bigger scheme. I've already taken care of Searle." He saw her look of surprise. "Oh yes, he's gone. An unpleasant death, cigarettes laced with cyanide, such a greedy man. He enjoyed all the vices; I knew he wouldn't resist the few cigarettes I slipped through the peephole in his cell door."

Dear God, she hadn't liked Searle, but she wouldn't have wished that death on her worst enemy.

"As for Jellic, I'll have to create an even more unpleasant departure for him. He's the one who tainted my perfect sacrifice and *his* turn will come."

A scream raced through her head but she trapped it in her mind, wondering what venal plan he would concoct for Franc.

Wordlessly she prepared a speech to bring him to his knees. A plan demolished by the cell phone inside her purse ringing. The sound bounced round the stone-lined walls of the crypt like the knell of doom playing a rendition of "Greensleeves."

The sound of a tinny tune pealing out of the darkness was even more nerve-racking than wandering round a churchyard at midnight inside high walls where tree branches played a dirge in the breeze. Franc had been trying to call Jo, but her phone was set on vibrate. He looked down at the pale green screen of his phone and discovered it was Maria's number he'd picked out of his directory. He hit finish and the music stopped.

He spun his flashlight around the base of the church. Even

though summer was just at its height, a spongy carpet of leaves littered the grass; English trees gave up easy when lambasted by a tropical sun. On the base, a creeper had spread its grasping shoots through the cracked mortar, clinging so tightly he might have missed the door because the rusty red leaves licking round its frame softened its outline.

He tried it, fitting his fingers through the looped iron handle and giving it a twist. His heart missed a beat as it moved easily and the door swung open an inch.

He'd been warned not to go it alone, and after his interview by Jo's superior, Mike Henare, a detective inspector no less, he was wary about going down that road again. He punched up the directory again and he thumbed down through the list. Jo's number was last as he'd only just added it. The one before it was Maria's. His breath faltered as he pushed the call button.

His imagination hadn't gone haywire, for there it was again, the first few bars of ''Greensleeves,'' the haunting notes of the tune he'd set Maria's cell phone to ring came faintly through the opening. He pushed his ear up against the narrow crack but as suddenly as it had started the melody was cut off.

Bloody good, the bastard *had* returned to the scene of the crime. Thank you, Jo, for following in Milo's footsteps and having a nose for detective work. If he got to Maria in time, he would forgive his father. Damn straight he would.

Quick as a wink he raced through the directory again and got Jo this time. ''I've found her. Back left-hand corner of the base. It's shadowed by creeper but I'll leave the door open for you.''

''No, wait,'' Jo yelled in his ear.

''Too late, sis. I'm gone.''

His loafers had been expensive, and now he was glad of it. Soft as butter, they flexed with his feet as he started descending the stairs leading from the door. Jo might imagine he was the type to rush like a bull at a gate, but easy-does-it was the way to go when Maria's life was at stake.

Underfoot, desiccated mortar went off as loud as a bullet in his ears. He stopped halfway, listening at the edge of a yellow ball of light, his heart riding a roller coaster inside his chest. When the rush of nervous energy hushed in his ears, he heard voices, two, male and female.

His muscles tensed as adrenaline flooded his veins in ready for danger. He fought off the need to rush down the last few stairs, to confront the devil in priest's garb that had stolen Maria from him. Surprise was his greatest weapon, his only weapon come to that. No need to nullify its effect by racing into a situation even a fool would look at sideways.

One step, two steps, the glare of light enveloped him, but if he couldn't see them, then same goes, he was hidden by the last foot of wall enclosing the stairs. He let his eyes get accustomed to the light and listened.

"I can see hope in your eyes, Maria, sorry to disappoint you, it's useless. Jellic calling your cell phone is a last-ditch attempt to reach you after all other avenues have failed."

Something hard hit a wall and Franc heard Maria sob, "He won't give up. I know him as well as myself, he's not a quitter and neither am I. When Franc has something on his mind he gives it to you straight. He's not like you, he doesn't need to pretend to be something he's not to hide his inadequacies."

"You go, girl," Franc whispered under his breath and under the cover of Maria's rage. He crouched lower as he took the final step into the light and exposure. He had one moment's hesitation; almost faltering as he saw Maria, hundreds of Marias covering the wall. Some like the one Rosa had given him, only larger than life-size. Damn, so that was the connection.

The chaplain, or whoever he was, stood with his back to him, hiding Maria from Franc's view. Praying it would stay like that and that she wouldn't catch a glimpse of him and give him away, he crossed the last few feet. Crouched behind an old table, he waited in the shadow thrown by the oil lamp on the far corner of it and heard the chaplain say, "I'm not inadequate."

His voice was well modulated, concise even, but slightly higher-pitched than before, as if anger shimmered across the top of each word he pronounced.

"Oh, no...then why the necessity to prostrate yourself by turning me into a sacrificial lamb? You said you never raped me, I say you couldn't manage it. Inadequate!" she taunted.

From under the table, Franc could see her legs; she wasn't standing behind the chaplain. Like Franc, she was half crouched, but there the likeness ended. She was chained to the wall.

Biting his tongue on a howl of rage that erupted inside him, he watched the chaplain move closer. Franc knew he would have to charge soon. Then he heard a click, caught the gray gleam of steel in the chaplain's hand and knew it had to be sooner.

He stood, urgency flooding limbs that seemed unable to move as fast as time expanded like elastic at its farthest stretch.

Maria was at her most acerbic, her words snide and hurtful as if goading the chaplain to do his worst. "Oh *big* man, look at the knife. Is it the one you used to disfigure me or the one that emasculated you?"

Did she know Franc was there? Know he was hurtling toward the chaplain as if the thread of time had snapped?

The blade rose. Franc could see it gleaming above them as he tackled the chaplain, taking him down with his shoulder behind the knees, twisting the knife's momentum as it swung at Maria.

One minute the brute was facedown, the next he was rolling over in desperation. Franc launched at him from his knees, hand locking round the wrist holding the knife. Another roll and Franc looked up into the red eyes of madness.

Maria was wrong about the guy being emasculated, for he

certainly felt it when Franc drew up his knee. A woman's trick, but who gave a damn when Satan was breathing fire in your face.

Maria had known Franc wouldn't fail her. Buoyed by his arrival, she turned back to the lock and let them get on with their fight. But it hadn't been as easy a mark as she'd thought, unless it had clicked back into place as she'd hurled home truths at the chaplain's head. But then, he wasn't a chaplain, he'd been the photographer who had come to school in her last year to record each class, as well as take individual photos for the yearbook.

Her hand scrabbled on the gritty floor. Where was that hairpin? She emptied her lungs of air in a hissing sigh of reprieve as her fingers found the bent strip of metal beside her hip. This time she was sure she could make the tumblers release the lock. A glance over her shoulder promised that time wasn't on her side.

Franc rolled across the floor with a lock on the chaplain's hand that sent the knife clattering. Suddenly the fight drained out of the chaplain like air in a balloon. Franc was winning. She went back to her task with greater heart. She would get out of there…this time with Franc.

It had all come back to her, all her dreams of blood and knives in full Technicolor. Maria breathed through her nose as her mouth went dry as a bone. Remembering wouldn't get the lock open.

The chaplain's head hit one of the carved table legs, sending it swaying. Franc looked at the lamp, leapt to his feet and hauled ass away from there, away from the inevitable.

Shaking his head, and looking unsteady on his pins, the older guy tried to follow, but his weight was too much for the rickety table. The overhanging lip he grabbed came down on him as wormy wood sighed under the extra pressure, the leg snapped, toppling the table as it bowed inward, and the oil lamp hit the wall.

Paraffin dripped down the dank stonework onto the floor,

its fumes curling in swirls of blue above flames dancing tall, dancing higher, greedy for photographic paper.

The dark boundaries of the crypt melted in a flurry of light as it pushed back the walls to expose the once-impressive last resting places of an earlier colonial society. Empty now, they stared out of the walls like hollow eye sockets.

Franc leaped back from the flames. He had to free Maria.

Locked in Franc's arms, Maria's relief mixed with trembling exhaustion as he hugged her, groaning, "Thank God, you're free." He'd been terrified the flames would get them both before he could release her.

He swung her into his arms just as a keening howl surfaced above the crackle of flames. Through the pall of smoke, the chaplain scrabbled armfuls of photographs off the wall.

As if she weighed nothing, Franc lifted Maria over the burning table. "Run up the stairs, don't stop and don't look back. Jo should have found the entrance by now; tell her to call the fire department."

She saw him turn back as her feet hit the foot of the stairs. "Noooo, you have to come with me!"

"Sorry, hon. I can't leave him to roast."

She couldn't obey; couldn't leave him. She took three steps then turned back. It was the stuff of nightmares. The chaplain screamed as the photographs in his arms caught fire, turning him into a human torch. And worse, as Franc tore her crumpling images from his arms the chaplain clasped him in a bear hug.

Maria couldn't breathe, couldn't find the air to carry the scream in her throat, and just as she passed out, huge hands caught her and a voice, Rowan's voice, said, "Get her outside, Jo."

# Chapter 18

When Franc woke, someone was caressing the tips of his bandaged fingers. "Maria?" His throat was dry as a bone from the drugs they'd given him and her name came out in small pieces. Then, turning his head, he saw his sister.

"Sorry to disappoint you, kiddo, it's only little old me."

He gave her a smile that made his face hurt, his skin felt so tight. "Jeez, that smarts. Feels like I fell asleep on the beach and got me a sunburn." The top sheet on the hospital bed lay around his waist. It looked as if he'd lost all the hair on his body from the neck down—well, not that far down.

"You're lucky it isn't more than that, there are one or two bad spots on your hands, but the doctors say they will heal without skin grafts. Hell, Franc, what were you thinking?" Tears welled in her eyes. "God, I wish I could hug you, but since I can't, I have to scold you. Don't ever do anything like that again. It just seems like yesterday since we really found each other again. And I can tell you, brother. We were without family for *too* long, I don't want to lose you again."

"Quit, sis, you'll have me bawling like a calf needing its

ma if you keep that up.'' Then he grinned, sheepish like. ''Yeah, I've discovered family isn't such a bad thing. And what about the chaplain?''

''He didn't make it. He didn't deserve your help, either. Trying to pull him out was carrying humanity too far.''

Franc was silent for a minute. He'd always carry the picture of the guy going up in flames, but he wasn't going to let it make him an emotional cripple. That would mean the bastard had won. With Maria's family's help, the guy had almost succeeded in creating a victim last time round, it wouldn't happen again.

Franc chased the image out of his mind; there were more important issues at stake. He lifted the sheet between the finger and thumb of the hand his sister hadn't appropriated to peek under it. ''So, what's the rest of the damage, anything major?''

Jo shook her head and gurgled with laughter, it was a sweet sound. ''You men. Honestly, at a stretch I'd say everything's working as well as it ever did, depending on how good you are at boasting. And the Jellic men never were modest.''

''When can I see Maria?'' He paused midthought. ''She's okay, isn't she…you got her out of there?'' He watched Jo lick her lips and imagined the worst.

''She's fine,'' she replied. ''Her parents arrived in the wee small hours and took her home.''

''Damn, they're not going to do that to her again. I won't let them.'' He went to throw the covers back then remembered his naked state. ''Do you mind leaving a minute? I have to get dressed.''

She threw up her hands as her eyebrows shot skyward. ''Into what? Your clothes were singed and that's putting it mildly. Your shirt disintegrated.''

''Hell, I don't care, get me a hospital gown, anything to cover my ass so I can get out of here.'' And he didn't care, he had to get to Maria before Pietro and Rosa swamped her again in a huge wave of concerned parental love.

Jo's silence was broken only by the cogs he could see turning inside her head. ''Rowan should have a gym bag in the back of my car. Should be some sweats and a T-shirt in it. The T-shirt might drown you, but will be all the better for that. You don't want anything clinging to your chest.''

Yes he did.

He wanted Maria clinging to it and the sooner the better.

Jo paused in the doorway and for the first time he took in the room and realized she must have paid for a private one. ''Wait a minute,'' she said. ''How are you going to drive?''

''I don't care. Call me a cab.''

''To Matheson's Bay? No way, I'll drive you.''

Maria was packing. She remembered the last time she'd done this, less than two weeks ago with Franc standing watching. It wasn't the same, she missed him already. How could her parents have bundled her home and left Franc behind in hospital?

How could she have let them?

It was no good blaming them, she should have stood up to them, instead, and because of the trauma she'd gone through she'd let the old ways take over. Mamma's voice saying hush and Papa holding out his arms in the way he'd done when she was little when he'd thought he could solve all her problems and kill all her dragons for her.

No more. She had to get back to making her own decisions about her life, and if her dreams ever came to fruition, hers and Franc's lives together.

He just had to love her.

All morning she'd imagined him waking up and not finding her beside him. The palpitations she'd been experiencing on and off were nothing to do with last night. Each time she thought of him, her breath thinned, faded away until a large fist took her heart in its grip and set it racing. Racing toward Franc.

Toward the man she'd told Mamma she loved, and as the saying goes, Come hell or high water, he was going to be hers.

Rowan's feet weren't much bigger than Franc's, though his brother-in-law's shoes slipped down the backs of his heels as he bounded up the steps of the house at Falcon's Rise.

Rosa stood at the top, the blue shutters behind her making a picture with her red dress and white apron. She actually looked pleased to see him. "Franc, let me look at you." She gave him the once-over she'd given Maria on Christmas Eve, but this time her hands didn't touch, just fluttered over him. "Should you be out of bed?"

"I'm perfectly fine, Mamma. Where is she?"

She raised her eyebrows as he called her Mamma. Well, hell, why not? It was how he'd come to think of her.

"Up in her room, packing to go to you." Rosa spent a moment smoothing the creases out of her white apron, as if she needed to keep her hands busy. When she raised her eyes, there was a question in them just for him. "She told me if we wanted to find her, she'd be at your apartment."

"Damn straight! That's where she belongs, with me."

She nodded. "Good, you know where her room is."

He went across the hall and had a foot on the bottom step when he remembered his sister. He turned, wincing as he automatically reached for the ball gracing the foot of the banister. "Mamma, this is my little sister, Jo. She takes her coffee black with two sugars."

Rosa smiled and held out her hand to Jo. "Not so little, but I'll look after her."

What was it with women? The smile on Jo's face had the same about-to-burst-with-pleasure creases as Mamma Costello's. "Don't mind me, kiddo. Mrs. Costello and I have a wedding to plan, take your time."

"I intend to take more than that. See you later."

* * *

Maria closed one case and zipped it up. If she hadn't been half-dead with exhaustion last night, Papa wouldn't need to make another trip in to Auckland.

She'd grabbed the last of her clothes from the closet. The drawers she had already emptied, now she rolled up the clothes in her hands, hangers and all, and stuffed them in the second suitcase. There, she was done. She didn't live here anymore. She heard footsteps on the stairs, hurrying. "I'm almost done, Mamma."

The door opened behind her and when she recognized the face in the dressing-table mirror, her heart flipped in her chest and began racing again. The only voice that could do that to her said, "Well, I'm far from done, Maria."

She ran to him, went to throw herself into his arms, then came to a dead stop as the white bandages stood out against the baggy navy sweats and T-shirt he wore, so unlike himself, as Franc never looked sloppy. "Can I touch you?"

"You betcha! I'll go crazy without your touch. Come here, hon, and I'll show you how crazy life can get."

She ran her hands up the top of Franc's arms and onto his shoulders. She touched his jaw, gently running a fingernail against the brush of the dark stubble that was already growing on his face.

She reached up, his eyebrows needed the singed tips trimmed away, but apart from what looked like a brush with the sun, she liked what she saw. "You'll do."

Franc held her loosely in his arms. "Stings a bit, but I'd better *do* for you. What you see's going to have to last the rest of your life."

"Say that again." Now she really felt shocked. It didn't matter that this, this moment was what she'd longed for all along; the reality far outweighed her imagination. She wanted to lean on him and press her body against his, but feared she'd hurt him. Maria placed her palms on his shoulders and held the rest of her body clear in case she scraped the burns hidden under his T-shirt. Last night when Rowan and his team had pulled Franc out of the crypt, the medics had cut the tattered clothing off Franc's chest before closing the ambulance door with them both inside. All she'd needed treating had been her bruised wrist.

"I want you with me."

"I didn't want to leave you, big guy, not if you still want me. I was packing to go home…to see if you'd still have me."

His swathed hands came up and framed her face in white, like the wedding dress she'd always dreamed of having. "Where else would you go? You're mine, hon, for better or worse."

"Is that a proposal?" She held her breath waiting for the answer.

"I guess it is, better be since Mamma and my sister are downstairs planning a wedding. Want me to get down on one knee?"

Why was she hesitating? Say yes, her heart screamed, but her conscience said, "One last thing, Franc. One last shadow to sweep away. The chaplain, or should I say James Arblaster, his name was on the back of the photo." She nodded in the direction of the bed. "I took it out of the frame to throw it away."

"I don't blame you, hon. He was a talented photographer but misguided. Arblaster thought of the image he created as the end product, while I know you're a work of art in the making. The older you get, the more beautiful you'll grow in my eyes. I love you, Maria."

"Thank heavens, for I love you, too, Franc. But I have to tell you, although I asked Arblaster, and he said he had never raped me, I can't be certain he was telling the truth."

The line of his mouth flattened and his jaw thrust forward. Maria dreaded what he might say.

"Do you think that matters to me? I said I love you, Maria. And I know, no matter what happened before we met that the first time we made love, you surrendered your innocence to me. And no one can tell me any different. Or change my mind. Will you marry me, hon, be my family for as long as we live?''

''Of course I will. Looks like that summer fling you promised me will be stretching out some.'' She stood on the tips of her toes, stretching to meet his kiss.

''An everlasting summer, a promise is a promise.'' Those were the last words spoken for a while, as Franc bent his head and kissed her, the way he'd wanted to from the moment the goddess gate-crashed his life and turned it upside down. What more could an ambitious guy ask for but to be happy for the rest of his life?

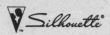
**Silhouette®**

# INTIMATE MOMENTS™

# An Order of Protection
### (Silhouette Intimate Moments #1292)

## by
# KATHLEEN CREIGHTON

### A brand-new book in her bestselling series

STARRS OF THE WEST

Jo Lynn Starr's best friend is missing but no one will believe her. No one except police officer Scott Cavanaugh—and even he has his doubts. But as they work together to unravel the mystery, one thing becomes perilously clear—their growing attraction for each other!

*Available May 2004 at your favorite retail outlet.*

Visit Silhouette Books at www.eHarlequin.com

SIMAOOP

# INTIMATE MOMENTS™

## A brand-new book in the bestselling WINGMEN WARRIORS series by
# CATHERINE MANN

### Joint Forces
(Silhouette Intimate Moments #1293)

Rena Price's once-solid marriage was on the rocks after a mission-gone-wrong had made her air force husband, J. T. "Tag" Price draw away. But with a deadly threat against the family—and an unexpected pregnancy—pulling them together, would the strength of their joint forces be enough to save their lives... and their love?

*Available May 2004
at your favorite retail outlet.*

Visit Silhouette Books at www.eHarlequin.com

SIMJF

# eHARLEQUIN.com

Looking for today's most popular books at great prices?
At www.eHarlequin.com, we offer:

- An **extensive selection** of romance books by top authors!

- **New** releases, Themed Collections and hard-to-find **backlist.**

- A sneak peek at Upcoming books.

- Enticing book **excerpts** and **back cover copy!**

- Read recommendations from other readers (and post your own)!

- Find out what everybody's reading in **Bestsellers.**

- **Save BIG** with everyday discounts and exclusive online offers!

- Easy, convenient **24-hour shopping.**

- Our **Romance Legend** will help select reading that's *exactly* right for you!

**Your purchases are 100% guaranteed—so shop online at www.eHarlequin.com today!**

INTBB1

If you enjoyed what you just read,
then we've got an offer you can't resist!

# Take 2 bestselling love stories FREE!

# Plus get a FREE surprise gift!

---

**Clip this page and mail it to Silhouette Reader Service™**

**IN U.S.A.**
3010 Walden Ave.
P.O. Box 1867
Buffalo, N.Y. 14240-1867

**IN CANADA**
P.O. Box 609
Fort Erie, Ontario
L2A 5X3

**YES!** Please send me 2 free Silhouette Intimate Moments® novels and my free surprise gift. After receiving them, if I don't wish to receive anymore, I can return the shipping statement marked cancel. If I don't cancel, I will receive 6 brand-new novels every month, before they're available in stores! In the U.S.A., bill me at the bargain price of $3.99 plus 25¢ shipping and handling per book and applicable sales tax, if any*. In Canada, bill me at the bargain price of $4.74 plus 25¢ shipping and handling per book and applicable taxes**. That's the complete price and a savings of at least 10% off the cover prices—what a great deal! I understand that accepting the 2 free books and gift places me under no obligation ever to buy any books. I can always return a shipment and cancel at any time. Even if I never buy another book from Silhouette, the 2 free books and gift are mine to keep forever.

245 SDN DNUV
345 SDN DNUW

| Name | (PLEASE PRINT) | |
|------|----------------|---|
| Address | Apt.# | |
| City | State/Prov. | Zip/Postal Code |

\* Terms and prices subject to change without notice. Sales tax applicable in N.Y.
\*\* Canadian residents will be charged applicable provincial taxes and GST.
   All orders subject to approval. Offer limited to one per household and not valid to current Silhouette Intimate Moments® subscribers.
   ® are registered trademarks of Harlequin Books S.A., used under license.

INMOM02                                ©1998 Harlequin Enterprises Limited

## LUNA

**Bestselling Harlequin Historical™ author
Deborah Hale has created a beautiful world
filled with magic and adventure
in her first fantasy novel.**

**"An emotional richness and depth
readers will savor."**
—*Booklist* on *Carpetbagger's Wife*

*On sale March 30 at your local bookseller.*

www.Luna-Books.com                    LDH205

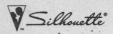

# INTIMATE MOMENTS™

### National bestselling author
# RUTH LANGAN
### presents a new book
### in her exciting miniseries

**Beneath the surface
lie scandals, secrets…
and seduction.**

# Wanted
**(Silhouette Intimate
Moments #1291)**

Someone wants to hurt
Hannah Brennan. But
it can't possibly be
handsome, single dad—
and murder suspect—
Ethan Harrison.
Or can it?

*Available May 2004
at your favorite retail outlet.*

Visit Silhouette Books at www.eHarlequin.com

SIMW

From *USA TODAY* bestselling author

# CANDACE CAMP

Lady Kyria Moreland is beautiful and rich, but when she receives a strange package she is confronted by danger and murder—not things that she can dispatch with her beauty or wealth....

Rafe McIntyre has enough charm to seduce any woman, but behind his smooth facade hides a bitter past that leads him to believe Kyria is in danger. He refuses to let her solve this riddle alone.

But who sent her this treasure steeped in legend? And who is willing to murder to claim its secrets and its glory for themselves?

## BEYOND COMPARE

"Readers looking for a good 19th-century ghost story need look
no further than this latest charmer...A truly enjoyable read."
—*Publishers Weekly* on *Mesmerized*

*Available the first week of April 2004
wherever paperbacks are sold.*

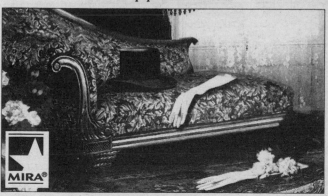

**MIRA®**

Visit us at www.mirabooks.com

MCC2030

 Silhouette®

# COMING NEXT MONTH

**INTIMATE MOMENTS®**

SIMCNM0404